The Scandalous Sisterhood

Sisterhood

of Prickwillow Place

The Scandalous Sisterhood

of Prickwillow Place

JULIE BERRY

Piccadilly
PRESS

First published in Great Britain in 2015 by Piccadilly Press
Northburgh House, 10 Northburgh Street, London EC1V 0AT

First published in the USA in 2014 by Roaring Brook Press,
a division of Macmillan Publishers

A CIP catalogue record for this book is available from the British Library.

ISBN: 978-1-84812-437-0

2

This book is typeset in 11pt Sabon using Atomik ePublisher

Printed and bound by Clays Ltd, St Ives Plc

www.piccadillypress.co.uk

Piccadilly Press is part of the Bonnier Publishing Group
www.bonnierpublishing.com

For my own scandalous sisters,
Sue, Jane, Beth, Sal, and Joanna,
and all the sisters I've gained
along the way

PRESENTING

the Students at Saint Etheldreda's School for Young Ladies

Young Ladies Whom You Shall Be Pleased to Meet
in This Narrative

SMOOTH KITTY
HEATON

STOUT ALICE
BROOKS

DOUR ELINOR
SIEVER

DISGRACEFUL
MARY JANE MARSHALL

DEAR ROBERTA
PRATLEY

POCKED LOUISE
DUDLEY

DULL MARTHA
BOYLE

Persons

Whom You Will Not Meet in This Narrative:

*Relations and Acquaintances of the
Aforementioned Young Ladies*

Mrs Maybelle Pratley, whose first act upon marrying
Benson Pratley was to enroll his daughter, Roberta,
at Saint Etheldreda's School for Young Ladies in
Ely, Cambridgeshire, forty miles from home. Mrs
Pratley believed firmly that a maiden so tall and
gangly who was always tripping over her long feet,
and possessing such a weak brain, needed intensive
molding into young womanhood. The late Mrs
Pratley's indulgent parenting had left Roberta soft,
but the new Mrs Pratley aimed to correct this.
Saint Etheldreda's School's reputation for stern
discipline and strict moral guidance satisfied Mrs
Pratley well. Never mind that anyone else who
knew Dear Roberta could only describe her as
adorably gentle and kind; Stepmother knew best.

Mrs Lloyd Marshall, mother of Mary Jane Marshall,
whose greatest fear was that her daughter might
elope much too young and make a scandalous
marriage with the wrong sort of man. Disgraceful
Mary Jane had ways of escaping even her mother's
strictest supervision, and young men, particularly
those of the young, reckless, penniless variety,

buzzed about her like flies round a honey pot. In the watchful of eye the headmistress of Saint Etheldreda's School for Young Ladies, the anxious mother placed all her hopes.

Leroy, Rupert, Alexander, and Chesterfield Boyle, the younger brothers of Dull Martha Boyle, who tormented her ceaselessly because it was so easy. Frogs appeared in her porridge. Mice scampered out from under her sheets. Her spectacles would go missing, time and again, only to resurface in the potato bin or the butter churn. To be fair, most boys believe their sisters are stupid. These young men were, one regrets to say, correct. At any rate, her former governess, if pressed, would concur, though she would add that Martha was a sweet, lovely girl with a gift for piano and the voice of an angel.

Isabelle Brooks cousin to Alice Brooks. Isabelle ate candied nuts, fruit jellies, and petits fours from midmorning till teatime, then buttered toast with fig preserves and cheese croissants from teatime till supper. Yet with all this, and because there is no justice in the world, she never added an ounce to her slender, graceful figure and wore Paris's latest dressmaking fashions to perfection. Their grandmamma held Isabelle up to Alice in comparison on a daily basis. The fact that Stout

Alice, who tended towards poundage, managed not to hate Isabelle was a testament to her great heart and her remarkable self-control.

Mr Maximilian Heaton, prosperous mill owner in northern England, vice-chairman of the British Railway Committee, and father of Smooth Kitty Heaton. His wife died when their only child was four, leaving Mr Heaton to anticipate no male heir to the great estate he built through his tireless industry. This was his one great sorrow. He boasted often that he'd never stood in a room with a man who was his equal at managing an enterprise. (Had he stood more often in a room with his daughter, he might have noticed a rival for his talents growing up right under his nose.) Supremely effective Mr Heaton may have been, but not even the shareholders in his mill, who became wealthy men by aligning their financial stars with his, liked the man.

Dr Matthew Dudley, London surgeon, and paternal uncle to Louise Dudley. He was admitted to Cambridge University on a scholarship to study medicine and later trained at the University of Edinburgh in Scotland. When his young niece, Louise, contracted smallpox at age eight, he attended her night and day, leading her safely to recovery, and became her idol and mentor forever. He encouraged her interest in science, chemistry, and medicine by supplying her with books and inviting her to lectures. He claimed she'd make a great physician. In fear of this prophecy coming true, when Pocked Louise turned twelve her parents confiscated her chemistry set and sent her to Saint Etheldreda's School to learn ladylike arts rather than medical ones.

Old Jim Clitherow, grave digger, of Newark-on-Trent, Nottinghamshire. He buried the dead at his parish church for forty years, and sometimes dug them back up again, if they had wedding rings or sturdy boots or lungs and livers worth a surgeon's silver. One night, as he loaded a recently exhumed German widower onto his cart, he found young Miss Elinor Siever watching from behind a tree. Her pale face looked ghostly in the moonlight. He thought she was an avenging angel sent to punish him for grave robbing. Old Jim's heart nearly gave out with shock. The young woman peered over his shoulder at the corpse of Hans Marx and reached out to touch the cold grey face of the dead. Old Jim Clitherow shooed Elinor Siever away, threw Hans Marx back where he belonged, shovelled dirt over him, and ran. That night he told the barkeep at the town pub, the Bubble and Brisket. When rumour of Dour Elinor's nightly wanderings reached the ears of Mr and Mrs Siever, they enrolled her at Saint Etheldreda's School for Young Ladies in Ely faster than you can say "necromancy."

Ｅｎｇｌａｎｄ

1890

Chapter One

Each Sunday afternoon at Saint Etheldreda's School for Young Ladies on Prickwillow Road in Ely, Cambridgeshire, the seven enrolled young ladies were invited by custom to join Headmistress Constance Plackett while she entertained her younger brother, Mr Aldous Godding, at the dinner table. The privilege of watching the headmistress and her regular Sunday guest consume the veal that they, the young ladies themselves, had prepared, more than compensated for the lack of sufficient veal for all the table to share. The girls had learned to be content with buttered bread and hot beans, Sundays upon end. Such self-denial would serve them well in their future callings as wives. This was Mr Aldous Godding's firm belief, and his sister, the widow Mrs Plackett, with years of matrimonial experience behind her, could only agree.

On one particular Sunday evening in May, midway through the meal, Mrs Plackett sopped her plate with her bread, took a bite of it, and let the morsel fall to the floor, while her head lolled back upon her shoulders, and her eyes gazed blankly at the ceiling. She shuddered. She shook. She let out a choking cough, then fell silent.

"What's the matter, Connie?" her brother demanded between mouthfuls. "Speak up, woman. It isn't decent goggling about like that. Pass the pepper, Missy." This he addressed to Disgraceful Mary Jane, who sat nearest to him, but he neither knew her name nor the source of her disgrace. All the young ladies were "Missy" to him.

Disgraceful Mary Jane passed the pepper. Mr Godding used it liberally, ate a bite of veal, lay down his knife and fork, touched his beard with his napkin, and rose from his seat. He made his way around the table to where his sister sat, raised his arm to thump her back, then choked, clutched his throat, fell forward, and landed on the floor with a thud that reverberated up the legs of the chairs upon which the seven young ladies sat.

"Dead, I imagine," Dour Elinor observed.

Smooth Kitty slipped from her chair and went softly to the headmistress's side. She plucked the spectacles off Dull Martha's nose, polished them on her sleeve, then held them in front of Mrs Plackett's limp mouth. She watched and listened closely. The other girls hung poised for the verdict, their forks frozen in mid-bite.

Smooth Kitty, satisfied that no breath had fogged the glasses, nodded and placed them back on Dull Martha's nose. "Dead as a kipper," she pronounced.

"Eugh," Dull Martha sputtered. "You made a dead person breathe on my glasses!"

Pocked Louise opened her mouth to correct Dull Martha,

2

but Smooth Kitty shook her head slightly. Pocked Louise, the youngest of the girls, was accustomed to her older schoolmates bossing her about. She kept still.

Dear Roberta covered her face with her hands. "But this is awful! Hadn't we ought to call Doctor Snelling?"

"Bit late for that," Dour Elinor said. "Louise, check the other one."

Pocked Louise, the resident scientist, approached the fallen form of Mr Aldous Godding cautiously. As his face was mashed against the floor, it became clear to her that she must touch him in order to turn him over, a thought which wrinkled her pox-scarred nose into a fright of disgust.

"Go on," Dour Elinor urged. "He won't bite."

"But he's a *man*," Pocked Louise protested. "And such a greasy one."

"Don't be a ninny. Of course he's a man," said Disgraceful Mary Jane. "Believe me, there are many far better."

"Think of him as a specimen in a jar," Smooth Kitty said, "specially killed for the purpose of examination."

Dear Roberta dabbed her eyes with a handkerchief. "Killed?" she squeaked. "Did you say *killed*?"

Pocked Louise by this point had managed to upturn her specimen and proclaim him dead. The gush of blood from his broken nose spread a ghastly crimson all over his already unpleasant face, and threatened to eternally stain the Persian rug. The girls gathered round in a circle, leaning over the body.

"*Killed*," Dour Elinor said. "*Murdered*." She savoured

3

the *R*'s in her pronunciation: *murrrrderrrred.*

"Oh. Oh my." Dear Roberta began to gasp. "A murder. Oh dear. I think I shall faint." She fluttered her hand before her face.

"Not now, Roberta, there's a dear," interjected Disgraceful Mary Jane. "Why bother swooning when there are no young men about to see you do it?"

"Balderdash," said Pocked Louise. "If *I* wanted to faint, which I wouldn't, I'd go right ahead and do it. I wouldn't give tuppence for whether or not there were males present."

"Sturdy stuff, Louise," said Stout Alice. "To thine own self be true. Now, if we can return to the matter at hand . . ."

"At foot, you mean." Dull Martha glanced at the corpse on the carpet.

"Something has killed Mrs Plackett and Mr Godding." Stout Alice dabbed at the blood spot on the rug with her napkin. "But it may have been a mere piece of meat lodged in the throat. We mustn't run away with ourselves with this talk of murder."

"The odds of both of them accidentally choking within seconds of each other seem infinitesimally small," said Pocked Louise. "The facts suggest poison, which clearly points to murder. Someone murdered them."

An angelic smile spread across Smooth Kitty's pretty face. "Ah," she said, "but the question is, who?"

Silence hung over the dining room. The glass-domed clock on the mantel ticked. Flowered chintz curtains swam in the sweet May breeze. Mrs Constance Plackett

4

sat straight and slack-jawed in her dining chair as seven young ladies each looked at the others as though seeing them for the first time.

"Surely it couldn't have been one of us," said Dear Roberta.

"Why not?" said Disgraceful Mary Jane. "I say hurrah if it *was* one of us. Finally someone showed some good sense and got rid of those two."

Dear Roberta's eyes filled with tears. "But that would be dreadful! How could we go on living here, wondering which one of us was a poisoner?"

"Grab his feet, won't you, dear?" Stout Alice addressed Dull Martha, and bent to lace her arms underneath Mr Godding's, which seemed now to be made of cement. Dull Martha complied, and the other young ladies pitched in, shifting and sharing the weight as best they could, taking special care to keep blood off their dresses. Together they hoisted their dead headmistress's dead brother up into the air.

"Now what do we do with him?" asked Disgraceful Mary Jane. "Dump him on the sofa until the constables arrive? I suppose we'd better send someone to fetch them." This thought seemed to please her. "Say, I'll go. There's a new constable up from London who's ever so tall, with such lovely square shoulders, and the most adorable little gap between his front teeth. I'll just get my new shawl . . ."

"Hold a moment," Smooth Kitty said. "Before we run off flirting with constables and calling physicians, I say we think carefully. Dear Roberta has asked a very sensible question."

Dear Roberta blinked. "I have?"

Stout Alice shifted Mr Godding's torso uncomfortably. "Do you mind if we have our little chat after we've put Mr Godding down somewhere?"

"Oh, just drop him there where he is," said Smooth Kitty. "He's beyond help now."

For the second time in minutes, Mr Godding crashed to the floor.

"Bother," Stout Alice said. "Now we'll just have to hoist him up again."

"As I was saying," Smooth Kitty began, then paused. "Oh! Check his pockets, will you, Louise?"

"Why?"

Kitty shrugged. "If he's got any money, we'll have better use for it than he will."

"Like the Achaeans in the Trojan war," murmured Dour Elinor, with a strange light in her eyes, "stripping armour off the bodies of their fallen enemies."

Smooth Kitty coughed. "Yes. Well. Something like that."

"I still don't see why *I* have to do all the dirty work," grumbled Pocked Louise.

"Because you're the youngest, and we say so," said Disgraceful Mary Jane, earning a kick in the heel from Stout Alice.

"Because you're so thorough, dear," said Smooth Kitty.

Pocked Louise grimaced as she reached two fingers gingerly into each of Mr Godding's trouser pockets. Her search yielded a cigar, a snuffbox, a coin, a key, and a folded bit of scribbled paper.

"Is it a note?" asked Alice, peering at the scrap. "Does it mean something?"

Louise frowned. "More like an inkblot," she said. "Perhaps a triangle. Nothing of interest here." She dropped the items on a table.

"You don't call a sovereign a thing of interest?" Smooth Kitty, ever one for figures and ledgers, nabbed the coin, then reported on their headmistress's pockets. "Mrs Plackett has a sovereign, a few shillings and pence, a handkerchief, and mint pastilles."

"Would to heaven she'd used the pastilles more often," said Disgraceful Mary Jane.

"Mary Jane!" Dear Roberta cried. "To speak so of the departed!"

"Well, she had foul breath, dead or alive," Mary Jane replied. "Her odours won't improve from here on out."

Smooth Kitty gathered what change they'd found in both sets of pockets and slipped it into her own. Then she gathered the other small items and dropped them into a small crockery urn on the sideboard.

"As I was *saying*," Kitty resumed her original query, with a touch of exasperation in her voice. "What Roberta so wisely asked, several moments ago, was, 'How shall we go on living here?' She has a point. Once we notify constables and so forth, we'll all be sent home."

"Of course we'll be sent home," Dear Roberta said. "It's the only logical thing." She sighed. "I suppose I must learn to love Stepmother somehow. It was so much easier here when I didn't have to look at her. It made it much easier to pray for her, as the vicar said we must do for all our enemies."

"But why, Roberta dear?" Dull Martha said. "Why should you go home to your nasty stepmother? Can't we stay here, and we'll all just go on like we do?"

"They won't let us," Pocked Louise protested.

"Who's 'they'?" Dull Martha asked.

"Coroners," Dour Elinor intoned. "Undertakers. Police. School overseers. All the people who'll descend upon us like a flock of ravens once it's known that these two are dead."

"You sound almost glad of their coming, Elinor," Smooth Kitty observed.

"Only the undertakers," Elinor admitted. "I've always wanted to witness an embalming."

"Bother and more bother." Disgraceful Mary Jane flopped back into her chair at the dinner table. "With those two nuisances gone, we might actually have had some fun. This whole place is suddenly *much* more interesting. And now we shall have to leave it."

"And each other," Pocked Louise added.

Stout Alice put an arm around Pocked Louise. Louise rested her head on Alice's shoulder.

"I don't want to go home, either," Dull Martha said. "My little brothers torment me so. They pull my hair and stick it in ink, and paste my piano pages together."

"Mother won't let me out of her sight for a minute," Disgraceful Mary Jane said. "She swears I'll elope if she leaves me unguarded for half an hour. I ask you, have you ever heard such rubbish?" She grinned. "Ten minutes and a willing man are all I'd need."

"You've never had a shortage of willing men," Smooth Kitty said.

"Correct, but under Mother's watch, there's an absolute dearth of minutes."

Stout Alice was uninterested in Mary Jane's chances for hasty marriage. "If I go home, all I shall hear from Grandmamma is how fat I am compared to Cousin Isabelle," she said. "*She* should talk. It takes two maids to tie Grandmamma's corsets, but that doesn't stop her from goading me."

Dour Elinor stared at the black coals on the grate. "My mother will tell me all day long that a young lady should radiate *sweetness* and *good cheer*." She spoke the words the way others might pronounce *maggots* and *black rot*.

Smooth Kitty clucked a sympathetic tongue for poor Elinor.

"I suppose they'll find other schools for us eventually," Pocked Louise said. "New mistresses, new nasty girls to make us miserable."

"We have all gotten along so beautifully here." Dear Roberta sighed. "It's something of a miracle, really. We aren't simply boarding-school mates. We're like a family."

"We're better than family," Disgraceful Mary Jane corrected. "Families are full of aunts and brothers and parents. We're *sisters*."

"I always wished for a sister," Dull Martha said.

"Me too," said Dear Roberta.

"Not me," Dour Elinor confessed. "But I don't mind your company."

Pocked Louise sat up. "None of us here has a sister at

9

home, have we?" she said slowly. "I never realised that before. Not a single one of us."

"That's why I'd hate to leave." Dear Roberta had begun to cry. "We have our own sisterhood."

Elinor handed Roberta a black silk handkerchief.

"You want to know what I say?" Smooth Kitty asked no one in particular. "*I* say we don't tell these . . . ravens and what-do-you-call-ems . . . coroners. Let's not tell *anyone.*"

They stared at each other. Smoldering coal settled in the fireplace, sending up low sparks. Each girl was alone, for a moment, with her private amazement. Smooth Kitty counted her heartbeats as she waited for their responses.

"But the bodies will smell," Dull Martha said at length. "Sooner or later they're bound to."

Disgraceful Mary Jane, whose green eyes had lit up wonderfully at Smooth Kitty's suggestion, gave Dull Martha a little rub on the back. "No, darling, they won't," she said. "We'll bury them. Right in the vegetable beds."

"They'll make a lovely compost," Pocked Louise added. "Perhaps not so much this season. But next season the marrows and squashes will burst with juicy goodness." She scratched her nose thoughtfully. "We'll just have to be careful this fall when we go digging for potatoes."

Smooth Kitty's eyes darted from young lady to young lady, watching to see how well her idea had taken hold. She didn't dare congratulate herself yet. She must be sure where they stood.

"Never mind potatoes. There'll be a scandal," she said. "An investigation. Each one of us could be under a cloud of suspicion for the rest of our lives."

"A *black spot*," Dour Elinor intoned. "A blemish upon our maiden purity."

"Oh no, surely not," Disgraceful Mary Jane replied. "Not for such a trifling thing as neglecting to mention the death of a headmistress and her nasty brother. No one could really be upset over that. It takes much more fun to leave a blemish upon one's maiden purity."

"They'll think one of us murdered them," Pocked Louise warned.

Smooth Kitty slipped an arm through Louise's elbow. "What I'd like to know, love, is whether or not one of us actually did."

Chapter Two

Evening breezes began to blow chill through the chintz curtains. The white roses in the dining room wallpaper took on a reddish hue from the setting sun outside, as did Mrs Plackett's ever-pallid complexion. In fact, that rigid and upright lady (who, to be frank, had never been more rigid nor more upright than at this moment) looked positively mauve, as though reflecting the sunny warmth of a summer afternoon.

The rosy sunset made even the mud of Farmer Butts's vast acres of meadowland blaze with heavenly glory as far as the eye could see out the western picture window. His sheep radiated like bright angels. High above and far beyond the Butts farm, Ely Cathedral pressed its two great towers up into the violet sky. The dining room would be rosy for only a few minutes more, and then they'd need to light the lamps, so Stout Alice went down into the kitchen and returned with the kerosene and matches.

"Let's all sit in the parlour and make our plans," Smooth Kitty said.

"Let's all sit in the parlour and drink Mrs Plackett's

medicinal wine, and eat her tinned biscuits," was Disgraceful Mary Jane's reply.

Smooth Kitty opened her mouth as if to reply, then paused. It hit her then, as it had hit all of them, that there was really and truly nothing barring them from the biscuits or the wine, nor from any other hidden treasure at Saint Etheldreda's School.

There was a general stampede to Mrs Plackett's bedroom where, it was well known, the former headmistress kept her medicinal wine and a supply of glasses hidden in a small cupboard next to her bed.

"The bottles are all empty!" Pocked Louise cried. "Worse luck."

"But not the tins of biscuits," Stout Alice sang from the back of the closet, from which she pulled two whole boxes full of Scottish shortbread, and one of Parkinson's Butterscotch.

"We can at least drink the fancy tea with these," Smooth Kitty said. "Come on."

In no time Stout Alice had the kettle heating on the stove, while Pocked Louise lit the lamp. By this time more light was necessary, as both Dear Roberta and Dull Martha had tripped over Mr Godding in the dining room. Dear Roberta, who though not yet fully grown was still the tallest of the bunch, toppled right down onto his body, which was now cool to the touch, and she required a sniff of Mrs Plackett's smelling salts and several extra biscuits before the threat of another faint was averted and her temperament restored to its usual calm sunniness.

"Loosen your corset strings, girls," sang Mary Jane. "Free from rules forever! Elinor, you're rid of that horrid posture back-board. Mrs Plackett can never strap it on you again."

"Let's burn it," said Louise, and before anyone could advise otherwise, she flung the brace Mrs Plackett had insisted Dour Elinor wear, with her elbows looped through its rings, to make her perennially slouching posture straight, into the coal fireplace. Elinor, it must be said, sat erect and alert to watch it burn.

"A toast," Smooth Kitty cried, feeling almost giddy, "to self-government. Saint Etheldreda's School *for* Young Ladies will be run *by* young ladies from this point forward. Hear, hear!" Great applause.

"To independence!" added Pocked Louise. "No fussy old widows telling us when *not* to speak, and how to set the spoons when an Earl's niece comes to supper. And telling us to leave scientific experiments *to the men*." Teacup toasts in support of Louise.

"To freedom!" chimed in Disgraceful Mary Jane. "No curfews and evil eyes and lectures on morals and propriety." Loud, if nervous, cheering.

"To womankind," proclaimed Stout Alice. "Each of us girls free to be what she wishes to be, without glum and crotchety Placketts trying to make us into what we're not." Tremendous excitement.

"To sisterhood," said Dear Roberta, "and standing by each other, no matter what."

This inspired three cheers, and then three more, followed

by many butterscotches and biscuits. They were a merry party indeed.

The west tower bells of Ely Cathedral tolled their rolling chorus for eight o'clock.

The front door bell rang. The girls froze and stared at each other.

"We're ruined!" Dear Roberta cried softly.

"Sunday night callers?" Mary Jane whispered. "Rather late for high tea. Whoever could it be?"

"Look at us, carousing, with bodies strewn about as though we live in a mausoleum," hissed Stout Alice. "How shall that look?"

"Interesting," said Dour Elinor, but no one paid her any heed.

"We shall be caught and blamed for their murders!" Dull Martha sobbed.

"I feel weak . . ." Dear Roberta gasped. "Lightheaded . . ."

Smooth Kitty sprang from her seat. "No, we shan't be caught and blamed," she whispered. "Not unless we behave stupidly. Roberta! Pull yourself together. Louise. Alice. Mary Jane. Get the bodies into Mrs Plackett's room. Wipe the blood off her brother's face and hide him in the armoire. Tuck Mrs Plackett into bed like she's having a little rest. Just to be safe. We must all rally round and work together."

The bell rang again. Stout Alice dimmed the lamps in the parlour while the others each grabbed a cold, stiff arm or leg and helped hoist their corpse down the hall to the bedroom. Smooth Kitty swept biscuit crumbs off the cushions and walked slowly towards the front door.

It was a long, narrow corridor; Mrs Plackett's was a long, rambling house, larger than she had any need for, which was one reason she opened a school. Tonight, it seemed to Kitty, hundreds of doors to hundreds of rooms stretched between her and the ringing doorbell. She shook her head, and the illusion passed.

Kitty could see a silhouette through the sheer window curtain. It was a man, though it might as well have been a barrel with a head on top. For a brief moment she thought of her own father, and paused to steady her nerves. She opened the door to find the massive, stooped, but imposing figure of Admiral Lockwood peering down at her through thick spectacles.

Kitty took an involuntary step back. Admiral Paris Lockwood, once famous for his exploits in Her Majesty's Navy, generally kept to his house in the village, surrounded by relics of his many travels, and, some believed, sacks of money. He had a fearful reputation as a tyrant in Ely. Fishermen claimed they could hear his bellows halfway to Saint Adelaide along the River Great Ouse.

But his voice tonight was a low and gravelly whisper. "Connie?"

Connie? Smooth Kitty had no time to marvel at what this could mean.

"Mrs Plackett has gone to bed," she responded gravely.

The old man shuffled his feet and squinted at Kitty. "That poorly, is she?" He clucked his tongue. "Poor thing. Bit strange, though. O-ho, I see! It's all part of the game!"

Kitty was at a loss. It was a rarity, for her, but it must be noted.

Admiral Lockwood entered and began removing his coat. "Well, we can all still toast the young man's birthday even if the hostess is unwell." He winked. "Here, hold this." He thrust a heavy bottle at her, which she took obediently.

"The . . . young . . . *man's* birthday?"

"Her brother," Admiral Lockwood explained. "Connie invited some friends over to surprise him. Must be I'm the first to come."

Kitty thought perhaps the ground had begun to buckle underneath her feet. That nasty Aldous Godding could be thought of in anyone's estimation as a 'young man' was the least of the shocks poor Kitty now faced.

"Connie said we're to wait in the parlour," the admiral went on, heading down the hall. "It's a surprise party she has in mind. Resting in bed must be part of the ruse." He hung up his coat in the hallway and retrieved his gift from Kitty. "I'll take that. It's a fat bottle of the best Taylor's Vintage Port. You won't find *that* for sale anywhere in Ely, nor even Cambridge. My contribution to the party."

They reached the parlour, and Admiral Lockwood unwrapped and uncorked the bottle. A side-table tray was stocked with glasses, so he took a convenient seat between the table and the fire. He gave Smooth Kitty a shocking wink.

"Tell your headmistress she can stop 'resting' now," he said. "The party's all arriving. Ah! Shortbread biscuits!"

The doorbell rang. Smooth Kitty backed away like one trapped in a nightmare and slipped back down the corridor. The other girls popped their heads out of doorways like anxious rabbits.

"What's happening, Kitty?" Stout Alice whispered.

"Birthday party for Mr Godding!" was Kitty's terse reply. Her schoolmates' eyes widened with terror. The sight of it put some steel back in her spine. Yes, this was an unforeseen inconvenience, but she was not about to throw away her freedom, now that she'd glimpsed it, for fear of a handful of old people sipping birthday wine on a Sunday evening, be it ever so expensive. Fate had failed to reckon properly with the Saint Etheldreda girls.

Kitty reached the door once more. There could be no mistaking this silhouette. Only one person in Ely had such a tall, stout frame and such a long, bald, peanut-shaped head. Feeling as reckless as a condemned criminal, she pulled open the door.

"Good evening, Reverend Rumsey." Smooth Kitty gave a little bow. "How can I help you?"

The vicar at Saint Mary's parish church crouched his great body down to Kitty's level and whispered moistly in her ear. "I've brought *fudge*! I'm not too late for the surprise party, am I?"

"That depends on your point of view."

"Eh? What was that you said?"

Kitty dabbed her ear with her handkerchief and smiled for the vicar. "Not too late at all, Reverend. That was an inspiring sermon you offered today."

Reverend Rumsey beamed. "Ah, yes. 'Nine Tips for Helping Youngsters Pilot Their Vessels Clear of Babylon's Waters.' Second Sunday in May sermon. It's one of my more popular addresses."

"Understandably so. I especially appreciated the warnings about the evils of drink." Kitty led the way to the parlour. "Please excuse Mrs Plackett this evening. She's unwell, but you and your fudge are more than welcome to join Admiral Lockwood in the parlour."

The two men greeted each other. Reverend Rumsey's gaze went immediately to the bottle on the sideboard. He seated himself in the chair nearest to it.

The doorbell rang.

Kitty left the vicar smacking his fishy lips and gazing happily at the glass of port Admiral Lockwood had poured him. She met the other girls in the corridor, each looking frantic.

"How are those bodies coming along?"

"Mr Godding is putting up a fight," Stout Alice whispered.

"Perhaps he knows his birthday party is gathering without him," Kitty muttered.

This time the shadow showed a man in a round hat, apparently checking his watch. Kitty took a deep breath and opened the door.

"Good evening," she said to the figure standing there, stamping his feet on the mat. "How nice to see you, Doctor Snelling."

"That's not what people usually say," the doctor said. "When I come around, people think of sickness, death, and medical bills. The apothecary is my only friend." He pushed past her into the hallway and handed her his hat. "Here."

Kitty moved to block the stout, sweaty man from travelling further in. "Death! What a thing to say. How may I assist you, Doctor?"

Dr Snelling waved impatiently at the hat. "By hanging that up and letting me pass. I'm here to see Mrs Plackett, so we might as well get on with it."

A new terror faced Kitty now. "You mean, you're here for the party, correct?"

Dr Snelling snapped his fingers. "Party! Yes. Forgotten clean about that. Mrs Plackett did mention toasting her brother." He examined his watch again impatiently. "Truth is, your headmistress asked me to stop by a bit before the party to examine her liver complaint. I'm running late, and odds are seven to one Mollie Bennion will deliver her baby before the night is over, or I'm no doctor. I'm giving three to one odds it'll be a boy. I'm always glad to have a friendly word with Mr Godding and wish him a convivial birthday, but tonight I'd better just see Mrs Plackett, and be on my way. Where's your housekeeper tonight?"

"Miss Barnes has the Sabbath day off. I wasn't aware Mrs Plackett was unwell." A bit of a falsehood, her conscience pointed out, but then, Mrs Plackett never had seemed *particularly* unwell. She appeared to pass instantly from her normal irritable state to death.

Dr Snelling waited irritably. "Yes? Well? Are you going to lead me to her?"

Kitty took her time responding. "She's resting." She handed Dr Snelling his hat. "Resting in . . ." She thought to say, *in her bedroom*, but checked herself, ". . . in peace. Perhaps you can stop by again tom—" Again she caught herself. "Stop by again if she summons you in the future. I will be sure to tell her you kept your appointment faithfully."

Dr Snelling peered down at Kitty through his gold-rimmed spectacles, sighed, and attempted a fatherly smile, failing utterly. He patted Kitty on the head, flattening her curls. "Now, my girl, I know you mean well to let your headmistress rest, but she is my patient, and she asked me specifically to inquire after her this evening, so I must be allowed to examine her. Never mind showing me in, I know the way." And with that, he pushed resolutely past Kitty and disappeared into the darkness.

Kitty ran along behind, trying to think of a new plan. She prided herself on plans. But now no plan presented itself, and so she must improvise. Improvisation made her feel cross. She passed the parlour, then the door leading down to the kitchen and larder, and just beyond them she saw Dr Snelling enter the rear room that Mrs Plackett had converted to a downstairs bedroom.

Stout Alice met her in the hallway with a saucer and cup of tea, still steaming from their tea party only a few moments ago, though it felt like hours to Kitty.

"Perhaps you'll need this." Alice offered Kitty the cup.

Smooth Kitty's eyes lit up. "You're brilliant, Alice!" She grabbed the cup. "Come on!"

Both girls entered the dead headmistress's room. The sight of Mrs Plackett's dead form stretched out on the bed, with the covers pulled up to her ribs as if she were merely asleep, gave Kitty a start. Only one candle lit the room, and in its flickering glow Mrs Plackett might indeed only be resting. The flame's motion mimicked the movements of a sleeper's breath. An oil portrait of the late Captain

Martin Plackett, which Mrs Plackett had been known to address in life as though it could answer her, frowned down upon the scene as if only he remained unconvinced by this charade.

The doctor had set his black leather bag on the table next to the bed and reached inside it for gloves and a stethoscope.

"Perhaps you'd like some tea, Doctor?" Smooth Kitty said sweetly, holding out the cup.

Doctor Snelling harrumphed. "Kind of you, but no time for that now." He placed the paddle end of his stethoscope on Mrs Plackett's breastbone.

Kitty pressed the cup against Dr Snelling's free hand. "Sugar?" Some hot tea splashed onto the doctor.

"Ow!"

"Oh, I am most terribly sorry," Kitty purred.

"You burned me!"

Kitty pretended to be flustered, which she felt to be a great sacrifice to her well-ordered reputation. "Clumsy me! I do apologise. Mrs Plackett always told us to offer tea a second time in case guests refused it out of politeness."

Dr Snelling grunted in disgust. Smooth Kitty nearly baptised his waistcoat with the remainder of the tea. Pocked Louise slipped into the room and appeared at the doctor's side.

"May I watch you, Doctor Snelling?" She spoke in low, earnest tones. "I'd love to see a body examined."

Dr Snelling jumped at the sight of her. "A body, did you say?"

"Surely." Pocked Louise never took her eyes from his face. "As a doctor, you examine the bodies of the sick, do you not?"

"Yes, but not with prying schoolgirls watching. What are you, nine years old?"

"I'm twelve," said Louise with great dignity.

"Hmph," said the doctor. He inserted the stethoscope arms into his ears. Kitty held her breath. This was it. Discovery was seconds away. Then Kitty had an idea. She waggled her eyebrows meaningfully at Stout Alice, who looked at her quizzically, then deduced her friend's meaning and hovered directly behind the doctor, breathing loudly.

The doctor frowned and removed his stethoscope. Alice took a quick step back while the doctor tapped the earpieces against his palm. "Odd," he said. "I can hear her, but it's not quite . . . something . . . perhaps these need repair or cleaning."

He turned suddenly and found Alice lurking at his back. He gaped at her. She, not knowing what else to do, folded her hands and stared at the floor.

Kitty's own pulse pounded in her throat. The game was up now. She was out of ideas. This charade was too absurd for words. Any second now Dr Snelling would learn the truth. They would all end up going home. There'd be an inquest and ghastly questions. Admiral Lockwood and Reverend Rumsey would be on the spot as witnesses. She watched the sweat on the doctor's head gleam in the candlelight and waited for the dreaded words to fall from his lips.

The doorbell rang.

Doom was upon them; failure howled at the gate; but there was nothing for Kitty to do but carry out the charade and carry out the summons. She wasn't sure if any of her ancestors had fought in the Battle of Hastings, but there was stern stuff in the Heatons, and Kitty wouldn't let a doorbell defeat her.

Dull Martha, Dear Roberta, and Disgraceful Mary Jane appeared in the doorway to Mrs Plackett's room. "We'll see who it is," Roberta announced.

"More party guests, undoubtedly," Kitty told them. "I think, though, in light of Mrs Plackett's illness, we'd better cancel the party. We'd hate to infect anyone else if her complaint is catching. Will you ask the newcomers to return another day?" The girls nodded knowingly and disappeared.

"Oh, come now, liver complaints aren't catching," Dr Snelling said irritably. "Can we *please* have a bit less hullabaloo in here?"

"Are you sure liver complaints don't spread, Doctor?" Pocked Louise inquired. "I read a fascinating pamphlet from the Royal Society about germs and how they're all around us, too small to see, feeding upon our very bodies, spreading contagion like . . . well, like contagion."

"Liver complaints are not caused by germs. They're caused by weak livers." Dr Snelling wagged his finger in Louise's face. "I don't care what pamphlets you've gotten hold of. Those Royal Society folks do nothing but dither in their laboratories and drink champagne. If you want science, stick to facts, to good trusty medicine."

Pocked Louise pulled a notebook and pencil from her pocket. "I agree completely, Doctor," she said. "It's refreshing to speak to a true man of science. I don't suppose you know my uncle, Doctor Matthew Dudley, the great London surgeon?"

"No, I do not know your blasted uncle! Would you please run along and leave me to my . . ."

"Well, never mind my relatives." Pocked Louise acted as though she couldn't even hear the doctor's rant. "Now, where might I find better liver pamphlets?"

While this scientific discussion was underway, Smooth Kitty elbowed Stout Alice. "Where is Elinor?" she whispered.

Alice pointed towards the bedroom armoire. "In there."

Kitty's jaw dropped. "You don't mean—"

Alice nodded. "Inside. With Mr Godding. He wouldn't stay put otherwise."

Chapter Three

Down the hallway, Dull Martha opened the front door to find Miss Letitia Fringle, the spinster choir mistress, leaning on her polished oak cane.

"Miss Fringle!" Dear Roberta said, with genuine delight. "How nice of you to stop by. Won't you come in? Oh!"

Disgraceful Mary Jane had trodden hard upon Roberta's toe. Dear Roberta's sweet and generous impulses could be a trial at times, especially when they so utterly eclipsed her brain. No power under heaven could evict nosy Miss Fringle from a house where she intended to stay, not once she'd been invited past the threshold. She had that in common with vampires.

"Good evening, girls." Miss Fringle squinted at them as she wobbled over the flagstones. "I'm here for the birthday party. I brought elderberry cordial and a rhubarb tart. *And*, I brought the sheet of practice music I promised to your headmistress. Patricia Rumsey says she's to sing at the social on Wednesday, and *I* say her voice wants coaching."

"I'm so sorry, Miss Fringle," Mary Jane said. "Mrs Plackett is unwell and has taken to bed for the evening."

"Nonsense," Miss Fringle replied. "She invited me for a party, and I expect a party. My niece spent all afternoon baking this tart. Where is Mrs Plackett's brother, anyway? Why she cooked up the idea of a surprise party, I don't know. Surprises can give heart attacks. Well, no matter. Let's go inside. If she's unwell, I shall condole with her."

"I think you really ought not to," Mary Jane persisted. "You could catch a fever."

"Which one are you? Can't see well in this poor light." The choir mistress peered at them each in turn, then addressed Mary Jane. "You're one of the pretty ones. A sight too pretty, I'd say, and that leads to vanity. Give me a plain, clean-living girl any day, like this one." She gestured to Dull Martha, who gasped in wounded astonishment.

"Fringles don't take fevers," the choir mistress continued. "Step aside, girls." Her cane thumped against the floorboards as she advanced down the hall. "How is your tablecloth for the social coming along? The girls at Mrs Usher's school are already done with theirs. *Such* fine work."

Mary Jane sniffed disdainfully. Those Usher girls might stitch well, but they had no sense of style.

"What do we do?" Dear Roberta whispered to Dull Martha. "She mustn't come in."

"Then let's stop her." Without any pause, Dull Martha pursued the old woman and plowed into her side, knocking her cane out from under her.

Mary Jane gasped. "Martha!"

Miss Fringle shrieked. The thin old woman wobbled like a sail in a tempest. Martha caught her before she could truly fall.

"My ankle!" the old woman cried. "Sabotage! Violence! Oh, my poor ankle!"

Doctor Snelling poked his head out from the bedroom. "What's all this? Miss Fringle, what are you doing here?"

"Being attacked by this great oaf of a girl," Miss Fringle answered. "You! What's your name?"

"Martha, Miss Fringle," that young lady obediently replied. "I played the pianoforte at your recital last autumn."

"Then I should think you'd have the cultivation not to gallop like a savage. Doctor, what a mercy you're here. Help me to the sofa in the parlour, and see to this ankle, won't you? Constance won't mind waiting for my sake."

Miss Fringle disentangled herself from Martha, calling her stupid and clumsy and giving her ear a good hard twist, then yielded herself like a frightened damsel into Dr Snelling's knightly care. He guided her into the parlour and called for the girls to fetch him his bag. Admiral Lockwood and Reverend Rumsey leaped to their feet and shouted advice at Dr Snelling. Admiral Lockwood called for splints while Reverend Rumsey determined that the elderberry cordial in Miss Fringle's basket would do just the thing.

Smooth Kitty, still in the bedroom, gathered up Dr Snelling's bag. "Rescue Elinor if you can," she whispered to Stout Alice, then fled from the room where the corpses were and made her way to the party in the parlour.

Disgraceful Mary Jane caught up with Dear Roberta and Dull Martha in the corridor. "Martha, what were you thinking, tackling poor Miss Fringle like that?" Mary Jane hissed. "Just because she called you plain! Women her age are made of eggshells and cobwebs. You could have killed her. Then we'd have yet another body to dispose of."

Dull Martha's eyes filled with tears. "I didn't do it because she called me plain," she sniffed. "Kitty said she mustn't come in. I was trying to help. It wasn't *my* fault Roberta invited her."

Roberta's eyes grew red as well. "It's late at night! How could we not invite the dear old lady in?"

"Nosy old bat is more like it." Mary Jane sighed, then looked at the penitent pair. She put an arm around each of them. "Never mind, my chickadees," she said. "Forgive me for being cross. It's a trying time, and I know we're all doing our best." She steered them both into the bedroom, where they were rejoined by all the other girls, including Dour Elinor, who looked like she'd danced a quadrille with the Grim Reaper before finally managing to get out of the armoire and lock Mr Godding's body in.

Stout Alice brushed dust off Elinor's dress. "Are you all right?"

"Never better," Elinor said briskly. "I found Mr Godding remarkably fit, for a dead man."

Dear Roberta's face took on a greenish hue. "Do you mean you've encountered *other* dead men?"

"Oh, never mind that!" Stout Alice cried. "What's the plan? We need a plan, and soon."

"They have to go," Smooth Kitty replied. "One way or another, Doctor Snelling, Miss Fringle, Reverend Rumsey, and Admiral Lockwood have to go."

"I know where there's some rope," Dour Elinor said.

29

"Heavens! Not that way," Kitty cried. "Let's be sensible, all of us, and use our intelligence."

"I say that we simply do not let them in here," Pocked Louise ventured. "They can't come in, and that's final."

"It's not much of a plan," Disgraceful Mary Jane observed.

"Coo! Coo!"

"What was that?" Dear Roberta gasped.

The girls all froze. The sound, whatever it was, seemed to be coming from outdoors.

"Coo! Coo!"

"A pigeon?" Dull Martha ventured. "A dove?"

"No such luck," Stout Alice said. "A dove coos, it doesn't *say* 'Coo, coo.' It's a person. Out in the garden."

"Probably Henry Butts." Disgraceful Mary Jane tossed her head. "He's always doing idiotic things to get me to notice him. As if I ever would bother. So typical of a farmhand."

"He's not a farmhand. He's the farmer's son," Dull Martha said.

"Precious difference that makes," Mary Jane replied. "Either way, their boots smell like manure, and their hair is full of straw."

"Never mind Henry Butts." Smooth Kitty saw that the agenda of this meeting was in jeopardy, and she had firm feelings about agendas. "We've got to go break up the birthday party. They're bound to wonder where the hostess and the guest of honour are. I'll think of something to say."

"Yes, but keep in mind, when they leave and it comes time to bury Mrs Plackett and Mr Godding, we must make sure there are no Henry Buttses lurking around," Stout Alice said.

They filed back into the parlour where Dr Snelling was just finishing wrapping Miss Fringle's twisted ankle. He might have finished much sooner if she had not flinched and moaned and shuddered at every slight touch upon her stockinged foot. Her performance was stirring, but Dr Snelling, that old medical campaigner, seemed largely unimpressed.

"Just a slight sprain, nothing more," he said. "This bandage will help support it for a day or two. But you mustn't walk on it tonight. You shall have to stay here until a ride can be arranged for you in the morning."

"I could escort you home in my buggy," volunteered Admiral Lockwood, who sat averting his eyes from Miss Fringle's tempting ankle.

"At this hour? No, thank you." Miss Fringle pointed her toes and examined her wounded joint. Dour Elinor would have sworn the sight of it pleased her. "I shall pass the night here and return home in the morning."

Once again Kitty felt the earth sway beneath her feet. *Steady on*, she told herself. It was time to make a speech. She needed a plan, so she made one on the spot, considered it, and pronounced it good. Time to put it in motion. The wiliest member of Parliament could scarcely rival Kitty when it came to nimble thinking.

"If I might interrupt," she said in a clear, firm voice. All the adults present paused to look at her in some surprise. Reverend Rumsey's lips were stained burgundy from the port, and Admiral Lockwood had shortbread crumbs all over his chest. Somehow this helped Kitty feel confident.

She thought of her father, addressing the board of directors of his company, and screwed her courage to its sticking place.

"Thank you all for coming at Mrs Plackett's invitation to celebrate Mr Godding's birthday," she said. "This afternoon, after church, Mrs Plackett and Mr Godding received a distressing message from family members in India. Mr Godding left immediately for London to book passage to India, and Mrs Plackett was so concerned for her brother that she felt faint, and took to her bed to rest." From the corner of her eye Kitty saw Dr Snelling frown. *Liver complaint*, she could almost hear him objecting.

"The shock of the news, compounded with her already weak health, overcame her. I am sure she'll be much better in a day or . . . a week."

"But what was the distressing news?" Reverend Rumsey inquired. "Has someone left this world for a better?"

Two someones have, Kitty thought, *but not the someones you're thinking of.* She racked her brain. She'd overheard a name pass, once, between the headmistress and her brother about a relative in India. But who was it?

"It . . . was . . ."

"Please don't say it was Julius," Miss Fringle implored. "The poor child!"

". . . Julius," Kitty said smoothly. "Yes, the poor little thing. The doctors are gravely concerned for him."

"What does he have?" Dr Snelling asked.

Kitty's eyes met Pocked Louise's. *Help me,* she asked silently. "He . . . has . . . pneu—"

32

"Malaria," Pocked Louise said swiftly.

"Pneumaria?" Admiral Lockwood asked.

"Malaria," Smooth Kitty said emphatically.

Admiral Lockwood stoppered the bottle of port wine. "That's a bad business," he said. "I've seen sailors drop like flies from malaria."

"We shall pray and hope that Mr Godding does not expose himself to infection on this journey," Reverend Rumsey said gravely. "He has been prone at times to overindulge in drink, which can weaken the body."

"Her brother's safety is Mrs Plackett's fervent prayer," Kitty said.

Dr Snelling shook his head. "I wouldn't have pegged Aldous Godding as one to race across the world to a nephew's sickbed."

"He's probably glad of a reason to avoid his bill collectors," Miss Fringle said.

Dr Snelling harrumphed. "Bill collectors have their ways of finding you and your money."

Kitty chose to ignore their speculations about Aldous Godding, Deathbed Sojourner. She'd spun her tale and she would stand by it. "Whatever his reasons, Mr Godding has indeed gone, and Mrs Plackett is . . . affected by it. Please excuse Mrs Plackett for failing to greet you personally. Thank you so much for coming this evening."

Reverend Rumsey and Admiral Lockwood each fortified themselves with butterscotches and rhubarb tart, then made their exits together, after both kissing Miss Fringle's hand with deep gallantry. The choir mistress basked in the attention.

"Oh, young lady?" Admiral Lockwood had poked his head back into the hallway, and now beckoned towards Smooth Kitty.

She went to him. He took several steps down the hall so that no one else could see or hear him, and pulled a small parcel from a pocket within his coat.

He handed it to Kitty. It was surprisingly heavy, about six inches by four, and wrapped in brown paper and twine a bit roughly, as if done by old and shaky hands.

"For your headmistress," he said. "You'll see to it that she receives this, won't you?"

Kitty took the parcel and nodded. "Instantly, the moment she wakes," she said, considering this to be essentially a truthful statement.

The admiral patted her on the head – the second time tonight that an older man had flattened her curls. "There's a good girl." He left.

Kitty resisted her curiosity about the parcel and stowed it in the drawer of a wooden hutch in the hallway, then rejoined the others in the parlour. She found Miss Fringle thumping her cane on the floor.

"Very well, girls. Show me to your headmistress's bedroom."

Dear Roberta began to cough loudly. Dr Snelling patted her vigorously on the back.

"Mrs Plackett is confined to her bed already," began Smooth Kitty.

"And sleeping deeply," added Stout Alice.

"Being seriously ill," said Dour Elinor.

"But nothing that a night's sleep won't cure," added Smooth Kitty, with a nervous glance at the doctor.

"We could help you to an upstairs room," offered Disgraceful Mary Jane.

"You've already helped me to this excruciating injury," Miss Fringle replied. "No, I shan't hazard the stairs. Constance's room will do. I don't take up much space. Captain Plackett bought her a much larger bed than necessary when they married, but I always said he was an extravagant man. There's room for us both." She paused, then lowered her voice as if confiding in the girls. "Captain Plackett bought her a house that was too big, come to think of it, then up and died leaving her in need of pupils to pay its upkeep. But men are never famous for thinking ahead."

Dr Snelling coughed suggestively. "If *you* don't think ahead, Miss Fringle, and give that ankle some rest, I shall order your charming niece to confiscate your shoes and so confine you to your bed. As for extravagance, I recently heard Captain Plackett's wealth from overseas was more than enough to leave Mrs Plackett comfortably off."

"Pah! What wealth?" Miss Fringle snorted. "If there was wealth, I'd know." The girls, exchanging silent glances, agreed. They ate their daily bread on Mrs Plackett's economy, and witnessed how she pinched and scrimped. They were quite certain she possessed no fortune to speak of.

Dr Snelling shrugged. "Idle gossip, perhaps." He gathered his instruments back into his bag and checked his gold watch. "Nothing more to be done for you, Miss Fringle," he said. "Mollie Bennion will have birthed *and* weaned her baby by the time I arrive if I don't leave now, and then how shall I collect my fee? As you say, Mrs Plackett sleeps soundly. I'll leave a sleeping draught for her if she should wake and have trouble settling. See that she gets this, won't you, young ladies?"

All seven young ladies nodded solemnly.

"She'll sleep like the grave," Dour Elinor said.

Disgraceful Mary Jane pinched Elinor where no one could see.

Miss Fringle's eyes narrowed at Elinor's remark, and Kitty worried a bit, but the spinster choir mistress only said, "Stand up straight, my girl. Posture is everything, and you've got a back like a camel."

"Good night, ladies," the doctor said. "I'll return in the morning." He showed himself to the door.

The door banged shut behind him, and the girls found themselves facing Miss Fringle.

"Well?" She banged her cane once more. "Help me up, one of you. Not that one." She glowered at Dull Martha.

Smooth Kitty clutched the packet of sleeping powder in her hand. A glimmer of an idea began to stir.

"Wait a moment, Miss Fringle," she said. "First, let us build up the fire in Mrs Plackett's room. We wouldn't want anything cold to disturb your sleep. I mean, the, er, cold night air. Or the sheets." *Or a cold corpse,* she managed to not say.

Pocked Louise's eyes met Kitty's in alarm. "Should I just go, er, tidy things up in that room a bit first? I left my, um, book in there earlier. When I was . . . reading to Mrs Plackett."

Stout Alice and Disgraceful Mary Jane made jerky movements with their heads in the direction of Mrs Plackett's room.

"No need." Smooth Kitty smiled sweetly at the others, enjoying their looks of terror. "Miss Fringle is aware she'll be sharing a bed with Mrs Plackett." She hoped her meaning would not be missed – they couldn't remove Mrs Plackett now or they'd have to explain her absence. "The two of them will be quite cosy together, once we build up the fire. Now, Miss Fringle, I know you've had a terrible shock to your nerves, being tripped and injured like you were. Let me bring a cup of chamomile to soothe you."

"Don't need soothing," the choir mistress barked. "Always sleep like a lamb. Only takes me half an hour or so to fall asleep."

"Wonderful," Kitty replied. "Did you know, Mrs Plackett's chamomile won a prize at the Ladies' Domestic Arts Council in Northampton last year?"

Miss Fringle's eyes narrowed. "What was she doing all the way over in Northampton? Cambridge isn't good enough for her?"

"It's just that there's such a demand for her prize chamomile." She smiled. "Wait right here. I'll be back in two shakes."

The other girls followed her downstairs to the kitchen. Once there, they shut the door and Kitty shovelled more coal into the cooking stove to heat water for Miss Fringle's chamomile tea.

"I thought she didn't want tea," Dull Martha said.

"She'll be itching to drink it now that you've made up this nonsense prize," Disgraceful Mary Jane said. "Good thinking, Kitty."

"But why?" Dear Roberta inquired. "Why all this fuss over tea?"

"The sleeping powders, obviously." Pocked Louise seized the packet from Kitty's pocket and read the dosing notes Dr Snelling had written. "Must be sure not to over-drug the old lady, or we'll have yet another body to deal with."

"And, oh, Saint Mary's church just wouldn't be church without its choir," Dear Roberta mourned.

"She's not dead yet," Dour Elinor pointed out.

Stout Alice collapsed into a chair. "Birthday party! Darling little Julius! What next?"

"Pish posh. Nothing to it." Smooth Kitty patted Alice on the head. Truth to tell, she was feeling quite smug at the moment. It had been rather a stroke of brilliance, cooking up a trip to India for Mr Godding. That got rid of him for now, and with pneumaria or dipthussis or malonia in the air – Kitty resolved to pay better attention in science class from now on; wait, there'd be no more science class, ever! – they could kill him off permanently from afar. If they could survive this horrendous night, Kitty was sure the young ladies of Saint Etheldreda's School could conquer anything.

"Elinor, will you go build up the fire in the bedroom?" she asked. "We want it nice and toasty so Miss Fringle won't need to snuggle next to a cold corpse for warmth."

"But the light of the fire will make her see Mrs Plackett more clearly," Mary Jane said. "Not if we swipe her spectacles when we tuck her in," Smooth Kitty replied. "We *want* her to see Mrs Plackett. We want her thoroughly convinced she's sleeping with a living Mrs Plackett. In the night, after the fire's died down and the drugs have made Miss Fringle quite unconscious, we'll make the switch and get the body out of there."

"Switch?" Stout Alice inquired. "What will we switch for Mrs Plackett's body, a scarecrow?"

Smooth Kitty studied Stout Alice.

The latter girl took a step backward.

"Oh, no, Kit. You wouldn't."

Smooth Kitty placed her hands on Stout Alice's cheeks and planted a little kiss on her forehead. "No scarecrow, dear," she said. "Promise you'll forgive me for what I'm about to say, but you're simply the best for the job. We shall switch *you* for our dearly departed headmistress."

Chapter Four

Stout Alice ran her hands about her thick middle and sighed. "I only have myself to blame for this, I suppose."

"You're the ideal fit for the task," Smooth Kitty said soothingly. "You're a natural actress. Last Christmas, when we did our tragedy plays, you were . . ."

"Lying in bed sleeping isn't playing Lady Macbeth," Alice said. "No need to try and make nice. I'm the best *fit* for the job because I'm the best *fit* for Mrs Plackett's clothes. I even have her horrid double chin." Stout Alice composed herself bravely. "Never mind. I'd better go find one of her nightgowns and caps, and try not to think about having the figure of a sixty-year-old woman."

"Your complexion's much nicer," Pocked Louise called after her retreating form, but Alice ignored her. Dour Elinor slipped away to build up the bedroom fire.

Pocked Louise handed Smooth Kitty a cup of chamomile tea. "Here you are. Brewed to perfection and laced with sleeping draught. Miss Fringle will snore like a hound in no time. I'll go clear up the dining room table. All our dinner things are still there."

Dull Martha stretched her arms high above her head and yawned. "I'm absolutely worn to death. Oh! What an unfortunate thing to say today." She poured hot water from the kettle into the dishpan. "I'd better get washing up so we can all get to bed."

"Never mind, Martha," Disgraceful Mary Jane said. "You cooked today, so I'll wash. Off you go to bed."

A lovely light filled Dull Martha's eyes as she gazed at the older girl. "Oh, would you? Thanks awfully. I'll owe you."

"Not a bit, my little mouse. Trundle off, now. You too, Roberta. Nighty-night."

When both girls had trudged up the stairs, Smooth Kitty took a long look at Disgraceful Mary Jane. "That was kind of you."

Mary Jane shook her head and scrubbed some soap onto her dishwashing brush. "Penance. I was a beast to them earlier when they let Miss Fringle in and then tripped her."

Kitty laughed and banked down the stove for the night. "We're lucky they did. They saved our skins. Dr Snelling was just about to discover Mrs Plackett was no longer with us."

"Bless that poor dear Martha," Mary Jane said. "She's gone and used every pan in the house to cook dinner, I think. Here's one for the beans, and here's another for potatoes. One for boiled onions, and three for the veal! A roaster, and . . . these tiny frypans look like a doll should use them."

"She's a bit of a doll herself. Pretty and . . ."

"A head full of fluff."

"Ssh!"

41

"You started it." Disgraceful Mary Jane grinned. "Miss Fringle called her 'plain' tonight."

"Of all the nerve!" cried Kitty. "Wait. Before or after Martha tripped her? Never mind. Don't answer that." She seized the teacup and headed for the parlour, where a fidgety Miss Fringle awaited her.

"What took so long?" she demanded. "Constance Plackett would never keep an injured guest waiting like this."

Kitty smiled with all her teeth. *Call our Martha plain, will you?* "I apologise, Miss Fringle. We were fixing some tea and warming up your room. Have a nice cup, now, why don't you, and then I'll show you to Mrs Plackett's room."

"I don't need to be shown. I just need someone's arm to lean on, since that idiot girl plowed me over." Miss Fringle took a deep draught of chamomile tea and smacked her lips thoughtfully. "First prize in Northampton, did you say? They must have strange tastes over that way. This has a distinctly bitter overtone."

"Perhaps life is bitter in Northampton," Kitty mused. "Bitter tea appeals to them."

"I shouldn't wonder."

Smooth Kitty helped Miss Fringle to her feet and steered her slowly to the bedroom. On their way to the bed, she spied some wads of cotton wool in a china dish on Mrs Plackett's dressing table, and had one of the bursts of inspiration for which she prided herself.

"Here, Miss Fringle," she said, handing two pieces of cotton wool to the choir mistress, "you'll want these for your ears. Mrs Plackett, truth be told, is quite a noisy sleeper."

Miss Fringle sat on the edge of the bed. "Help me with my boots, there's a good girl." She craned her neck to peer at Mrs Plackett. "She's quiet enough now, I'd say."

"She always starts her snoring phase after midnight," Kitty replied.

"Snoring! I detest snorers. My father, rest his soul, used to shake the roof." She wadded the cotton pads into her ears. "It's one of the reasons I thank the Lord I never married." She yawned deeply. Her eyelids began to droop. "Mercy, I *am* tired. Must be the shock of that vicious attack catching up with me."

Kitty smiled to see the sleeping powders take hold. With the cotton wool in Miss Fringle's ears, even if the sleeping drugs didn't do their job, the old biddy would be less likely to wake up when they moved the corpse.

"May I take your spectacles for you?" Kitty asked.

Miss Fringle folded up her eyeglasses. "See that you put them where I can reach them in the night," she said. "I'm quite blind without them."

"Of course," Smooth Kitty purred. She slipped them into her dress pocket. "They'll be right here on this night stand."

She waited upon the old lady until she was comfortably unbuttoned and tucked into bed, practically half asleep already, then blew out the lamps and bid her goodnight.

She found the other girls congregating in the parlour. Dear Roberta and Dull Martha had already gone to bed in the room they shared. Disgraceful Mary Jane, Pocked Louise, and Dour Elinor had all changed into their nightgowns, and poor unfortunate Stout Alice had changed into one of Mrs

Plackett's. She sat with shoulders rounded and a drooping lower chin, just as their former headmistress always used to.

"That's Mrs Plackett to perfection!" Pocked Louise giggled. "You really have a talent, Alice."

"Off to bed with you, Miss Dudley," Alice said in a spot-on imitation of Mrs Plackett's cross voice. "Remember: beauty, that jewel to which every young lady should aspire, and you in particular, Miss Dudley, comes from taking adequate rest."

Louise laughed. "I was so sick of her carping on about my ugly skin. What does a scientist care if her skin is pocked?" Her face grew worried. "Say, you don't mean it, do you? About bedtime? Because I can stay up as late as the rest of you, if I want to!"

Stout Alice ignored this and scratched her side morosely.

Disgraceful Mary Jane shuddered. "Ugh, her horrid scratching. It's a wonder she ever made a man want to marry her."

"Perhaps the Captain was also a scratcher," Dour Elinor said. "Those seafaring men catch fleas from rats. Perhaps they scratched one another."

"Coo! Coo!"

They gazed out the dark window towards the garden from where the sound came.

"Henry Butts will get an earful from me in the morning," Disgraceful Mary Jane said.

"First thing we should do, I think, in our life without adults, is get a bulldog," Stout Alice declared. "Someone to scare away farm boys and intruders, and bite policemen."

"Not if the policemen are handsome," Mary Jane said.

"But what if it isn't Henry Butts out there?" Dour Elinor said. "What if it's someone with more sinister intentions?"

Disgraceful Mary Jane began unpinning her braids. "If it was, they wouldn't coo their fool heads off."

Stout Alice shook her head. "I still can't believe it. Murders. Two of them, right under our noses."

"I know." Dour Elinor shivered. "Isn't it marvellous?"

Stout Alice sniffed in disgust. Then she sniffed again and pinched a fold of her headmistress's nightgown to her nose. "Eugh. This smells of Mrs Plackett. After a long afternoon in the vegetable garden."

"Take heart," Smooth Kitty said. "By tomorrow Mrs Plackett and her odours will be resting in the vegetable garden permanently. We'll launder all her clothes."

"Shouldn't Louise and I perform an autopsy first?" Dour Elinor inquired. "I can handle the bodies, and Louise can test the specimens."

Disgraceful Mary Jane clutched at her stomach. "Really, Elinor," she snapped. "Sometimes you go too far. 'Handle the bodies'? Even Constance Contrary and her ghastly brother, Aldous the Arch-fiend, deserve at least enough respect not to be mangled by school-maidens before they reach their eternal rest. Chop them open to find . . . what? Daggers in their bellies?"

A wild light flashed in Dour Elinor's heavy-lidded dark eyes. "Poisons," she said. "Once they're buried in the gardens, crucial evidence goes with them, lost forever."

Pocked Louise sat upright. "Oh! What's the matter with me?"

They all stared at her. "I don't know, dear, what *is* the matter with you?" Smooth Kitty asked.

"Poisons. Evidence. Of course, of course!" She gripped the armrests of her chair feverishly. "The food. When we cleaned up dinner, what did we do with the food?"

"Scraped it into the slop bucket like always," Disgraceful Mary Jane replied. "Calm down, little Louise. I dumped it on the compost pile while Kitty took Miss Fringle her tea."

Pocked Louise sprang to her feet. "Come on! There's not a moment to lose!"

She grabbed a candle, lit it in the coal embers of the parlour fire, and ran downstairs to the kitchen and from there, outside in her bare feet. The bewildered older girls followed suit and brought candles with them.

Chill evening air caught the girls like a slap in the face after the drowsy warmth of the parlour. The grass was scratchy and damp with dew on their bare feet. When church bells rang out for ten o'clock, all the girls jumped. Their short walk to the compost heap suddenly felt pregnant with danger.

"Watch out for Henry Butts," Disgraceful Mary Jane warned. "If he tries to kiss me I'll stab him with a pitchfork." She paused. "Unless, perhaps, he's a nice kisser, in which case I'll wait a minute or two, and then stab him . . ."

"Hush with your foolish kissing talk," Stout Alice panted. "Louise, we all ate the food. If it was poisoned, wouldn't we all be . . . Oh! Of course. The veal!"

They stopped in their tracks, looking like a ring of ghosts in the dark night, with wavering candlelight playing over their pale faces and nightdresses.

46

"Martha cooked the veal," Smooth Kitty whispered.

Stout Alice shook her head slowly. "She *wouldn't*."

"She couldn't!" Disgraceful Mary Jane cried.

"By accident she could," said Dour Elinor ominously.

"She didn't!" Alice insisted.

"Come on." Pocked Louise urged them onward. "We must find that veal."

"It'll be revolting now, all mushed up with the compost and cold gravy and slimy beans." Disgraceful Mary Jane grimaced at the thought.

They reached the compost pile, hidden behind the woodshed, where its odours wouldn't reach the chairs by the flowerbeds in the sunny back garden. Here there was no trace of light from the parlour windows, and the girls' candles could scarcely penetrate the thick darkness. The compost pile was a blur of indistinct rottenness, and the smell made their stomachs clench.

"This won't do," Smooth Kitty exclaimed. "I can't see a thing in all this mush. Mary Jane, do you remember where you dumped tonight's bucket?"

"Never mind." Pocked Louise had squatted down some feet away from the edge of the pile. Dour Elinor crouched beside her. "We have what we need."

A frigid wind blew over them, snuffing out several candles.

"What is it?" Smooth Kitty cried, then immediately felt ashamed of the fear in her voice.

"A stoat, with a piece of veal in its mouth," Pocked Louise announced with scientific neutrality. "I trod on its fur."

Dour Elinor supplied the vital detail. "It's dead."

Chapter Five

"Poor little thing," Stout Alice said. She dabbed her eyes with Mrs Plackett's nightgown sleeve.

"Hardly," Disgraceful Mary Jane said. "That stoat's probably the one that's been making off with our baby chicks."

"Justice will find you in the end," Dour Elinor declared.

"Just like it did Mrs Plackett and Mr Godding?" Pocked Louise asked.

"Oh, let's go inside," Disgraceful Mary Jane exclaimed. "I'm sick and tired of this whole business. It's a wretched dead rodent, for heaven's sake."

"Technically it's not a rodent." Louise pried the stoat's jaws apart and wrestled the morsel of meat from its vicious teeth. "It's a member of the weasel family." She peered over the rest of the compost pile, snagged the other piece of slimy fried veal, and wrapped it in a handkerchief. Then they trudged back towards the house, by now with only one lit candle, Kitty's, among them.

"Hsst!" Kitty threw an arm back to block the other girls from advancing, and quickly blew out her light. "*Don't move.*"

They waited, silent and watchful.

Stout Alice felt a curious tingly terror run up her spine and wondered if she might lose control of herself and start to scream. *Odd*, she thought. *I'm not the fanciful sort. Could it be ghosts? Rubbish. But what, if not?* How would Mrs Plackett's ghost feel to discover Alice impersonating the dead and making off with her clothes? *Any more of this, my girl*, she scolded herself, *and it'll be the sanatorium for you.*

They waited. A thin crescent moon peeked through a gap in thick-covering clouds. Pocked Louise listened to the silence till her ears itched. What had Kitty heard or seen?

Then they heard it. A snap, sharp as a drumbeat. A breaking twig.

Something moved in the dark. They sensed rather than saw it. Then there was no doubting it. Footsteps ran away, crashing through brambles and brush, helter-skelter towards the Butts farm.

Tension drained from the group like sand from a broken hourglass. "It's only stupid Henry," Disgraceful Mary Jane said. "We had nothing to fear."

"But did he hear us?" Dour Elinor whispered. "*We spoke freely of death!*"

Smooth Kitty kicked at a tuft of grass with her bare toes. She should have known better. She should have foreseen this. As someone who prided herself on leadership, on management, on remembering every detail, this whole business had grown terribly sloppy.

"Those footsteps sounded fairly far away," Stout Alice said. "I think we can comfortably assume Henry didn't hear us. If he did, he probably wouldn't have understood it all."

"See? I told you he's stupid," Mary Jane said.

"I didn't mean that," Alice said. "I meant, without context, our words would make little sense to him . . . oh, never mind."

They reached the door and went inside. Their nightgowns were wet to the knees with dew from the tall grasses. The young ladies sat by the coals in the parlour fireplace for several minutes to dry out. No one spoke.

"Well, here I go," Stout Alice said at last. "Time for me to crawl into bed with Miss Fringle, on the very spot where a dead woman has lain. At least I'm spared your job of hauling her away somewhere and hiding her. Where will you stuff the old girl?"

Smooth Kitty was happy to stop worrying for a moment whether or not Henry Butts had heard all. "Oh I already have that figured out," she said. "We'll carry her upstairs to your bed."

Pocked Louise and Dour Elinor retired to the bedroom they shared with Stout Alice while the older girl remained downstairs in the parlour, waiting to change beds with Mrs Plackett's body. Louise crawled in between her chilly sheets and wrapped her arms around her knees. "Are you worried a bit, Elinor?" she asked her roommate.

Dour Elinor combed slow strokes through her long black hair. "About what?"

Louise shrugged. "Oh, I don't know. About murder, I suppose."

Elinor's comb caught upon a snarl. "I don't think so," she said. "Murder doesn't pay much heed to who's worried about it or not. The Grim Reaper always collects his prize in the end."

Pocked Louise rolled her eyes. It was so frustrating, sometimes, trying to talk to Elinor. "What if it was one of us?" she asked. "Do you think it's possible?"

Elinor rose and stretched. "Of course I do." Her nightgown rustled as she blew out their candle and climbed into the upper bunk of their bed. "Anything is possible."

"Then who?"

"I don't know. Whom do you suspect?"

Louise shuddered. "'Suspect'! It's such a serious word. I wouldn't dare to suspect anyone. Not without evidence."

Elinor lowered her head down over the edge of her bed. Her hair hung down almost to the top of Louise's bed, a swaying curtain that glistened in the wavery moonlight. "I won't tell a soul what you say," she said. "It's not suspecting. It's just asking the question. A scientist asks questions to find the truth, don't you think?"

Louise slid down under her covers. "Yes . . . naturally."

"Then what questions occur to you?"

This, Louise felt certain, was one of those times when saying nothing would be the wisest policy. But Elinor *did* promise to keep her words secret. And it wasn't often that the older girls seemed this interested in Louise's opinions. This was murder, after all. What if she said nothing, and then poor Elinor was the next to fall? Louise could never forgive herself.

"I don't know anything," Louise whispered. "Not a thing. Not a single clue." She took a deep breath. "But doesn't it seem rather strange to you how quick Kitty was to take charge of things?" She heard Elinor's soft intake of breath and plowed ahead. "I mean . . . this idea of running the school all by ourselves. It seemed so . . . almost premeditated. Almost as if Kitty had been thinking of and planning this for a long time."

Elinor nodded her dangling head, sending her hair undulating.

"That's not suspicion, of course," Louise said. "It's just a question I have."

"I know." Elinor pulled her head back up and lay down upon her bed.

Footsteps down the hall made them both pause. Someone creeping down the hall after dark, and tonight . . . Louise's pulse raced. She slipped out of bed to listen at the door. She breathed a sigh of relief. "It's only Kitty and Mary Jane," she said, then blushed to think of all she'd just said. "They're bringing us the body."

Smooth Kitty woke at four o'clock in the morning, when nothing but a sable stripe along the eastern horizon suggested morning would come. After a late evening spent deep in calculating thoughts and plans, she'd had less than three hours of sleep, but Kitty was blessed with the knack of waking whenever she had predetermined to – to the precise minute. Any less control over her person would have been unacceptable to her well-ordered mind.

She shook Disgraceful Mary Jane awake. The older girl did not rouse easily. Her chestnut curls spilled over her pillow like a waterfall. *It's a shame she's so disgraceful,* Kitty thought. *She really is quite lovely. Then again,* Kitty considered, *perhaps moral rectitude and dazzling beauty could scarcely coexist in the same person. Not, at any rate, in a person like Mary Jane.*

"Mary Jane," Kitty whispered. "Time to go grave digging."

"Whatever you say, Reggie," Mary Jane murmured. "Mamma will never know."

"Not Reggie. *Kitty,*" said that young lady firmly. "Wake up!"

"Hmph?" Mary Jane's eyes opened reluctantly. She squinted at Kitty's offensive candle, scowled, and rolled herself out of bed. "Did I hear you say 'grave digging,' or was I having a nightmare?"

Kitty pulled her gardening frock over her shift and reached for yesterday's stockings. No use soiling today's before the sun was even properly up. "This whole excursion is a nightmare, I suppose," she said, "but we must keep our eyes on the prize. Independence! Freedom from tyranny at home and at school. We shall form a perfect utopia of young womanhood right here at Saint Etheldreda's School. It's fitting, don't you think? Saint Etheldreda, the Maiden Saint?"

"Fitting for some," Mary Jane grumbled. "Though why someone who was married twice should be sainted for remaining a maiden is more than I can figure out. *I* think she must have had revolting breath, and that's the real explanation for her virtue." She buttoned her gardening frock. "I thought one usually hired experts with stooping shoulders and strong backs to dig graves. Not young ladies studying French literature and social dancing."

It was slow going, rousing Dull Martha and Dear Roberta from their sleep, and Martha required explanations and re-explanations of what had transpired the prior evening, as she had convinced herself in her fitful sleep that it was all a terrible dream. The revelation that it was not a dream brought new tears afresh, and hinted hysterics from Dear Roberta. All in all it took another three quarters of an hour to get all the girls ready to begin their funereal task.

Dour Elinor and Pocked Louise had shown remarkable fortitude in sharing their bedroom with dead Mrs Plackett without complaint. Louise was much too scientific and rational to be affected by a corpse in her room, whereas, truth be told, Elinor rather liked the experience. It held for her an aesthetic appeal akin to that which connoisseurs appreciate in an exquisite cheese. "Death is ever near," she was often wont to say, and it now brought her great satisfaction having Mrs Plackett join their dormitory as a specimen of dying proof.

All the girls but Stout Alice joined the grave-digging party, as she was still bravely occupied in Mrs Plackett's bed, maintaining illusions for Miss Fringle. The rest tiptoed down the stairs in their stocking feet and out the kitchen door, slipping on their wellingtons as they stepped outside. Dear Roberta rubbed her bare arms and shivered. The morning was grey and damp, with a mist rising off the fields and baptizing the grasses with water droplets. No houses or buildings nearby could be seen, except the mighty cathedral's towers, rising through the fleecy fog as though surrounded by heavenly clouds of glory.

The girls caught a rabbit unawares in the vegetable garden, chewing dandelions. It stared at them as if in a dream, then bolted for the cover of nearby bushes. Mr Shambles, the school's resident rooster, stalked his way towards them through the damp grass and paused to crow indignantly.

"Quiet, Mr Shambles!" Pocked Louise whispered. "The sun's not up yet, and neither are the neighbours, so keep still!"

Mr Shambles, not the least perturbed, pecked a fat slug and ate it.

The girls found their shovels in the shed, one for each of them, as Mrs Plackett had been a great believer in the wholesome virtues of gardening for young ladies. They selected an out-of-the-way corner behind the kitchen, near a stand of shrubs, and stood in a loose rectangle enclosing an area Smooth Kitty reckoned ought to accommodate two corpses, side by side.

It seemed a solemn occasion to Dear Roberta. The pearl-grey dawn air felt thick with significance. "Oughtn't someone to say some words?" she asked.

"Yes," Disgraceful Mary Jane replied. "How about these: 'Let's get this over with quickly.'" She plunged her shovel blade into the ground and wrenched away the first load of heavy red clay.

They rallied round and followed Mary Jane's example. After some confusion about where to throw the dirt, they soon made excellent progress, though Smooth Kitty couldn't help worrying that the scrape of the shovels against the soil sounded much louder, really, than it ought to, and mightn't they be heard? Dear Roberta's shovel sliced a fat worm in half, and she cried a little for the poor creature, until Dour Elinor pointed out that dead human beings were the purpose of this hole, and oughtn't she to grieve more for them than for worms? At which Dear Roberta realised that their dead headmistress and her dead brother would be laid to rest in the immediate vicinity of many worms, which would make breakfast, luncheon, tea, and supper off their moldering flesh for weeks to come, without so much as the satin lining of a coffin to protect them, and she declared that she'd lost her appetite forever.

"Never mind your appetite," Disgraceful Mary Jane said. "Dig quickly and dig deeply, for pity's sake."

Soil in springtime is stubborn and claylike soil all the more so. After the first layer of sod had been spaded off, they found deeper levels to be rough going, with gnarled roots from a pear tree some feet away snarling up the operation, and the sheer weight and composition of the soil vexing their work. Despite the cool foggy morning air, Smooth Kitty found perspiration running down her face and sides, but she ignored this stoically and urged the other girls to do the same. They could bathe soon enough.

"Can you imagine what Mrs Plackett would say if she could see us now?" asked Smooth Kitty.

"'Put your backs into it, you lazy girls,'" mimicked Disgraceful Mary Jane.

"'But mind your dresses,'" Kitty said.

"'And stand up straight,'" Dour Elinor added for good measure.

"She did like to see us gardening," offered Dear Roberta.

"Correct." Mary Jane heaved an unruly load of soil. "She liked us to weed and plant her flowerbeds. It saved her the trouble of hiring someone."

"Here's what she can't say to us afterwards," said Kitty. "'Only half a slice of toast per girl.' From now on, ladies, she can't starve us anymore."

The digging progressed at a discouraging pace. Their hands blistered, yet still the hole seemed far too shallow.

So engrossed were they in their task that they barely noticed when Mr Shambles flapped up off the ground in alarm. A lanky lump of curly brown fur shot past where he'd stood pecking a moment before.

"Good morning, Brutus," Dull Martha said, stopping to scratch the panting Bingley terrier under his bearded chin. "Did you catch any rats today?"

"Oh, no!" Pocked Louise moaned. "Where Brutus is, Henry Butts cannot be far behind."

And sure enough, a young man in thick leather boots and a wide straw hat strolled into the gardens a moment later. He paused at the sight of them all, stumbled back, and flushed violet in the cheeks. Pocked Louise and Dear Roberta hid their shovels behind their backs. Dour Elinor rolled her eyes and went on digging. Brutus joined in the fun and sent a spray of soil flying out from his paws. Dull Martha's glasses somehow fell from her nose and landed in her dress pocket, out of sight.

"I'll handle this," Disgraceful Mary Jane whispered, and curtseyed sweetly. She gestured to Elinor to halt her digging. "Good morning, Mr Butts. What brings you out so early on this lovely May morning?"

"I . . . uh . . . morning . . . I . . . message . . ." Poor Henry eyed the onlooking females like a cornered mouse might eye a bevy of cats.

Disgraceful Mary Jane laid her slim white hand on his shoulder. "My, but you are a hard worker. Up before dawn to pitch straw for the cows?"

"Hay." This topic of conversation drew nearer to Henry's expertise. "Milking's first thing."

"How charmingly rustic." Mary Jane flashed a dimpled smile at Henry, a calibre of weapon that had brought much stronger men to their knees. "What brings you all this way over to see us this morning?"

Dull Martha watched Mary Jane perform with something almost like envy. Mary Jane had a knack for saying "to see us" in a way that clearly implied "to see me." These powers were the reason, Martha felt, Mary Jane was certain to die a duchess.

Henry Butts swallowed several times until he was ready to give his answer. "I needed to tell you. Last night. Someone. In your garden."

Kitty, Mary Jane, Louise, and Elinor exchanged sly smiles. "Indeed," Smooth Kitty said. "What were you doing in our gardens last night?"

Henry shook his head adamantly. "Not me," he said. "I'm not talking about me. Someone else."

Disgraceful Mary Jane tapped Henry playfully on his shirt buttons. "But in order to know about it, you must have been in our gardens as well."

His violet cheeks went straight to fuchsia. "It was B-Brutus," he said. "Chasing coneys. I didn't want his barking to disturb you young ladies." Henry looked about him for help, and his eyes fell upon less intimidating faces. "Good morning, Miss Roberta, Miss Martha," he said, nodding and doffing his hat. He suddenly realised he hadn't removed it as soon as he met the ladies, and thrust the offending headgear behind his back to hide its shame.

There they stood, six young ladies with shovels behind their backs, and one young man with a hat behind his.

They looked at one another.

Henry looked at Brutus, still digging at a furious rate, for which Pocked Louise inwardly blessed him. She wondered if treats and table scraps might induce him to excavate the entire grave.

"What are you doing?" Henry asked.

Several voices responded in chorus.

"Doing?"

"Doing," Henry insisted, "with the shovels."

"Oh these," Mary Jane answered.

Quick-thinking Kitty supplied an answer. "Digging," she said.

"Yes, but why?"

Once more the answers tumbled out in a simultaneous heap.

"Exercise," said Disgraceful Mary Jane.

"Worms," said Dour Elinor.

"Soil research," said Pocked Louise.

"Gardening," said Dear Roberta.

"Kitty said to," said Dull Martha.

The girls exchanged nervous glances. Henry's brow furrowed in deep concentration.

"Exactly." Smooth Kitty nodded.

Henry Butts blinked. "Exactly what?"

"Exactly as I said," she replied. "We're planting a tree."

Henry scratched his scalp. "Did you say that?"

"Naturally." Smooth Kitty found Henry Butts to be easy prey. It didn't require Disgraceful Mary Jane's charms to manipulate him.

"Autumn's a better time to plant a tree," Henry Butts pointed out.

"I knew we should have consulted with you, Henry." Disgraceful Mary Jane beamed at him.

"Nevertheless, we are planting a tree now." Smooth Kitty laid the matter to rest. "We are planting a cherry tree."

This galvanised Henry Butts into excited action. "Then you'll want manure," he cried. "I'll be back in a few minutes with a heaping load." And, whistling to Brutus, he turned and bolted off down the brambly stretch of Prickwillow Road that connected Saint Etheldreda's with the Butts Farm.

"Isn't that thoughtful of him to fetch us manure?" Dull Martha said wistfully. "He's a generous person."

"Oh yes." Disgraceful Mary Jane sneered. "So generous he's going to bring us boatloads of smelly manure for our very own."

"In which we will bury Mrs Plackett and Mr Godding," Pocked Louise pointed out.

The girls froze.

Disgraceful Mary Jane was the first to snort.

Dear Roberta tried hard not to laugh but even she couldn't help it.

"Farewell, Old Stinky Face," Smooth Kitty declared. "If you hadn't been such a sourpuss to us, we would have said no to Butts Farm manure as your eternal rest. Come, girls. We must finish quickly."

They heaved into the work once more with grim determination.

"Do you suppose Henry really did see someone here last night?" Dear Roberta inquired.

Disgraceful Mary Jane laughed lightly. "Certainly he did. His own shadow."

Dull Martha pushed her hair out of her eyes, which left a muddy smudge across her forehead. "If he only saw himself, why would he bother to come and tell us?"

"Maybe," Pocked Louise said, "he saw us last night and thought we were the intruders."

"That makes sense." Smooth Kitty nodded.

"But we heard the cooing sound the first time well before then," Dour Elinor pointed out.

Mary Jane, who was stronger than she looked, heaved a heavy rock loose from the claybed. It released its hold on the soil with a loud *schlock*. "I'm certain it was him," she declared. "He spies on us all a good deal more than you realise. I've even seen him point his mother's opera glasses our way." She wrestled the melon-sized stone out of the hole, which was finally beginning to look like a grave. "Who else could it have been?"

Dour Elinor's spade sliced through a shaft of pear tree roots. "The murderer."

Chapter Six

The grave was nearly dug when Henry Butts returned with his wheelbarrow heaped with pungent manure.

"We are truly in your debt, Henry." Smooth Kitty curtseyed for his benefit. "I wonder if we might trouble you for one more favour?"

Henry fumbled his hat off his head, leaving his sandy hair sticking every which way. "What can I do for you, Miss Katherine?"

Kitty slipped her arm through his and steered him towards his home. Farming, she noted, does no harm to one's muscles. "You know dear Miss Fringle, of course? The choir mistress?"

Henry nodded.

"She visited us last evening and twisted her ankle. She passed the night at the school with us because she was in no state to walk home. I wonder if you'd be willing to drive her home in your handsome little cart."

"Of course." Henry looked relieved once again to have something to do other than visit with the young ladies. "Let me go wash and hitch up your pony, and I'll be right back."

Henry and Brutus bolted off through the leafy path towards the farm, and the young ladies put their shovels away for the moment.

"Time to wake Alice up, before Miss Fringle rouses and begins asking her questions," Smooth Kitty said.

They left their muddy boots at the door, hurried softly indoors, and washed their hands in the kitchen. Kitty went upstairs and slipped into Mrs Plackett's bedroom, prepared to whisper Stout Alice into wakefulness, and found to her surprise that Alice and Miss Fringle were deep in conversation.

"Oh! Excuse me, I didn't mean to intrude," Kitty stammered.

"Not at all, young lady," Miss Fringle said. "Your headmistress and I were just having a bit of a chitchat about poor Julius and his uncle, Mr Godding."

"I see," Kitty said slowly. And she did see. Stout Alice lay with her back turned slightly towards Miss Fringle, and her face pointed towards the doorway where Kitty stood. Alice appeared to be working hard not to laugh. Miss Fringle looked like another creature altogether with her grey hair rumpled on the pillow, and her spectacles missing.

"Reach me my glasses, young lady," Miss Fringle ordered. Smooth Kitty slipped them from her pocket before the choir mistress could discover that they'd never been on the nightstand.

Kitty returned to Alice's side of the bed. "Now, Mrs Plackett, dear," she said, "do let me help you up. There's a

64

matter in the kitchen that I wish to discuss with you before Miss Barnes arrives for her day's work." Kitty pretended to assist Stout Alice up and out of bed, making sure that Miss Fringle, whose powers of vision were restored, had no opportunity to see her face.

They made it out of the room, and Kitty closed the door. Stout Alice shook with suppressed laughter.

"Lady Macbeth, am I?" she declared once out of hearing range. "I don't care what Grandmother says. I *will* pursue a career on stage!"

The other girls clustered round Alice in the downstairs kitchen to hear how she'd managed it. Alice told them how she and Miss Fringle had carried on a conversation for nearly an hour, ranging in subject from Mrs Plackett's dead husband, Captain Plackett, to her two brothers, Geoffrey and Aldous, and Geoffrey's dear son Julius. Miss Fringle had shown no shortage of scorn for Aldous – he was known to gamble! – and Alice's parody of the choir mistress's diatribe on his vices was highly amusing.

"She kept saying, 'I know he's your brother, but it's my duty to warn you of his dissolute ways, and I don't mind saying it to your own face!' Yet all the while she never had a glimpse of my face. Smart old puss!" Stout Alice shook with laughter.

"Oh, well done, Alice, well done!" Disgraceful Mary Jane cried. "Bravely executed."

Alice took a bow.

"A gambler, was he?" Smooth Kitty mused. "How very interesting. You don't suppose . . ."

"Suppose what?" inquired Disgraceful Mary Jane.

"Well, he was murdered, after all," supplied Pocked Louise.

"Sssh!" Kitty hissed. "She'll hear us!"

Louise ignored this. "He was murdered. Could there be a connection? Over gambling debts, perhaps?"

"Only if Mrs Plackett was a gambler, too," snorted Mary Jane. "I can see her now, all dressed in silks and feathers, at the casinos on the Riviera . . ."

Pocked Louise considered this most unlikely image. Mrs Plackett, a gambler? Mary Jane, on the other hand, fit perfectly into the glittering splendour of the roulette table.

"At any rate, now we know who Julius is," Stout Alice observed. "That's bound to come in useful."

"Hurry now, girls, we have no time," Kitty said, catching sight of the kitchen clock. "Amanda Barnes will be here before we know it, and we need a plan. For right now, Roberta, dear, would you fix some bread and butter and preserves for Miss Fringle? And Martha, would you heat some water for tea in case there's time before Henry returns? Alice, you run upstairs so there's no chance Miss Fringle will see you, and change into your own clothes. Elinor, Louise, find some old sheets we can use to wrap up the bodies. We need to get them out of sight the minute Henry's taken Miss Fringle home."

Each young lady ran to follow Kitty's instructions. Dull Martha and Dear Roberta prepared breakfast for Miss Fringle, and Disgraceful Mary Jane, not quite trusting them fully, delivered it to the invalid. Alice changed quickly, glad to be rid of her headmistress's nightgown, and was downstairs as her own person when Henry Butts arrived to collect Miss Fringle. He led the choir mistress on his own strong arm to the cart and seated her comfortably. Pocked Louise appeared and announced her intention of riding along as far as the village. She had some purchases to make at the chemist's shop, she said.

"Fine, fine," Kitty pulled Louise aside and whispered into her ear. "Purchase a young cherry tree if you can."

"Where?" Louise asked. "What if they don't sell them at this time of year?"

"Try the nursery shop, and if that fails, think of something," was Kitty's unhelpful reply. "We're stuck now. We've got to plant a tree this morning."

Louise climbed in the cart behind Miss Fringle, and the party set off for Ely. Disgraceful Mary Jane had lugged and toppled Mr Godding out of the armoire before the pony's tail was gone from sight.

"He's stiff!" she gasped.

"Of course he's stiff. He's dead," Dour Elinor said.

Mary Jane was unsatisfied with this excuse. "He's seized up all crooked!"

And indeed he was. His repose in the armoire had not allowed him to rest flat like a respectable corpse should. Rigor mortis had sealed his fate, with legs and arms bent every which way.

"We'll just have to bury him in a seated position," Smooth Kitty said. "With . . . let's see . . . one hand thrown over his forehead. What difference does it make? Let's get wrapping."

They swathed the body in old cotton sheets. Stout Alice didn't mind a bit when his gruesome face was out of sight behind the makeshift grave clothes. Mary Jane and Kitty worked as fast as she-spiders. Dour Elinor seemed rather put out by this. She apparently had cherished hopes of relishing this macabre experience.

"Egyptian slaves spent weeks mummifying the pharaohs," she grumbled. "At the very least, we should insert a probe up the nose to agitate and liquefy the brains. They'll drip right out the nostrils."

"And that will benefit us how, exactly?" Disgraceful Mary Jane inquired. "Keep your revolting heathen suggestions to yourself, please. Can't you see we're in a hurry?"

Dull Martha and Dear Roberta hung back from touching the bodies, so Kitty, Mary Jane, and Elinor went upstairs to wrap up Mrs Plackett. Soon two bodies lay wrapped like laundry parcels at the rear kitchen door.

"This is the most dangerous part of the whole game," Smooth Kitty told the girls. "We've got to get them in the ground before anyone comes along and sees us doing it. Alice, you stand guard, and if anyone comes along, distract them somehow. Don't let them anywhere near the gardens or the windows overlooking them. Most especially, keep Barnes at bay. She's bound to turn up any minute. In fact, she's nearly late. Mr Godding first. Fly, girls, fly!"

Stout Alice made a pretence of picking lilacs in the front gardens while Kitty, Mary Jane, and Elinor each hoisted up a protuberance belonging to Mr Godding and waddled out to their cherry tree grave. They deposited him in the cavity, only to discover that his irregular shape meant that the grave needed to be a good deal deeper. Kitty and Martha remained behind to dig while the other girls hurried back for Mrs Plackett. Alice watched all this from a cautious distance, so intently that she failed, at first, to hear footsteps approaching up the path to the house.

Her heart sank into her boots. In their hour of need, she had faltered at her post! She had to get this unwelcome person away somehow. Then she saw who it was, and her heart leaped up into her throat and nearly choked her. It was Leland Murphy, the youngest junior law clerk ever employed by Mr Wilkins, the village solicitor with offices on High Street. Short, pale, with sparse whiskers, facial pustules, and a chin that sloped straight down to his Adam's apple without any trace of jawbone, Mr Murphy was Lancelot to Alice's Guinevere. She found no flaw in him. The great and abiding question of her tender heart was whether he found a flaw in her. Thus far in his presence fear had made her keep a shy and modest distance, almost to the point of muteness, but at this critical moment, she had not the luxury of such reserve.

She ran to him along the gravel path. "Mr Murphy! What a pleasure. What brings you here on this fine morning?"

Poor Leland Murphy was so startled that he seemed to shrink within his skin to little more than bones wrapped in a greasy black coat. One hand, tucked underneath his lapel, clutched a leather folder of papers tightly.

"Miss . . . Alice Brooks, is it?" he managed to say.

That young lady obliged him by curtseying. "Kind of you to take notice of my name."

He nodded stiffly, looking quite miserable. "May I come in?"

Poor Stout Alice suffered agonies over the outrageous boldness which circumstance now forced upon her. She slipped her arm through his and led him back along the front garden walk. "Why go indoors on such a fine morning as this? Surely whatever business brings you here can be transacted outdoors, can it not?"

Leland Murphy regarded Alice with a look that might have been terror, or loathing. Perhaps both, mingled. She couldn't be sure. Whatever it was, he remained frozen in that gaze for far too long. His elbow, Alice observed, quavered, no doubt with revulsion.

They stood there. Leland pondered the roof tiles, and Stout Alice examined the hedge. "I have papers for Mrs Plackett," the youth finally managed to say.

How Stout Alice's heart fractured into shards of mortification! Whatever hope she'd ever cherished of forging a closer acquaintance with Mr Leland Murphy evaporated. The perspiration beading on his cheeks was proof of his distaste for her. This should come as no surprise. Was she not, this very morning, cast in the role of a sixty-two-year-old woman? What charms could she hold for a dashing and eligible young man like Mr Murphy, whose arm even now she brazenly clutched?

"Excuse me." He cleared his throat noisily. "Perhaps you did not hear me. I said I had papers for Mrs Plackett."

"Of course," Alice murmured. "I apologise. Why don't you give them to me, and I will deliver them to her personally?" If all her hopes were dashed, Stout Alice would at the very least not abandon her mission. Her stoutness of person in no way eclipsed her stoutness of heart.

Mr Murphy's Adam's apple bobbed in anxious agitation. "I'm instructed to hand-deliver them to her only," he said. "Mr Wilkins was quite strict on that point. These are important papers."

"I comprehend you," Stout Alice said. "Unfortunately, Mrs Plackett has been unwell since last evening. She is resting now and cannot under any account be disturbed."

"Then I shall have to return." Creases of worry appeared on the junior law clerk's forehead. "Mr Wilkins will be displeased with me."

Alice, ever the actress, set her shattered hopes aside and gazed directly into Mr Leland Murphy's eyes. "You can trust me, Mr Murphy," she said. "I will spare you Mr Wilkins's displeasure, and any need to make a second trip. I will make sure that these papers go directly to her private desk, and that she is notified as soon as she wakes." *At the Day of Judgement*, she added inwardly, *and not a moment before.*

She reached out her hand for the papers. Mr Murphy's hand trembled in indecision.

Just then a footstep sounded further up the road. Alice looked up to see Amanda Barnes, their daily domestic woman, walking slowly towards the house. It wouldn't do for her to see Alice here like this, but more to the point, here was the true threat to the girls' attempts to bury the bodies. If Amanda Barnes entered the house, it wouldn't be two minutes before she looked out of a kitchen window and saw the burial in progress.

Oh, the exquisite pain in Stout Alice's broad heart! She must wrench herself away from Mr Murphy, ending their first and final conversation, prevail upon him to give her the papers, forever sully his image of her as a well-mannered young lady, and evict him, in twenty seconds' time, so she could face the imminent domestic servant threat.

"Trust me, Mr Murphy," she repeated, her voice tremulous with intensity.

As one under a darkly magical spell, Leland Murphy drew forth his hand and slowly surrendered the papers.

"Thank you." Alice curtseyed. "I must go. I will deliver the papers immediately, and I must greet our daily woman." She turned to flee from Mr Murphy's side, where her presence caused him so much awkwardness.

"Miss Alice." Leland Murphy's voice had a strangled quality to it as he spoke her name.

"Yes?" She paused, fully mindful of Amanda Barnes's footsteps bringing her ever nearer.

"There is a parish strawberry social on Wednesday evening," the junior law clerk croaked. "Will you be in attendance?"

Poor Stout Alice's head was a jumble of confusion now. What could it mean? He must – surely he must – only intend to use that occasion as an opportunity to check to see that the papers had been properly delivered . . .

Mr Murphy's face was paler than chalk, yet his cheeks and pustules flamed vermilion. "Could I . . . would I . . . might I anticipate the pleasure of further conversation with you then?"

Rhapsodies of roses and violins flooded Alice's senses. "You may," she breathed, then ran towards the house.

Chapter Seven

Back at the grave site, Smooth Kitty, Disgraceful Mary Jane, Dour Elinor, Dear Roberta, and Dull Martha were having a much harder time than anticipated. Not only had Mr Godding's irregular posture forced a deepening of the grave, but the awkward spread of his limbs required a widening as well. He was like a little boy sharing a bed with his brother and refusing to keep to his half. The girls dug and manoeuvred their cocooned contraband as fast as they could, but the stubborn bodies would not submit.

"How on earth is it so wretchedly difficult to bury something!" Mary Jane fumed. "We'd have an easier time of it wrestling living persons into a grave."

"Hush," Smooth Kitty whispered. "Footsteps! And talking. Someone's come to the house."

"All we can do is trust Alice, and hurry," Mary Jane whispered. "That's the way, Roberta Dear! Wedge this rock on top of Mr Godding, won't you, and then we can pour on the manure."

"They look like pupae," Dour Elinor noted. "I'm sure

that's what Louise would say if she were here. Let's hope they don't hatch into gigantic insects."

"Really, Elinor!" Mary Jane rolled her eyes. "The things you say!"

They finished wedging the bodies into a position that seemed likely to stay below ground at last, then they dumped an avalanche of manure over the shrouded bodies. Dear Roberta gagged into her handkerchief, but Dull Martha didn't seem to mind. "It smells wholesome," she said. "Like ponies."

"Rest in peace, Headmistress," Dear Roberta said, bowing her head for a moment.

"Very touching, and befitting the occasion." Disgraceful Mary Jane patted Dear Roberta on the back. "And rest in peace, Her Ugly Rude Brother."

"Oh, oh, oh." Dear Roberta began to moan. Her breathing accelerated anxiously.

"What's the matter?" Smooth Kitty cried. She recognised a faint was afoot.

Mary Jane rolled her eyes. "Not again. And not now, for the love of heaven!"

"It occurs to me," Dear Roberta said between panting breaths, "that it's not a very Christian thing we're doing, burying them in this way."

No one spoke. Glances shifted from side to side until all eyes rested expectantly upon Kitty. This, she felt, was a test of her leadership.

"That's true, Roberta," she said. "It isn't."

"*Ohhhhh,*" wailed that conscience-stricken young lady. "I knew it!"

"But," Kitty went on firmly, "their heavenly reward is in no way linked to their burial. Think of all the poor sailors who die at sea."

Disgraceful Mary Jane nodded encouragingly. *Keep going, Kit.*

"Mrs Plackett and Mr Godding have . . . burst the confines of this mortal prison," Kitty continued, proud of herself for having salvaged some use from one of Reverend Rumsey's tedious sermons. "And we are brought to this unhappy pass through no fault of our own. *We* didn't kill them." Kitty glanced around the group to see what private thoughts, if any, this statement revealed. "So we shall pray for them, and from this point on, we shall reform ourselves and turn over a new leaf. I feel confident that fate will never present to us such a morbid dilemma again. No more bodies shall we ever bury in this garden."

"I should hope not," muttered Disgraceful Mary Jane.

Kitty coughed disapprovingly.

"All right, Roberta?"

Dear Roberta's mournful expression softened slightly. She took a deep, sniffling breath, and finally nodded.

Feeling the worst of the danger was behind them, Kitty, who had stayed well away from the manure, left the other girls to smooth over the mound, and risked peeping around the corner of the house. She ran back to the girls. "That young law clerk – what's his name, Murphy? – he was just here, talking to Alice," she whispered. "And Amanda Barnes is coming up the road."

"Eugh, do you mean that greasy salamander of a clerk?"

Disgraceful Mary Jane shuddered visibly. "Poor Alice. She has suffered much for us all."

"Why can't people leave us alone?" Dour Elinor muttered. "Suddenly we're a tourist attraction."

"Let's pray Louise returns swiftly with a tree for us to plant. Everyone hurry in and clean up. You smell like stables, I'm sure. I'll go help Alice deal with Amanda Barnes."

"Good luck," Disgraceful Mary Jane said. "I have a feeling she'll be even harder to dispose of than Mr Godding."

"Morning, Miss Alice." Amanda Barnes's voice drifted across the driveway to where Stout Alice stood, still quivering inwardly at the recollection of Leland Murphy's words. The clerk had fled the moment Alice headed towards the house, so she deemed it safe to turn about and greet the daily woman. She slipped her handful of legal papers behind her back.

"Oh. Good morning, Barnes," she said. "I trust you are well this morning?"

"Well enough, thank you," Barnes replied. "Bit of a headache, but at my age sleep isn't what it once was." Though shot with a few streaks of grey, the bulk of her thick hair was still butter-blonde. Alice had wondered more than once why a woman so pleasant looking, who had always been in service with respectable families and cooked as well as any housekeeper in Ely, had never married.

"I'm sorry to hear it," Stout Alice replied mechanically, then saw an opening. "Would you have any wish to return home and rest?"

"Oh no, no, no matter in the slightest. I shouldn't have mentioned it."

"I'm *sure* Mrs Plackett wouldn't mind," pressed Alice.

"Then you're far more sure than I am." Barnes cocked her head to one side. "Was that the young law clerk I just saw hurrying away from here?" She waited for Alice to reply, then rightly took Alice's awkward silence for a yes. "I wonder what could have rousted him out of bed so early. Lawyers drink the night away and sleep in late, or so my sister tells me. She's in service to a chamber of barristers in London. How they smoke!" A new thought seemed to strike her. "Or did the young clerk come to see *you*?" She winked. "It's awfully early in the morning for him to have come a-courting."

"Courting!" Alice wondered if her voice was too shrill, or her cheeks too red. "What a thing to say, Barnes."

The daily woman eyed the door to the house. "Never mind me, Miss Alice," she said. "I'm all chatter. Not a word I say is worth worrying about. I'm sure the young gentleman had some perfectly ordinary papers for Mrs Plackett."

Alice felt the papers clutched in her hidden hand. It seemed silly to her now to have hidden them – *that's the kind of folly a guilty conscience leads one to*, she thought – but having done so she balked at displaying the papers now. "No, no papers."

Barnes waggled her eyebrows. "Then I stand by my other theory that it's *you* the young gentleman found a reason to visit. Oh come now, Miss Alice! I'm only teasing. If you'll excuse me, it's time I tend to the kitchen and set its affairs to rights."

Alice's mind jolted back to her original mission – to keep Amanda Barnes away from the house, and for as long as possible. If she'd had any plans for how to accomplish this great feat, her conversation with Leland Murphy had wiped them clean from her head.

She clutched the housekeeper's arm. "The kitchen will keep," Alice said breathlessly. "Miss Barnes. Do tell me. How is your mother?"

The expression on Barnes's face could not have been more startled if Stout Alice's head had chosen that moment to fly off her shoulders. "My *mother*, Miss Alice?"

Alice wished her mouth weren't so painfully dry. "Yes. Your mother."

"Well," Barnes began, still eyeing Alice strangely. The truth was, the students at Saint Etheldreda's School *never* inquired after Barnes's mother. Whether the school's domestic even had a mother was not a subject of general conversational interest. "Well, Miss Alice, my mother is well enough. Much the same as ever."

Stout Alice would not be put off so easily. Each moment she prolonged this conversation helped the girls finish their digging. Having remembered the mother, Alice now clung to her like a life-saver in choppy waters. "Didn't you tell Mrs Plackett, just a few days ago, that you were worried about an ill turn in your mother's health?"

Barnes blinked. "Did I?"

"Yes," Alice cried, warming to her theme. "Yes, I remember. Mrs Plackett said, 'What's the matter with you, Barnes? You're moping around here like the walking dead.

You burned the toast, and you haven't put your back into your chores all day long.' And you said, 'Pardon me, Mrs Plackett. I do apologise, and I'll set it to rights. It's just that my poor mother has caught a touch of the rheumatism, and she won't eat like she should. It pains her to get about the house, and I worry about her so.'"

Barnes peered at Stout Alice through narrowed eyes. "That's quite a memory you've got, Miss Alice."

Alice blushed. "Well, naturally, I was concerned for her."

"And a knack for voices, too. You sounded just like Mistress there for a moment. Well, I expect I was worried that day, but Mother's getting well on in years, and her rheumatism – it's been coming on for a while now. Mrs Plackett, well, we both know that now and then she can be, shall we say . . ."

"Say no more, Barnes," Alice said loftily. "I understand you, but let us not speak of her in words we might later regret."

Barnes looked at Alice strangely, then shrugged. "I suppose. Given her moods, though, I'd best not keep her waiting. If you'll excuse me . . ."

Alice, who, for both girth and courage, was called Stout with good reason, could see she faced a formidable opponent in Barnes. Though she had run out of weapons, she had not lost the will to fight. "Come with me to the henhouse, Barnes," she said desperately. "Let's see if the latest chicks have hatched."

Barnes's mouth hung open. She stared at Alice, completely incredulous. "Chicks, Miss?"

Indeed! *Chicks?* Alice gulped and plowed onward – a habit that was becoming painfully familiar.

"Yes, chicks! Don't you love chicks? Most have already hatched, but there was a biddy sitting on a nest two days ago. I always say there's nothing in all this world so divine as a sweet, downy, fluffy, tiny, adorable, precious little chick. Like little puffs of . . . butter. Sunshine. Butter-coloured sunshine. Don't you think so, Barnes?"

Imbecile! Alice thought. *You're gibbering. Barnes will see through this charade. No one takes their domestic to see new baby chicks.*

"Chicks are nice enough, Miss Alice, but work won't wait, will it?" Barnes's tone was that of an adult speaking to a child or a person lacking some of their wits. "My workday doesn't end till all the chores are done, and I do need to get home to Mother, so if you'd just let me go in and get started, so I can get back home before *midnight*, after taking care of you all, I'd be obliged to you."

To Stout Alice's immense relief, Smooth Kitty emerged from around the corner of the house, heading purposefully in their direction.

"Good morning, Barnes!" Smooth Kitty hailed the daily woman with unusual enthusiasm, and parked her body where it obstructed Barnes's access to the door. "How was your Sunday?"

"Good morning, Miss Katherine. It was a Sunday much like any other. And yours? You had your weekly dinner party with Mrs Plackett's brother?"

"Yes, dinner, yes, and then a birthday party for Mr Godding later on," Kitty replied. "It was quite an exciting evening for us all."

"Was it Mr Godding's birthday, then? I wonder why Mrs Plackett never asked me to bake a cake?" Barnes looked genuinely put out, as though this lack of cake requests was a personal slight upon her baking skill. "And it was a surprise party, you said? That must have been a surprise indeed for Mr Godding. I'm not sure I'd be glad of a surprise party. I heard once of a man who died of shock when all the guests jumped out and surprised him. He was probably elderly, but all the same. Now, if you'll pardon me, I'd best get on with my work. A party means dishes, and I wouldn't want Mrs Plackett to accuse me of shirking, out here visiting with you young ladies. And you'll need to get on with your lessons before long, won't you?"

Stout Alice began to feel a headache pressing against her temples.

Smooth Kitty pressed her arms against the door lintels, forming a friendly barricade.

"Lessons have been cancelled for today," she said. "Mrs Plackett has taken to her bed. She's unwell."

The change in Barnes's expression was immediate. "Heart trouble? Bad milk? Something she ate? Fainting spells? Bunions?"

"A tragedy in the family," Kitty replied. Stout Alice marvelled at her convincing performance. There might turn out to be two Lady Macbeths at Saint Etheldreda's. "Poor young Julius has . . . pneu—"

"Malaria," Stout Alice supplied.

"Malaria. Mr Godding has departed for London to sail out on the earliest ship bound for the Indies. Mrs Plackett is . . . prostrated . . . utterly prostrated by concern for her brother and her . . ."

"Nephew." These details of pedigree were fresher in Stout Alice's mind after the morning's pillow-top tête-à-tête with Miss Fringle.

"Nephew. Naturally Mrs Plackett is in no position to teach lessons, nor will she wish to be disturbed by housework noises, so she has asked us to pay your day's wages but to excuse you from your duties." Here Kitty pulled money from her pocket and counted out a shilling and thruppence. All eyes watched her count, for even in anxious moments, metallic money has its hypnotic appeal. Alice thought she saw Kitty frown at the money left in her hand, then close her hand quickly. She held out Barnes's wages, but the daily woman ignored them.

"My land!" Barnes declared. "What a turn of events! A nephew ailing in the colonies. No wonder Mrs Plackett's in shock. And Mr Godding, gone off like that so suddenly, without even time to pack." Deep furrows of concern creased the daily woman's forehead. "I just can't picture him gallivanting off so suddenly. He scarcely seems the adventurous type."

"I see what you mean," Kitty said sagely. "It was a stirring moment, after Mr Godding read the telegram. 'Constance,' he said, 'I must be off at once, and brook no delay. I *will* be at young Julius's side as soon as I can. He is the last to carry the Godding name into futurity, and I must go render any assistance that I may.'"

Stout Alice began to fear Kitty was taking her performance a bit too far. Still, Barnes seemed to hang upon her every word.

"'The last to carry the Godding name'. He said that, did he?" Miss Barnes reached into her pockets for a handkerchief and dabbed her eyes. "That was noble of him, then, wasn't it? Of course, if Mr Godding were ever to marry, young Julius needn't be the last, but that's none of my affair."

"Mrs Plackett worried about her brother's safety," Kitty went on, "but Mr Godding declared that he'd give no sway to cowardice or womanly fears. He would not shirk his family duty to his dead brother's only living son."

Amanda Barnes blew her nose with great emotion. "Well, that's very good of him," she said, "even if it is uncommon sudden." She tucked her handkerchief back into her pocket, and pushed the proffered money back towards Smooth Kitty. "I won't take money from Mrs Plackett like this without working to earn it," she said. "You know how she is with her economies. If she paid me now for no labour, I'll wager she'd regret it later. I'll just tiptoe inside and make up some soup, and some tea, for Mrs Plackett. She'll want nourishment eventually, and I can tidy up as quiet as a ghost."

Barnes started towards Smooth Kitty as if determined to march straight through her. Kitty blocked her move with a forward thrust of the money.

"*Dear* Barnes! You are too, too good, and far too generous of heart. But I must insist, I really must. Mrs Plackett herself was quite vehement. She says you deserve a bit of holiday."

"She said that?"

Kitty gulped. Considering Mrs Plackett's usual demeanour towards her hired help, perhaps she was stretching belief too far.

"We girls can tend to all that's needful today. We shall keep a quiet vigil in the parlour, studying our lesson books and remembering our headmistress, her brother, and her . . . nephew in our prayers."

Smooth Kitty bowed her head in a touching display of pious concern. Stout Alice followed suit, counting heartbeats and waiting for Barnes to *leave*, for the love of heaven. But still the daily woman hesitated. Never had a tenacious work ethic proved so irritating.

Finally Barnes curtseyed in acquiescence. "Well enough, Miss Katherine," she said. "If Mrs Plackett insists, I'll take my holiday. But first let me just nip inside for a pan of mine I left here last week. I need it for a recipe for my poor mother."

"Tell me what it looks like, and I'll get it for you," Alice exclaimed, too eagerly.

Barnes cocked her head to one side. "If I didn't know better, I'd think you girls were trying to keep me out of the house," she said. "Remember, I was a girl once myself. You're not up to any mischief while your headmistress is unwell, are you?"

"None in the slightest!" Stout Alice exclaimed.

"Really, Barnes." Smooth Kitty looked quietly affronted. "At a time like this, what an insinuation."

Amanda Barnes bowed her head. "I apologise. There I go again, not thinking before I speak. Oh! And here's another thing I didn't think of." She reached into her bag and pulled out a large, thick, folded hank of cloth. "Mrs Rumsey asked me to bring this to you. It's three yards of linen for your strawberry social tablecloth."

Smooth Kitty reached for the fabric. It felt silky beneath her hands. "Thank you, Miss Barnes. We'll have to make hasty work of it, but we shall do our best. Good morning to you."

Amanda turned to leave, then halted. "Is there hope the young nephew will recover?"

"Precious little," Kitty replied. "He's said to be a weakly child. His constitution is feeble." She sniffed tragically. "We fear the worst. Poor Mrs Plackett."

There was an awful pause. They waited. Barnes's shoes were rooted to the gravel of Saint Etheldreda's driveway. Stout Alice could see no end to this terrible impasse. She began to understand why her grandmother complained so often about dealing with hired help.

"Yoo-hoooo!"

A voice came bellowing from down the road, approaching Saint Etheldreda's at a rapid clip.

"Yoo-hoooo, I say! Alice! Kitty! Look what I've found!"

The shock of surprise zipping up Kitty's spine was positively electric. It was little Pocked Louise, dragging – or being dragged by – something on a string, waving what looked like a stick in the air, and galloping like a schoolboy.

"Kitty! Alice! Look!" the breathless Louise cried. "Oh, hullo, Barnes. Look, girls, what a jolly day we're going to have. I got us a tree to plant, just like you asked, but best of all, I got us a puppy!"

Chapter Eight

The streak of black and white speckled fur dragged Louise around behind the house and out of sight.

Smooth Kitty and Stout Alice avoided meeting Amanda Barnes's gaze. What Barnes must think now, Kitty couldn't stomach to guess. The awkward silence was broken by a trotting horse appearing far down the road, pulling a lightweight chaise.

"Doctor Snelling, making his rounds," Barnes observed.

"He's on his way to call upon Mrs Plackett," Smooth Kitty said. "Alice, perhaps you should go inside and change your clothes."

Alice blanched, then slipped indoors. The horror! It was one thing to pretend to be sixty-two-year-old Constance Plackett while sleeping in a darkened room with a blind, drugged, ear-plugged old choir mistress; quite another thing to play Mrs Plackett by the light of morning for the scrutinizing eyes of a man of medicine.

"I don't see why Miss Alice needs to change her clothes," Miss Barnes said. "You'll forgive my saying so, Miss Katherine, but *your* frock has quite a splash of mud around the hems. I'll tackle it on washing day."

Dr Snelling's gleaming chaise advanced slowly up the road, pulled by a well-groomed bay mare. Kitty watched it come with mounting dread. Oh, this aggravating Amanda Barnes!

The doctor stopped his chaise, climbed out stiffly, and tied it to a post near the front door.

"Morning," he called out. "Don't mind me. I'll show myself in."

"Wait!" Kitty cried. *Stall him, stall him!* "Er, tell me, Doctor Snelling, if you would be so kind, please, how Mrs, er, Benson? No, Bennion, fared last evening. At the birth of her child."

Dr Snelling scowled. "A daughter," he grumbled. "I lost my wager. Now, if you'll excuse me . . ."

And before Kitty could stop him, he pushed open the door and disappeared into the dark bowels of the house.

Kitty found herself in a moment of peril, and like all great women, she let the moment of crisis infuse her with strength she hadn't known she possessed. Summoning the very essence of her dear departed Aunt Katherine, that imposing force of nature after whom she was named, she drew herself up to her full height, which was not very great, and still managed to look down her nose at the daily housekeeper.

"Good *morning* to you, Barnes," she said with polite but decisive firmness. She seized Barnes's wrist and pressed the wages into her palm. "Enjoy your holiday. I must go inside now and tend to my late headmistress."

Barnes's eyes widened. "Your *late* headmistress?"

"Late," she replied with frosty dignity, "for her doctor's appointment." She turned abruptly, went inside, and closed the door behind her.

Kitty could not pause to revel in her triumph. *Late headmistress!* That had been a near catastrophe. She dropped the tablecloth linen into a chair and ran to the door of her headmistress's bedroom. Low voices inside, sounding male and female, and not the least bit animated, met her ears.

She pushed open the door and entered the dim room. The curtains were drawn shut.

Dr Snelling turned from examining Mrs Plackett to look up at Kitty. "Pardon me, young lady," he said. "I'm examining my patient."

"Yes," Mrs Plackett said in a frosty voice. "Kindly afford me my privacy, Katherine, and resume your studies in the schoolroom."

Smooth Kitty was so astonished, she nearly stumbled backwards, which would have been anything but smooth, so it is fortunate that she did not in fact do so. But there she was! Mrs Plackett, in the flesh, dressed in her customary widow's mourning, peering through a black lacy veil, and speaking in her unmistakable voice to Dr Snelling.

Kitty backed out of the room. She began to feel a bit faint.

Dour Elinor and Disgraceful Mary Jane appeared in the hallway. Mary Jane seized Kitty's elbow and dragged her into the parlour where Dull Martha and Dear Roberta were already seated. All the girls struggled to silence their mirth over some suppressed joke.

"Isn't she absolutely brilliant?" Disgraceful Mary Jane whispered.

Kitty was at a loss. "Who, Mrs Plackett?"

"No, silly." Mary Jane sank into a soft chair and kicked up her heels. "Elinor!'

Smooth Kitty turned a bewildered glance upon Elinor, hoping to find some explanation. She saw nothing outside the ordinary in the girl's stark, pallid, morose appearance.

Mary Jane sat up straight in her chair. "You don't comprehend yet, do you?" She laughed. "What, you goose, did you think it was Mrs Plackett in there?"

Kitty would have died before admitting as much to Mary Jane.

"Elinor made Alice up," Mary Jane explained. "She used her artist's charcoals to paint Mrs Plackett's face right onto Alice's. She did it like lightning, wrinkles and bumps and all. You should have seen it. Well, you did, didn't you? Bit of a shocker, wasn't it?"

Kitty clutched the armrests of her chair. "But . . . the clothes! And the hair, and . . . everything! She only went inside a moment or two ago. How could you possibly?"

Disgraceful Mary Jane preened before a small mirror she kept in her pocket. "We pounced on her, naturally."

"We all helped," Dear Roberta added. "She came running in, calling for assistance, so we all pitched in. Martha ran for Mrs Plackett's old clothes . . ."

"While I dumped talcum in her hair and twisted it up like Mrs Plackett's," Mary Jane added.

"Elinor used her pencils and pastels to do her face up astonishingly," Martha offered.

"And I adjusted Mrs Plackett's corsets so that Alice was . . . Plackett-shaped." Dear Roberta beamed with simple pride.

"I held Doctor Snelling at the door for a minute or two," Mary Jane said. "I'm rather better at it than you are, Kitty."

Smooth Kitty sank back in her chair. "Well. Nothing more can surprise me after this. Superbly done, girls. Now we can only pray that Doctor Snelling fails to recognise the difference between a sick and aged liver, and a young and healthy one."

"Shall he cut her open, do you think, for a closer peek?" asked Dour Elinor with genuine interest.

Kitty ignored Elinor. A smile began to spread across her face. "Do you realise what this means?" she whispered. "If Alice can trick Doctor Snelling into believing she's Mrs Plackett, then we can fool anyone!"

"Possibly," Dour Elinor said.

The bedroom door opened in the hallway, and heavy footsteps advanced out.

"I'm glad to hear you're feeling so much better," they heard.

"Thank you, Doctor." The voice floated down the hall as if straight from the grave. Smooth Kitty wasn't the only one to shudder. "I'm deeply indebted to you."

Dr Snelling moved towards the door, pausing within view of the girls. "As to that, there is the small matter of your account. I must remind you to respond to your most recent statement of balances due."

There was an awkward pause. Smooth Kitty and Disgraceful Mary Jane eyed one other.

"Of course," Alice-as-Mrs-Plackett replied. "I apologise, Doctor. I've felt too poorly of late to keep up with financial matters. I will attend to it directly."

"I'm obliged to you for that small consideration. Lord knows a country surgeon will never be a rich man. Still . . ." He checked his gold watch. "We all like to eat." He passed out of sight, and the girls heard the sound of the front door opening and closing, and shortly thereafter the sound of hoofs clopping and wheels rolling over the gravel drive.

Stout Alice, still as Mrs Plackett, peeped around the doorway and smiled. The girls flew to her side and tackled her with hugs.

"You did it!" Kitty exclaimed. "You made an examining doctor believe you were a sixty-year-old woman!"

"Sixty-two," Alice laughed.

There was another knock at the door. Stout Alice sighed. "I'll go change. We'd best not push our luck with two impersonations."

"No, don't," Kitty said. "Stay. I want to see if this will work. Mary Jane, get the door, will you?"

Mary Jane ushered Henry Butts into the parlour. Kitty watched him like a hawk to see if he spotted the counterfeit Mrs Plackett.

"Note for you, Ma'am," he said, handing Stout Alice an envelope.

"Thank you, young man," the false Mrs Plackett said. "Katherine, be so good as to reward Master Butts's helpfulness? I seem to have misplaced my change-purse."

Kitty fished in her pocket for a suitable coin for Henry, but the young gallant refused any payment. "No, thank you, Ma'am," he said. "It was my pleasure." He turned to go, then turned back. "Pardon me, Ma'am," he ventured. "If I may ask . . ." He bit his lower lip.

"Yes, Master Butts?" said Stout Alice. "What is it?"

Henry blushed. His gaze roamed around the room until it rested upon Disgraceful Mary Jane. He took a deep breath, then addressed the supposed headmistress once more. "There's a strawberry social Wednesday night at the parish. Will you be going?"

"No," Smooth Kitty said, while,

"Yes," Stout Alice said, and,

"Absolutely," Disgraceful Mary Jane said.

Kitty and Mary Jane glared at each other.

"We are going," Alice said in Mrs Plackett's most commanding voice. "Such an opportunity to socialise with our neighbours is one not to be missed."

Kitty had no choice but to curtsey in deference to her headmistress for Henry's benefit.

Henry couldn't hide his excitement. Disgraceful Mary Jane made matters worse by winking at him. He turned and bolted for the exit, colliding heavily with the doorway. At last the front door slammed shut behind him.

"Well, Mrs Plackett," Smooth Kitty said with a touch of asperity, "I'm glad to hear you're recovered enough from your shock and grief over young Julius to feel like venturing out into society."

Stout Alice plucked her widow's headpiece off. "I'm not going as Mrs Plackett," she cried. "I can't!" Her thoughts went racing to Leland Murphy, who had asked her specially if she was going. She hoped fervently that Smooth Kitty, whom Alice sometimes suspected of being a mind-reader, had no way to know it.

"You've no choice," Kitty replied. "You've committed us to attend the social, and it's inconceivable that Mrs Plackett would allow her charges out at an evening party unsupervised. Alice will have to remain home with a headache while Mrs Plackett chaperones us."

A knot of keen disappointment welled up in Stout Alice's bosom. She wanted to contradict Kitty – she *must* contradict her – but Alice saw in a terrible instant that she was right. Only as Mrs Plackett could she attend the social. "I think I *do* have a headache," she said. "It's been a ghastly twelve hours. I'm going to go lie down."

Before Alice could leave the room, they heard a whining and a scratching noise at the rear door that led from the parlour straight out into the gardens. The door opened, and in shot a black and white dog, followed closely by Pocked Louise.

"Is it safe to come in now?" she asked, pulling off her bonnet. "I planted our cherry tree, and watered it with a bucket from the pump. Aldous here wanted to dig the bodies right back up, didn't you, you naughty boy?"

She sank to her knees and kissed the puppy, which attacked her face with loving licks.

"*Aldous*?" Disgraceful Mary Jane cried. "You named him after nasty Mr Godding?"

"I thought we wanted a bulldog to protect us, not a silly spaniel," Stout Alice said.

"Aldy's not a silly . . ." Pocked Louise turned and noticed Alice's costume for the first time. She blanched for an instant, then smiled. "I say! Spot-on, Alice! You nearly made me consider the possibility of ghosts for a second." Aldous grew more passionate in his ardent licking, and Louise abandoned human conversation in favour of canine. "That's a boy, there, isn't he a good boy? We don't need any frightful bulldog, do we, Aldy? He's a *smart* boy, yes he is, yes he is."

Dour Elinor blinked languidly. "What is it about pets that makes rational people start babbling like infants?"

Dear Roberta and Dull Martha joined Louise on the floor to make Aldous's acquaintance. Even Stout Alice joined the party, and admitted readily that Aldous was a smart boy and a handsome fellow and not a silly spaniel at all. He had great curly ears that flapped and flew like windmill blades as he spun his head.

"I hope we can manage the expense of a dog," Smooth Kitty said. "And while we're on the subject of money, our independent feminine utopia can't exist long without some funds, or all this fuss over hiding the bodies will come to naught. Oh!"

Dull Martha looked up at Smooth Kitty's exclamation. "What is it, Kitty?"

Kitty reached into her pocket and pulled out the coins from her pocket. "Nothing . . . just that thinking of money made me remember . . ."

"Yes, do tell," Alice said. "I noticed you looked puzzled when you counted the coins in your hand this morning for Barnes."

"Hm, did it show?" Kitty held two gold coins up for a view in better window light. "I thought these were sovereigns, but that's not Victoria. She squinted at the coin to read the engraving. "*CAROL III, D. G. HISP. ET. IND. R.*" She turned the coin over and read the other side. "*Auspice Deo In Utroq Felix.*" Elinor? Louise? You're our Latin scholars. What does it mean?"

Both girls peered over Kitty's shoulder at the coins.

"Through the auspices – or the generosity, you might say, or grace, of God, we . . . live happily?" Dour Elinor ventured.

"Prosper," Pocked Louise said. "Charles the Third, 'R' for *Rex*, or king. 'Hisp' is *Hispania*, or Spain, in Latin, and 'Ind' is for Indies."

The three girls looked at each other.

"So these are Spanish coins?" Disgraceful Mary Jane inquired.

"Old ones," Kitty replied, peering again at the inscription.

"Doubloons, I should think," offered Dour Elinor.

"Ooh, how romantic!" Disgraceful Mary Jane sighed. "They sound like something from a pirate novel."

Pocked Louise ignored this interruption. "They're probably worth more than their face value," she said.

"I imagine collectors would pay extra for these."

Dear Roberta peeked in for a closer look. "But where did you find them, Kitty?"

Kitty's mind was so busy, she almost didn't hear the question. "Hm? Oh." She hefted them in her palm, and thought. "These are what I thought were sovereigns when we cleaned out Mrs Plackett's and Mr Godding's pockets. They each were carrying one."

Pocked Louise frowned. "That's odd."

"Family heirloom?" offered Dear Roberta.

Disgraceful Mary Jane threw her hands up in the air. "Maybe they each found one in the bottom of a drawer, or an old sea chest. Honestly, Louise, sometimes you severely overthink things. Let's leave off with this coin nonsense and find something to eat. I'm starving."

Chapter Nine

The students at Saint Etheldreda's School for Young Ladies breakfasted on bread and butter and milk, and lunched on eggs gathered from the henhouse. At teatime they had toast and tea. To an outside observer these might have seemed to be the only events of this quiet day at Saint Etheldreda's school. But as is so often the case with groups of young ladies, the real intrigue took place underneath the surface, in small domestic matters, in conversations, in whisperings, and in private thoughts.

Take, for instance, Pocked Louise's afternoon stroll outdoors with Aldous, ambling along the hedgerows that lined Prickwillow Road. She was still fuming over Disgraceful Mary Jane saying she overthought things. A dose of occasional thinking, she thought, would do Mary Jane a mountain of good. Pocked Louise pressed her lips together grimly. She didn't care what they said. She would never, never, never allow herself to grow to be a noodle-headed young lady whose brains had been sacrificed on the altar to boy-worship. Though Louise's experience with males was limited, she knew enough of what sticky-fingered fiends her boy cousins were to know that no male, be he ever so combed and shoe-shined, could tempt her to give up her intellectual pursuits. Never.

She wandered around a hedge, then Aldous let out a yap and dragged her headlong into someone.

"I say! Pardon me," that someone said, disentangling himself from the leash and from Pocked Louise. "So very sorry."

Louise levelled a look at him. It was a young man, a few years older, she would guess, than the eldest girls at Saint Etheldreda's. What's more, she deduced from his well-dressed look, courteous bearing, and rather excessive smiling, he was the sort of young man that Disgraceful Mary Jane or even Smooth Kitty might fall batty over. She was in such a pique with those overbearing young ladies, and with males in general, that she chose to hate this young man on principle.

"Do you mind telling me," said her new acquaintance, oblivious to the ill-regard in which she held him, "if this house here is the finishing school for young ladies? Saint Ethel's?"

Louise's gaze narrowed. What could *he* want with a finishing school? Nothing worthwhile, she was sure. Perhaps he was an old beau of Mary Jane's, and she'd posted a letter to him the moment their backs were turned. If Disgraceful Mary Jane thought the others would stand by while she invited flirtatious young men over, she had another thing coming.

"Ely has several finishing schools for young women," Louise said stiffly. "This house isn't one of them."

"Oh," he said, and knitted his eyebrows together. "I thought for certain this was the right place. When I met you, I assumed, naturally, you must be one of the students."

"I live here with my grandparents," Louise said, inwardly surprised to find what a liar she'd become. But the last thing any of the girls needed was more visitors. It wasn't her fault this person was so inquisitive.

He tipped the brim of his hat towards her. "My apologies, then," he said. "A very good day to you." And he headed off in the direction of town.

Louise watched him leave. Mary Jane and Kitty, she knew, would have fits if they knew such a well-dressed young man had come a-calling. All the more satisfaction, then, Louise thought with a private smile, she would take in forgetting she ever saw him.

Meanwhile, Dull Martha and Dear Roberta had volunteered to cook supper, but Disgraceful Mary Jane insisted on doing so herself. Mary Jane, who had never cooked a thing in her life, was certain that with the aid of Mrs Lea's famous cookery volume she would be perfectly able to conjure up something edible.

"She's acting like she doesn't trust me," Dull Martha whispered to Dear Roberta.

"Do you think so?" Roberta whispered back with deep concern.

"Ever since . . . what happened at Sunday dinner, I've wondered," Martha said. "I cooked, you know."

"But surely!" remonstrated Dear Roberta, who couldn't

imagine anyone suspecting ill of her dear roommate, Martha.

Martha tugged Roberta up the stairwell and into their bedroom. "Do you want to know what I think?"

"Of course!"

Martha lowered her voice to a hushed whisper. "With all this talk of murder, I think it's curious that Mary Jane . . ." Her voice trailed off.

"Yes? Go on!"

Dull Martha removed her spectacles and polished them on her skirt. "Oh, I don't know. I feel awful even thinking it."

Dear Roberta was practically beside herself. "Thinking *what*?"

"Well," Martha said, "I don't know. But she is so very risqué in her behaviour, wouldn't you agree? She's an absolute flirt! And I can't help but wonder whether she mightn't . . . Now that I speak it out loud it seems shocking, but I just wonder if she couldn't have conceived the idea of poisoning Mrs Plackett as a means of setting herself free."

Dear Roberta's jaw dropped. "No more chaperones, you mean?"

Dull Martha glanced from side to side as if fearing the walls might be listening. "It's probably only another one of my foolish ideas, isn't it? I should know better than to go guessing. She wouldn't kill Mrs Plackett just so she could go chasing boys, would she?"

Roberta thought of the many lurid crimes mentioned in the London newspapers, and shook her head. "Stranger things have happened," she said. "Of course, you might well be wrong. The scriptures say it's a sin to judge."

Dull Martha hung her guilty head.

"However," Roberta continued, "we can't overlook the fact that she's shown a shocking lack of reverence and respect for the dead. She's been absolutely flippant about it."

Dull Martha sat on her bedspread and twisted the tail of her braids nervously between her fingers. "Ohhh, dear," she said. "I feel terrible now. I feel so disloyal for thinking these things. And speaking them aloud, too."

"Never mind, Martha." Roberta slipped an arm around her friend. "I won't tell a soul. We'll forget it ever happened. But we'd both be wise to keep our eyes wide open. Just in case. We can't forget we've been witness to murder."

Disgraceful Mary Jane grew bored in midafternoon and went hunting for Smooth Kitty. She found her poring over papers at Mrs Plackett's writing desk, scratching figures on a blotter, and frowning.

Mary Jane sprawled upon Mrs Plackett's bed. "What's the matter, Kit?" she said. "Why the long face? These murders got you down?"

"Murders? Pah," Kitty replied. "I can't make head nor tail of these books. Mrs Plackett's finances are a mess. My father would burst a blood vessel if he saw them."

Disgraceful Mary Jane would not be put off from her chosen subject by something so mundane as bookkeeping. "Tell me, pet," she said, "which of us do you think polished the old duffers off for good?"

Kitty's eyebrow rose. "Which of *us*? Why do you think it was one of us?"

"Oh, I want it to be, desperately," Mary Jane said. "A nice private, domestic vendetta, and then we can all just go on happily. Someone else, someone *out there* makes matters a frightful nuisance. One of us? Cosy as anything."

Smooth Kitty laughed. "You really have no morals at all, do you?"

"Not a brass farthing's worth." Disgraceful Mary Jane lolled around on the bed, then propped herself up luxuriantly with pillows and bolsters. "Want to hear my choice for our little murderess?"

Kitty, whose mind was more occupied by totting up numbers, nodded. "Why not?"

"Elinor, obviously!"

Kitty paused to picture this. "Oh?"

"Of course, can't you see? The girl was born in a mausoleum. Or ought to have been. Death is all she thinks about. Why, in her warped world, there's probably nothing at all wrong with killing someone. She might have thought she was doing them a favour. You know . . . Mrs Plackett's liver complaints – just end it all, as a merciful gesture."

Kitty found this theory amusing. "And Mr Godding?"

Mary Jane wrinkled her nose. "What difference does it make? Perhaps she thought she'd spare him the trouble of grieving."

Kitty tried to picture Elinor tiptoeing into the kitchen and pouring poison over the veal cutlets. She couldn't. "If I were to picture Elinor in the role of murderess," she said thoughtfully, "I wouldn't think poison. Battle-axe, perhaps, or a scythe."

Mary Jane laughed. "I see your point."

Kitty returned to her arithmetic. "Seventeen . . . twenty-three. I don't like thinking it was one of us, so I'm not going to," she said firmly. "Carry the two, makes fourteen. But if I did, I wouldn't picture Elinor. I'd picture . . ."

"Me?"

"Don't flatter yourself."

Mary Jane pretended to pout.

"It couldn't be one of the younger girls," Kitty went on, now forgetting her accounting entirely. "Out of the question. I wonder . . . you know, I do. I wonder about someone like Alice."

Mary Jane sat bolt upright. "Not our Alice! She's so doggedly *decent*. And far too sensible. She doesn't fly off in rages. She'd be the last person *ever* to think of such a thing."

Kitty nodded. "I know. And that's why I *do* think of it."

"But . . . !"

"Still waters run deep, don't they say?"

Disgraceful Mary Jane shook her head. "Alice! I never. You know, sometimes you surprise me, Kitty Heaton."

Kitty grinned. "If so, I learned it from you. It's one of your gifts."

Mary Jane preened like a cat. "One of many."

Pocked Louise's trip to the chemist's shop that morning had equipped her with all the chemicals she needed to perform tests upon the veal. Now that she and her puppy – for she privately thought of Aldous as *her* puppy – were refreshed by their walk, she decided it was time someone took this crime more seriously. So Louise set about transforming the schoolroom into a science laboratory. She had to use drinking glasses as beakers, which distressed her scientific mind, but the pursuit of truth allowed her to overlook shoddy equipment. First she soaked the two remnants of veal in two different jars, each with just enough water to submerge the meat. After removing the meat she proceeded to swirl granules of potash into the water in each jar.

Dour Elinor watched her work.

"Where did you learn to do this?" she asked Pocked Louise.

"My uncle is a physician in London," Louise explained, peering at the water level in one of the jars. "He knows I want to be one myself someday, and *he's* not shocked by that. He lets me help myself to books and journals he no longer needs. I keep them in my footlocker upstairs. One is about medical research used in criminal cases. Fascinating reading. It lists symptoms of various poisons and methods for ascertaining their presence. Hm, I hope this isn't too much potash. It didn't say . . . but this amount seems sufficiently dissolved, I think." She glanced at Elinor. "Time for the iron sulphate." She wiggled a thin glass in which she'd mixed green crystals with water to produce a greenish liquid, then carefully dropped a bit of the green mixture off the end of a spoon into each jar. Dirty-looking granules began to settle to the bottom of both jars. "Ah! Just as I thought . . . see these brown precipitates? Time for the oil of vitriol." She mixed drops from a small dark bottle into yet another glass containing water, then tipped a small quantity into both jars.

"*Miss* Dudley!" Stout Alice entered the room and addressed Louise in Mrs Plackett's voice. "Let me hear no more of this indecent folly! Science? Young ladies, studying the body? What next? If you *must* devote yourself to studies, content yourself to become a respectable governess."

"I like you better dead," Louise replied cheerfully. "It's ironic, isn't it? Mrs Plackett, who was so dead-set against me studying science . . ."

Stout Alice giggled. "*Dead* set."

Louise grinned. "Very funny. She who opposed my scientific interests so strenuously is now the subject of my experiment." She shook her jars slightly, then held them both up to Dour Elinor and Stout Alice. "Now, what do you see?"

The other girls had all entered the room at the sound of Alice's headmistress impersonation.

Dour Elinor peered into the jars. "Blue," she said with some surprise. "Shocking blue."

"Prussian blue," Pocked Louise said. "Signifying crystalline prussic acid."

The other girls looked at one another. Louise's manner suggested this was a significant announcement.

"Meaning?" Disgraceful Mary Jane asked. "What is prussic acid?"

Pocked Louise folded her arms across her chest. "Cyanide," she said. "One form of cyanide is used for blue dye. Cyanide salts are one of the most potent and deadly poisons known to man. They kill almost instantly. And they're relatively easy to purchase at the chemist's shop. A common use is rat killer."

"But what does it all mean?" asked Dull Martha. "What has cyanide to do with us?"

Pocked Louise looked to Dour Elinor to translate. Elinor explained in her low, spectral voice.

"Poison," she told Dull Martha, "in the veal. Louise has just tested it and found cyanide in the meat."

The colour drained from Dull Martha's cheeks. "The veal was poisoned?"

Elinor nodded. "It was the only thing both Mrs Plackett and Mr Godding ate that we did not. And, last night, after you'd gone to bed, we found a dead stoat at the compost pile that had eaten a bite of leftover veal."

Martha wrenched off her glasses and hid her face in her hands. Loud sobs escaped her throat. "The veal!" she cried. "The veal killed them, and *I* cooked the veal!"

Smooth Kitty flew to Martha's side and placed her arm around Martha's shoulders. "We don't think *you* did it, dear," she said.

Dull Martha's hysterics could not be assuaged. "Did I use the wrong pan?" she wailed. "Is veal something that . . . reacts with iron . . . like tomatoes?" She snuffled loudly. "Did I use the wrong recipe in the book? Barnes said Mrs Plackett wanted fried cutlets. She left the marker in the book. I fried them in lard with salt and ground pepper. Was . . . the pepper actually . . . rat killer?" She removed her hands from her face, revealing shockingly red eyes, and tear tracks streaming down her cheeks. "I-I . . . I always do things stupidly! It's why everyone thinks I'm so dull. My brothers called me The Dunce. Father and Mother always said it's a pity I'm so unintelligent." Her sobs racked her whole body. "But . . . I'm sure . . . they always thought . . . I was h-harmless, and now I've gone and *murdered two people*!" She made no more attempt to hold back her tears.

Aldous ran to her and licked her face frantically, his bobbed tail wagging furiously.

"Hush, sweetheart," Disgraceful Mary Jane ordered, scooping up Martha and placing her head in her lap, where she could smooth Martha's wayward hair from her face. "It wasn't the pan or the recipe. Louise has just shown us it was poison. Hush! No one thinks you murdered those two old wretches. Someone else must have poisoned the veal before you ever got to it."

"That's right," Alice said stoutly. "You'd no more murder a headmistress than . . ."

"Conjugate a Latin verb," Dour Elinor offered.

"Hush, Elinor!" Smooth Kitty hissed.

". . . than fly to the moon." Alice glared at Dour Elinor.

"But who else could have poisoned the meat?" Dear Roberta asked. "Meaning no offence, Martha. But the meat came straight from the grocer's delivery boy, Saturday night. I remember the little packages, all wrapped in paper and string, along with the potatoes and beans and the other things Mrs Plackett had ordered."

"We were at church all morning," Pocked Louise said. "Half the town knows the larder door is never locked. Anyone could have slipped inside during church and poisoned the meat."

Dull Martha's eyes were wide. "You mean, anyone could have done it?"

"So it seems."

Martha drew a long, ragged breath. "If anyone could have done it, there's little reason to suppose I did, is there?"

"Not a smidgeon," Disgraceful Mary Jane replied. "Put it right out of your pretty head."

Martha sat up straight at these words. "Oh I'm not pretty," she said, and an objective observer noting her dishevelled hair, red eyes, and puffiness might have, at that moment, agreed. "Not like you. You're a great beauty."

"Perhaps," Mary Jane conceded, "but that doesn't mean you can't be as sweet as an angel yourself. When your nose isn't running, you're simply charming."

Chapter Ten

Louise dumped her noxious cyanide samples in the rhododendrons and opened the window to clear out any vapors. The other girls abandoned the schoolroom for the parlour, and Louise joined them there. Dull Martha sat curled in a ball on the sofa, heaping guilt on herself for ever suspecting Disgraceful Mary Jane after she'd been so kind to her. She hoped Dear Roberta would never divulge it to a living soul. Stout Alice sat in the rocking chair, lost in thought. Smooth Kitty browsed through a stack of papers on her lap. Dear Roberta dangled a bit of yarn for little Aldous, who cavorted and leaped about delightfully in his lust to snap it.

"Louise," Dear Roberta said, "why was one jar of liquid more blue than the other one?"

Pocked Louise frowned and considered. "That's to be expected, I think," she said after some thought. "Different specimen sizes, inexact measurements."

Smooth Kitty lay down her papers. "Everyone, I think we need to hold a meeting. If we are to remain here as independent young women, we need a source of funds on which to live. I have spent the afternoon looking through Mrs Plackett's papers, and . . ."

"Mrs Plackett's papers!"

The girls all turned in astonishment towards Pocked Louise, the source of this outburst.

"Funds!" the agitated young lady continued. She fixed each of them with a look of pure incredulity.

"Yes, Louise?" Kitty was clearly miffed. "Is something the matter?"

Pocked Louise threw up her hands. "Here we sit holding *meetings*, and discussing *funds* and *papers,* when I've just proven conclusively that there's a *poisoner on the loose*, who killed two people right here in this house. Who's to say he won't strike again and murder us all? Our time for dilly-dallying is past. This isn't a game of playing house. We have to solve this crime!"

Stout Alice smiled to herself. That Louise had pluck. Not many twelve-year-old girls could stand up to so many older girls like that. And clearly, she'd rattled Kitty.

But Smooth Kitty was not one to let anyone, much less a younger girl, discompose her for long. "No one is suggesting that we ignore the mystery, Louise," she said stiffly. "But if we don't attend to funds and papers, our attempt to remain here will fall to pieces, and we'll soon run out of food."

"If we ignore our poisoner, we'll end up choking on our food and sharing Mrs Plackett's fate," retorted Pocked Louise.

Dull Martha and Dear Roberta seized one another's hands and held on tight.

111

Disgraceful Mary Jane stretched and rose languidly to her feet. "There, there," she said, "let's not quarrel. You're both right. I propose that Kitty be placed in charge of funds and paperwork and Louise be appointed our resident Sherlock Holmes. All in favour . . ."

"Our resident *who*?" inquired Dull Martha.

"Sherlock Holmes," repeated Mary Jane. "He's the detective from *A Study in Scarlet* by A. Conan Doyle. Elinor, you've read it, haven't you? I thought you read everything."

Dour Elinor waved a dismissive hand. "That was popular a few years ago, but I was too deep into my Russian author phase to pay much attention to it."

Stout Alice had no wish for another of Mary Jane and Elinor's literary squabbles. Both were avid readers, but Elinor thought Mary Jane's romance novels were frivolous tripe. Alice coughed to gain the floor. "All in favour of Mary Jane's motion that we appoint Kitty as our chief financier and Louise as sleuth, say aye."

The room aye-d without delay. Kitty and Louise, seeing the consensus, aye-d also. Louise was inwardly thrilled at this vote of confidence from her friends, and if her ribcage swelled with a new sense of importance, she can be forgiven for that. She felt much more inclined to be magnanimous, so much so that she forgave Mary Jane for accusing her of over-thinking.

"I shall devise a plan of attack for my criminal investigation," she announced. "Meanwhile, Kitty, please proceed with the financial matters you wished to share with us."

Kitty had to hide her smile.

Dear Roberta, thinking a distraction might help keep moods tranquil, retrieved the linen Barnes had brought, and spread it out for everyone to begin working on the strawberry social tablecloth. She armed each girl with a skein of red or green or gold silk thread and a small paper of needles. They began to embroider strawberries around the edge of the cloth, as promised for the strawberry social. All the girls, that is, except Dour Elinor, who was much engrossed in her sketching, and Smooth Kitty, who was preoccupied by a lap full of ledgers and documents.

"I found a statement of accounts," Kitty began, "including copies of the bills she sends monthly to our families. Now, I'm a fair hand at penmanship, and Elinor does splendid work imitating others' hands. Between us two I believe we can continue producing the monthly statements, mailing them to our families, and collecting tuition on which to support ourselves. So that solves the money problem for the time being."

Mary Jane, Alice, Louise, and Elinor nodded, but Dear Roberta looked aghast. "You mean we shall deceive our parents and rob from them in order to live?"

Smooth Kitty had not anticipated this objection. Her mouth, it must be said, dropped open in a most un-Kittylike way.

"Nonsense, Roberta," Disgraceful Mary Jane replied. "Our parents support us financially regardless of where we are. It's their moral duty. Kitty is merely proposing that we take on the management ourselves."

Dear Roberta's conscience would not be so easily dismissed. "But they believe they're paying for us to receive an education," she said. "We will be taking their money under false pretences."

"Nothing of the kind," Smooth Kitty replied. "We shall continue our studies on an independent basis and help each other according to our individual strengths. You can teach music, Martha. Mary Jane was always a better dancer than Mrs Plackett. Elinor, you can teach French, from those years you lived in Paris as a child . . ."

"We shall read Victor Hugo," Elinor said, and Mary Jane groaned.

"That's the idea." Kitty nodded approvingly. "Louise, of course, will teach science, I can take math, and Roberta, needlework. See? We shall continue to be educated. Are you content, Roberta, dear?"

Roberta looked anything but content, but she nodded.

"Very good. Now I must return once more to the matter of money. As I said, I've been reviewing Mrs Plackett's papers, and her ledger has some mysteries of its own. I see line items for the grocer, for coal, for Dr Snelling, for the dry goods shop, for the chemist, for Farmer Butts for milk and for pasturing her pony, for Amanda Barnes's salary, and so on. All the school's basic expenses. The tuition money she receives ought to be enough to cover everything. But it isn't. I see several substantial checks drawn on her accounts which are labelled simply, "Cash." No explanation is given for these withdrawals. I can't account for it. But together, the withdrawals exceed the income."

Pocked Louise lured little Aldous back from Dull Martha with a biscuit. "Then why is Mrs Plackett not bankrupt?"

114

"Because she has a trunk full of Spanish doubloons buried in her cellar," announced Disgraceful Mary Jane.

"Really?" Dull Martha's eyes were wide.

Mary Jane laughed. "No, silly. I'm making a joke. Remember the coins Kitty found in their pockets? They were probably fakes anyhow."

"Yes, but didn't Doctor Snelling say Captain Plackett was said to have left his wife a fortune?" asked Dear Roberta.

Smooth Kitty nodded slowly. "So he did, Roberta," she said. "But remember what Miss Fringle said. If Mrs Plackett possessed a fortune, others would be sure to know. And Mrs Plackett would likely never have opened her school if she were rich, nor live on such spare economy."

Pocked Louise tickled Aldous's belly. "Then how does she get by with all these deficits?"

"I'm not certain," replied Smooth Kitty, "but here's a clue." She held up a folded piece of paper and opened it to review several five-pound notes. "This is the note that Henry Butts delivered this morning. It's from Admiral Lockwood."

The girls gazed at each other in astonishment.

Kitty began:

Dear C.,

   Hoping this finds you recovering smoothly. Was sorry to be deprived of your company yesternight. Enclosed are the results of an exchange merely for one. Better rates are likely in town.

"That's cryptic, to say the least!" said Kitty. She continued:

*I hope you enjoyed the little trinket I left
Sunday night. Its use will become clear before
long. I cherish the hope that your entrusting me
with these matters suggests you may, in time,
come to entrust more to my care. I await our next
visit with keen pleasure. Please allow me to be of
service in any way that I can.
Yours sincerely, Paris Lockwood, Admiral.*

Kitty looked at her schoolmates. "What do you suppose it means?"

"It means theirs is no ordinary friendship," Disgraceful Mary Jane said.

"'An exchange' . . . what did he say . . . 'merely for one' . . . 'better rates'?" Pocked Louise repeated. "What can that mean?"

"Is he doing some shopping for her?" wondered Dull Martha. "Exchanging merchandise?"

"If so, why would he *send* money?" Dour Elinor asked.

"It sounds to me like he's *selling* something for her," Stout Alice said. "Pawning off old bits of jewellery or furniture, do you think?"

"Possibly." Smooth Kitty frowned. This was a knotty puzzle to unravel.

"What was that bit about a trinket he left yesterday?" asked Dear Roberta. "Does he mean the wine?"

"I was wondering that myself . . . oh!" Kitty suddenly remembered. "Wait here, girls."

She raced to the hallway and pulled open the drawer to the hutch where she'd stowed Admiral Lockwood's package.

She brought it back into the parlour and slipped off its string. "He said it was a present for Mrs Plackett, just before he left," she explained. "I stuck it in a drawer and forgot all about it."

Disgraceful Mary Jane chided her. "How is it possible to forget a present?"

Kitty made a face at her. "If you'll recall, we had cooling corpses on our minds at the time." By now she had the paper off, and the other girls had gathered around for a better look.

It was a wooden box, cherry-stained and lustrous in its finish, but smooth and unadorned by carvings or embellishments. Kitty fingered the latch and opened the top. A black object lay upon a field of black velvet. She held it up to the light.

"An elephant?" Dull Martha asked.

"An elephant," Pocked Louise affirmed.

"Such a curious elephant!" said Dear Roberta.

"Why an elephant?" Smooth Kitty mused.

"The man has strange ideas about how to woo women," said Disgraceful Mary Jane.

"Oh, I don't know," said Dour Elinor. "I'm no expert. But that's ebony wood. Very rare and beautiful." She took the elephant from Kitty and studied it more closely. "The toenails – or whatever you call them on an elephant – are gold, and so are the tusks, and this necklace it has . . . That's a sapphire stone on the necklace! And the eyes, if I'm not mistaken, are rubies."

"Rather a lot of jewellery for an elephant," observed Pocked Louise.

"Perhaps it's a royal elephant," offered Dour Elinor.

Mary Jane took the elephant from Elinor. "Let me see that one more time." She peered at the admiral's gift. "Is the trunk gold, too?"

Pocked Louise shook her head. "Brass, I think. Much harder than gold. It's got grooves along the side, here, I suppose like a real elephant's trunk. Nostrils, too."

"How strange." Smooth Kitty reread the admiral's note. "Such an odd little trinket. 'Its use will become clear before long.' What *use* could an ebony elephant possibly have?"

"That's like asking, 'What's the point of earrings and bracelets?'" Mary Jane's righteous scorn took in Kitty and any who dared to agree with her. "'A thing of beauty is a joy forever.' Keats."

"You've changed your tone a good deal," observed Stout Alice. "What happened to 'strange ideas about how to woo women'?"

"Precious metals and gemstones happened, that's what," muttered Dour Elinor.

"But what does it all *mean*?" Smooth Kitty felt more frustrated than she cared to let on. "We already have one mystery to solve: who killed Mrs Plackett and her brother? And now here's another: what's the story behind this elephant and the money in Admiral Lockwood's letter?"

"Mrs Plackett's finances are a mystery in themselves," said Pocked Louise.

"Kitty, would you read us the bit again from the admiral's letter about the money?" Dear Roberta said. "It reminds me of something."

Smooth Kitty obliged her. "'Enclosed are the results of an exchange merely for one. Better rates are likely in town.' Any theories?"

Roberta nodded over the strawberry she was stitching. "Exchanges and rates sound like financial terms," she said. "I hear my uncle use those words when he talks to Papa. Exchanging money from different countries and whatnot. Apparently it's quite complicated."

Kitty paused, then scanned once more the admiral's note. "By gum, you're a marvel, Roberta dear," she exclaimed. "How do you do it?"

"Do what, exchange money?" Dear Roberta looked shocked. "*I* don't know. Ask my uncle."

Kitty laughed. "No, I mean, how do you keep unravelling mysteries for us?"

Dear Roberta's eyebrows rose. "Do I?"

"I think so," Kitty said. "Think of the coins we found. What if there are more of them? Perhaps the admiral exchanged one of the coins for Mrs Plackett, and that's where the money came from."

"One coin couldn't be worth so many pounds," Dull Martha declared.

"It could if it's old and rare," said Pocked Louise.

"I think it's all a sham," Disgraceful Mary Jane announced. "The real point is, he's giving her money and gifts because he fancies her, and she lets him do it out of necessity. He's probably been bailing her out for some time. 'Dear C.' 'Deprived of your company.' '*Keen* pleasure!' Our crosspatch of a headmistress was having an affair with the elderly admiral. The naughty old girl."

Dull Martha was aghast. "Surely not!"

"But he sent her twenty pounds," Smooth Kitty said. "*Twenty pounds*! He's rich. He must be near eighty, and she was sixty-two. I suppose to him, she was fresh as a daisy."

"How revolting." Pocked Louise shuddered. "Men are bad enough, but he's so horrid and *old*."

Disgraceful Mary Jane began to laugh. The other girls stared at her. She only laughed harder and clutched her sides. "Imagine his thrill when he gets a kiss from our Alice!"

Stout Alice heaved a sofa cushion at Mary Jane. "Eugh, don't even joke about it!"

Mary Jane wiped tears from her cheeks. "We may need you to, mightn't we, Kitty? Alice must sacrifice herself for the cause, no?" She pantomimed a kiss. "Ooh, Admiral, you look *dashing* with that cane. Your brass buttons send my heart a-flutter."

Stout Alice rose to her feet. "I'm already sacrificing plenty for this endeavour," she said, then bit her lip. A vision of Leland Murphy flashed before her eyes. "More than you'll know. And it can't last forever. We need a plan to put a stop to it, or else I shall spend the rest of my life as Mrs Plackett, with Alice nowhere in sight. I'm to disappear, apparently. It amounts to you covering up her death by killing me, and I'm not volunteering to die just yet."

"Oh come now, Alice," Smooth Kitty protested. "Let's not be melodramatic. We're just asking our Alice to stay home now and then with a headache. No one's asking you to *die*."

"We might be, though," Dour Elinor said softly.

The room went silent. All eyes turned to Elinor. She went on sketching as though nothing had happened.

Stout Alice's voice cracked as she spoke. "What did you mean by that, Elinor?"

Dour Elinor held up her still life to examine it at arm's length. An angel tombstone spread her wings over a slumbering churchyard beneath a waning crescent moon. "We seem to forget that someone tried to murder Mrs Plackett. That someone must now believe they failed. What's to stop them from trying again?"

Chapter Eleven

Dear Roberta began to quietly cry.

Stout Alice rocked in Mrs Plackett's chair. Anyone watching her closely might have noticed her face grow pale beneath her fading make-up.

Dull Martha seized Aldous and stroked his soft curly ear against her cheek. Aldous bit her nose lovingly in reply.

Disgraceful Mary Jane met Smooth Kitty's gaze. It was the first time Mary Jane had seen her roommate look afraid. She sidled next to her on the sofa and spoke in a low voice so the others couldn't hear.

"Have we waded in deeper than we can swim?" she whispered into Smooth Kitty's hair. "We can still back out, love. It's not too late."

Smooth Kitty stiffened. The hand holding Admiral Lockwood's letter curled in on itself tightly. How dare Mary Jane voice aloud all her own thoughts?

"It's all right, dear heart," Mary Jane whispered. "We have nothing we need to prove. Independence was a lovely dream."

Mary Jane was trying to reassure her, Kitty knew, but

her words fell like icicles. Kitty shivered. She would not, she would *not* submit to fear and lose heart now! She imagined herself returning home to Father and felt protest welling up inside her. The isolation of a desert island would be preferable to evenings in the drawing room with Mr Maximilian Heaton, Lord of All He Surveyed.

No, Kitty would not go back home. She'd worked too hard and risked too much to surrender now. But to put poor Alice in harm's way? Kitty felt sick. She couldn't. If only *she* were the one who could pretend to be Mrs Plackett.

"We shall find the murderer before he has a chance to hurt Alice," said Pocked Louise. "We must."

"And do what with him?" asked Dour Elinor. "Tell the police he killed Mrs Plackett, and we're all living here alone, we scandalous maidens? That would end the game."

"We're trapped," moaned Dear Roberta. "This is the price of our deceit. Our wages for dishonesty! We never should have buried Mrs Plackett in the vegetable garden."

"We'll find a solution." Pocked Louise was resolute. "If it's to be a battle of wits, we shall win!"

"In the meantime," Stout Alice said, speaking for the first time, "I'll be careful.

But somehow, we need a plan to kill Mrs Plackett off a second time – a plan that allows us to stay here – so I don't have to be her for the rest of my life. It's a cruel fate to be a widow before I've even been married."

"Alice is right," Louise said. "This is a rotten deal for her if she has to remain in disguise forever, anytime we leave the house."

"We could go on a journey," Disgraceful Mary Jane said. "To Egypt, perhaps. Or Turkey. And we could say that Mrs Plackett contracted an illness there and died. No one would be the wiser."

"That could work." Stout Alice nodded her approval.

Smooth Kitty poured water on this suggestion. "*If* we could afford it. Which we can't." She paced the room, thinking furiously. There must be a way to set them all free and rid themselves forever of the burden of Mrs Plackett, may she rest in peace in the vegetable garden.

"A school can't exist without a headmistress, so we need a Mrs Plackett," Pocked Louise mused aloud. "At the same time, we need to get rid of her so Alice need not keep on pretending."

"And so as not to have a murderer on our heels," added Stout Alice.

"If we pretend she dies in Egypt, would that satisfy the murderer?" Disgraceful Mary Jane asked. "Or mightn't he travel to Egypt to investigate? If he wants her dead badly enough, he might."

"It would depend on his reasons," Alice said.

"That's a mystery in itself," Mary Jane said. "Why would anyone want Mrs Plackett dead? She was a pompous, crabby old bird, but that's scarcely cause for the battle-axe."

"You're forgetting something," Dour Elinor replied. "We have two murders here, not one. Someone wanted Mr Godding dead, too."

"Well, that's no mystery in the slightest," Disgraceful Mary Jane said with a shudder. "He was revolting and rude.

He smoked vile cigars, and his whiskers were diabolical. He gave men a very bad name."

"Never mind his whiskers," Pocked Louise said. "Men don't need Aldous Godding to give them a bad name. The question is, who would benefit by the death of Mrs Plackett and her brother? Whose interests were served by their absence?"

"Besides ours, you mean," Dull Martha said. She tugged her needle up high above her head.

Dear Roberta paused to admire the ripe red strawberry she'd just finished stitching. "Do you suppose Mrs Plackett left a will? That would tell us who inherits her property after she's gone."

Mary Jane threw up hands. "What property?" she cried.

"This house is a valuable piece of property," Pocked Louise said.

Smooth Kitty shook her head. "I've gone through all her papers. I never saw a will."

"Her solicitor would have it on file, if there was one," Pocked Louise said. "That's what my father said when Grandfather died."

"The solicitor would never let us see it," Smooth Kitty said, "unless Alice fooled him into thinking she was Mrs Plackett."

Stout Alice clapped her hands. "Oh! Her solicitor!"

"Mr Wilkins, isn't it?" Mary Jane said. "He employs that pathetic milkweed, Leland Murphy. Why are you so excited?"

Stout Alice bristled. "He's no milkweed. And I'm not excited. But he – Mr Murphy – brought by some papers this morning. Let me go and find them."

Alice returned shortly with the papers Leland Murphy had brought. She had shoved them behind the coffee jar on a kitchen shelf when Dr Snelling arrived, and there they might have stayed forever. She handed the papers to Kitty, who riffled through them.

Kitty smiled at the other girls. "It *is* a will! Imagine the luck. We're genuine sleuths now, aren't we, girls?" She scanned the lines rapidly, searching for meaning. The language was formal and Latinate, and unravelling the meaning wasn't easy. Finally she looked up.

"Mrs Plackett's only beneficiary is 'Darling Nephew Julius', to further his education," she announced. "He inherits the school and all its contents in the event of Mrs Plackett's death."

"He can't be our murderer." Dour Elinor looked seriously disappointed. "How can a child in India poison his aunt and uncle in England?"

Dear Roberta picked up the ebony elephant and examined it. "Voodoo magic?"

Smooth Kitty ignored this. "He's too young, and too far away, to have done it."

"And too ill," Dull Martha added.

Disgraceful Mary Jane and Stout Alice exchanged looks.

"He isn't ill, darling," Mary Jane said. "That's just a story we made up about him."

Dull Martha's cheeks coloured. She wouldn't lift her eyes from her sewing. "Right. I forgot."

"Perhaps he had an accomplice," Mary Jane went on. "A partner in crime here in England."

"Which would make sense," Smooth Kitty replied, "if the crime was to pinch a jar of marmalade. No, girls. Honestly! Little Julius isn't our killer. We're meandering. And we have identified no one else who stands to benefit from the murders."

"I'll investigate," Pocked Louise declared.

Stout Alice spoke up. "I'm still puzzled over this matter of insufficient money. What if we find that we, too, need extra sums of cash, and we run out of funds in the same manner as Mrs Plackett?"

Smooth Kitty inwardly blessed Alice for shifting the subject back to matters within their control. She rose and struck a match to light several candles, as the twilight pulled its violet curtain over the parlour's eastern windows. Once she could see sufficiently, she produced a sheet of paper on which she'd written out a budget. "We shall economise," she said, "starting with the most obvious expense we can eliminate."

"Butterscotch and shortbread biscuits?" asked Stout Alice.

"Amanda Barnes," was Kitty's reply.

This was met with a shocked silence.

"Not Barnes," Dear Roberta protested. "She doesn't deserve to be let go."

"Who will do for us if she's not here?" asked Dull Martha. "Do you mean we should look for other household help?"

"We shall have to manage on our own," Kitty said. "We can't have her about the house all day long. We'd never be able to uphold the illusion that Alice is Mrs Plackett for the benefit of someone who was indoors all day."

Shock became horror.

"You mean to sack her!" Dull Martha cried. "Fire her on the spot, with no month's notice to find other employment!"

Disgraceful Mary Jane looked stunned. "I don't even know how to do brasses and silver."

"Oh, Kitty, you wouldn't be so awful," Dear Roberta said. "Leave her penniless, destroy her reputation, and break her heart all in one blow! It's too, too much."

Kitty had anticipated these objections, but not, perhaps, their vehemence.

"We can pay her a month's salary," she said. "It will pinch us, but we'll certainly do it. And we – I – shall explain that Mrs Plackett's resources are too strained by Mr Godding's trip to India, and funds needed for Julius's medical care. I shall apologise, of course, and say that it all came about so suddenly."

"If she's being paid for the month, she'll wish to work the month," Stout Alice said. "Remember how hard it was to persuade her to take today as a holiday?"

"We shall simply have to insist. I'll do it myself. First thing tomorrow morning. I shall walk into the village to meet her at her home and deliver the news." Smooth Kitty spoke bravely but felt her mouth go dry. It had seemed simple enough to dispose of Barnes when looking at ledgers, but now, the real prospect of looking her in the eye and sacking her felt more terrifying than grappling hand-to-hand with the unknown murderer. Poor, plucky Amanda Barnes, who worked so hard to provide for her elderly mother. Again nagging doubt hovered at the corner of Kitty's mind. Was she doing the right thing? She chased those thoughts away. Of course she was. There was no other option.

"What did you fix for supper, Mary Jane?" Stout Alice asked. "I'm famished already."

Disgraceful Mary Jane gave a self-satisfied little toss of her head. "Mansfield muffins and rice pudding," she declared. "I'll go check to see how they're coming along." She ventured from the parlour and down the hallway towards the kitchen stairs. She'd not gone far when the doorbell rang. "I'll get it," she called.

Stout Alice heaved herself off her chair. "Not again," she moaned. "Come with me, would you, Elinor? Just in case I need my face painted again for *this* unwelcome visitor."

The other girls listened as Disgraceful Mary Jane opened the door and greeted the newcomer. The voice was unmistakable.

"Lord, Kitty," Pocked Louise said. "Speak of the devil. You can save yourself a trip in the morning. It's Amanda Barnes."

Chapter Twelve

"Good evening, young misses." Amanda Barnes greeted the young ladies in the parlour. She carried a dish of something mounded high and covered with a napkin. "Look at you all, hard at work on your tablecloth for the social. It's coming along grand. That's a fine berry you've just sewn, Miss Roberta. Think you young ladies will be able to finish by Wednesday?"

Smooth Kitty pulled a length of tablecloth over the strange jewelled elephant. Her stomach sickened. If she had to do this ghastly thing, best to get it over with. She rose to her feet.

"Don't get up on my account, Miss Katherine," Barnes protested. "I'm just here to collect the pan I forgot. In all my chattering this morning, I left without it. And I had so much free time today, I baked your headmistress an eel pie, seeing as she's unwell." She twitched the napkin off her hot plate, revealing a tall, brown, crumbling pastry crust with savoury fragrances wafting from its slits.

Smooth Kitty groaned inwardly. On the very day she had to sack Amanda Barnes, that good soul had spent her holiday baking them a pie. It was too cruel.

Kitty grasped Barnes by the elbow and took a candlestick in her other hand. "Mary Jane is cooking in the kitchen. Won't you join me in the schoolroom for a moment?"

"Certainly," Barnes replied, and set down her pie on an end table. "Is something the matter, Miss Katherine? Your mistress – is she worse?"

Dull Martha met them outside the schoolroom. She held out a tiny skillet. "Is this the pan you're looking for, Barnes?"

"The very same," Miss Barnes replied. "Thank you kindly."

Kitty closed the schoolroom door behind Martha, set her candlestick on a desk, and gestured for Barnes to be seated in a student chair. She did the same. Now, how to begin?

"Miss Katherine?"

Kitty forced herself to meet Barnes's expectant gaze.

"Is there something you wished to say to me?"

"There is," Kitty said. Her voice suddenly felt, to her own ears, weak and young. "Barnes, there is no pleasant way for me to say what I now must. I regret this most profoundly."

Barnes's expression did not change. She was perfectly composed, and yet something in her eyes made Kitty feel utterly exposed, and wish she could whisk herself away to any place but here, with the daily woman seeing straight through her.

"I am afraid I must – Mrs Plackett has tasked me with the unhappy burden – of dismissing you from your position here at Saint Etheldreda's School."

There was a moment of terrible silence. Kitty looked at Barnes, and looked away again, reproaching herself for her cowardice. Her eyes fell upon the blackboard at the side of the room, where Mrs Plackett's deliberate and flawless hand still spelled out the imperfect conjugation of *vouloir*, 'to want,' in white chalk curves. *Je voulais, tu voulais, il/elle voulait . . .*

When finally she spoke, Barnes's usually firm voice wavered. "You're giving me notice, Miss Katherine?"

Kitty nodded.

"A month from now I shall have to leave?"

Kitty shook her head. "Sooner," she said. "Now."

There was a slight intake of breath.

Nous voulions, vous vouliez, ils/elles voulaient. We used to want, you used to want, they used to want. What, Kitty wondered, had Mrs Plackett used to want?

"Might I be permitted to ask why?"

Barnes's words jolted Kitty back to the present. She struggled to think of how to answer.

"Has my service been found lacking?"

Kitty feared she might begin to cry. This was worse than burying dead bodies, a thousand times worse. Amanda Barnes gripped the handle of the skillet that lay in her lap, and for an instant Kitty imagined Barnes striking her with it.

"If I have failed to give satisfaction to Mrs Plackett, I wonder why she has never said so." Barnes held herself straighter and taller than before. "I've been in service twenty-four years, Miss Katherine, since I was younger than you, and seven years here with Mrs Plackett. In all that time I have never had a word of real complaint from any of my employers."

132

Twenty-four years – a career older than Kitty herself. Who was she to put the first stain upon it? *I did not kill Mrs Plackett,* she told herself sternly. *Whether or not we hid the bodies, Barnes would have lost her job today.*

"Barnes," Kitty said, "you've done a fine job. The simple truth is that the costs of Julius's medical care and Mr Godding's trip threaten to deplete her resources to the point where she can no longer afford household help. She has just enough to pay you a month's salary."

Ordinarily Amanda Barnes had a soft, comfortable aspect, but now her backbone was a sword. Kitty wished she could crawl into the bookshelves and hide among the French grammars. She began, absurdly, to resent Barnes's resolute strength. In some perverse way, Kitty felt, it would almost be better if she showed some human weakness.

"Miss Katherine."

Kitty made herself face the former daily woman.

"You have been the bearer of strange tidings twice today," Barnes said. "To be dismissed in this way – sacked from my post by a student! – is strange, to say the least. I do not wish to impose, but my years of service here entitle me to some small consideration. I feel I should at least be allowed to hear the reason for my dismissal from my own employer's lips." She punctuated her speech with a little nod, as though her choice of words had pleased her.

Kitty hesitated. The request was fair. To refuse could attract suspicion. Was Stout Alice up for this ordeal? She would have to be. "Well. Yes. I can see that that would be a natural request to make. Will you wait here while I go see if she is in a position to speak with you?"

Barnes paused a brief instant, then nodded brusquely. *Aha!* Kitty thought. There it was. That first wrinkle in her armour. She was nervous about facing Mrs Plackett, Kitty would swear it. "Please remain here while she prepares to receive you." Kitty closed the door behind her, and hurried down the hallway. At least, she thought with grim satisfaction, as she peered through the dining room to its western windows, the sun was now fully set, and darkness could only help.

Stout Alice peeped out from behind Mrs Plackett's bedroom door. "Is it done? Did you sack her? Is she gone?"

Smooth Kitty sighed. "Dear Alice. You will despise me now."

Alice shrugged. "I already do. What do you need?"

Kitty briefed her on her conversation with Barnes. Alice pulled Mrs Plackett's frilly night cap down low over her forehead and climbed under the covers of the headmistress's bed.

A fit of hilarity overcame Smooth Kitty. She may be excused for this; she had had a trying day. "Oh, Grandmother," she giggled, "What great ears you have!"

"The better to listen to sacked housekeepers with, Little Red-Cap." Alice rolled her eyes.

"Remember, you're sickly. And heartbroken that things have come to this sorry pass."

Stout Alice pointed imperiously towards the door, just as Mrs Plackett herself might have done. "Shoo! Bring me Amanda Barnes, and let's get this behind us."

Smooth Kitty ushered Barnes into the bedroom. Only one candle burned on the far mantelpiece, leaving Alice shrouded in darkness. She seemed to slump weakly against her pillows, as though she hadn't the strength to sit up in bed but had done so heroically, at great personal sacrifice.

Amanda Barnes seemed to crumple at the sight of her employer. She declined the chair Kitty offered her. She peered at Mrs Plackett, then rapidly turned away.

"I . . . I'm sorry to see you brought so low, Mrs Plackett." Barnes voice faltered. "It was wrong of me to disturb you."

"No." A sombre voice emerged from under the ruffled nightcap. "It is I who must apologise for this sorry state of affairs. I'm cut to the heart to think of what this will do to you."

Barnes seemed at a loss. "Your brother's really gone, then? To India, so sudden?"

Stout Alice nodded slowly. "Gone. And may he speedily return with good news. But, oh! Barnes!" Alice raised a handkerchief to her eyes with a trembling hand. "I fear for him. I do. My heavy heart tells me I shall not see my brother again in this world."

Amanda Barnes gulped. "Now," she said. "You mustn't say things like that. It'll weaken *your* health, and we can't have that."

Stout Alice dabbed her nose with her kerchief. "As soon as I am up from bed I shall write you a letter of reference, explaining fully the circumstances that brought your employment here to a close. It will do you credit as you apply for new positions."

"I'm obliged to you, Ma'am." She kept her head bowed low. "And I hope that you and the young ladies will be able to manage all right on your own."

Kitty became conscious of an unpleasant smell wafting into the room from the kitchen below. Footsteps could be heard, as could voices lamenting the fate of the Mansfield muffins.

Amanda Barnes spoke quietly. "I'll take my leave now."

"We will send you the letter and your upcoming month's pay," said Stout Alice.

Barnes nodded and opened the door. A cloud of burnt flour fumes entered the room, but the daily woman had too much pride to cough. She showed herself down the corridor and out of the house. Smooth Kitty felt her whole body deflate when she heard the front door close.

Disgraceful Mary Jane poked her head in the door. "How'd that go?"

"Badly enough," Stout Alice said. She pulled off her nightcap. "How goes the cooking?"

Mary Jane shrugged. "The muffins weren't a total success, but the rice pudding looks decent. A little lumpy, maybe. But come and eat Barnes's eel pie. She made it specially for you."

"Did you test it for poison?" Alice asked.

That's when the tears caught up with Kitty. "We don't have to test Barnes's eel pie," she lamented. "It'll be right as rain. Poor, poor woman." She buried her face in a pillow.

Chapter Thirteen

The students enrolled at Saint Etheldreda's School for Young Ladies set out the following morning for a walk into the village of Ely, armed with baskets and parasols, on a mission to complete several errands of vital importance. It was a fine clear day, with warm sun balanced by cool breezes blowing in across the fens. Saint Mary's church bells were just ringing ten o'clock as they closed the front door to the school behind them, and Mr Shambles, the rooster, crowed as they closed the gate.

"This is fine, for a change," Disgraceful Mary Jane declared, as they set off down Prickwillow Road towards Ely. "That house was beginning to close in on me."

The cry of the train whistle greeted them from the far-off station.

"Someday let's board that train and go somewhere interesting," Stout Alice said.

"Agreed," said Disgraceful Mary Jane. "Someplace exotic and far away."

"In the meantime," Kitty said sternly, "until we can board

that train, we've got business to attend to. Today we'll shop, tomorrow we'll wash clothes. We've got some terribly muddy frocks, and we promised Alice we'd launder Mrs Plackett's things."

"*Things*," Stout Alice repeated, "Speaking of Mrs Plackett's things, Kitty, dear, where did you put Admiral Lockwood's elephant?"

"I put it in the curio cabinet in the drawing room," Kitty said. "Why do you ask?"

Alice frowned. "I can't say, really. It's certain to be quite valuable, don't you think?"

"I locked the cabinet." Kitty felt defensive, which made her cross. "It's safe enough there. I'm sure that's what Mrs Plackett would have done."

"I'm just thinking about our murderer," Alice said slowly. "He let himself into the house to poison the meat. It makes me wonder, is all."

"Maybe we should conceal the elephant somewhere no one would ever think to look," Dull Martha ventured.

"I'll think about it," Kitty said, rather loftily. Secretly she suspected Alice was right to be concerned. But taking precautions was *her* role in their little tribe. Anything she didn't think of first, she couldn't consider to be valid, on principle.

Before long they reached the bustle of the city of Ely itself. Because it had a cathedral it was considered a city; by any other measure it was a small, bustling market town. But even a hamlet feels like a metropolis to bright, social young ladies who have been cloistered far too long in one house. The shopkeepers in their aprons, the tradesmen in their boots, and the housewives with their caps and babies were an invigorating sight. They proved the world was more than seven maidens, two corpses, and a puppy. Even Dour Elinor took notice of other living creatures with curious interest.

They stopped first at the post office on Market Street, where they mailed a stack of written bills, one to each of their families, as well as polite notes in Mrs Plackett's counterfeit hand to Miss Fringle, inquiring after her health; to Mrs Rumsey, thanking her for the tablecloth linen; and to Admiral Lockwood, thanking him for his solicitous inquiries and generous gifts.

"That one was the most horrid one to write," Dour Elinor muttered, dropping it in the letterbox. "Kitty made me redo it twice. She said my writing wasn't *alluring* enough."

"Disgusting," Pocked Louise said.

"But necessary," added Smooth Kitty.

"And wonderfully scandalous," said Disgraceful Mary Jane.

Elinor was unappeased. "How does one make 'Thank you for the elephant' sound alluring, I'd like to know?"

Each letter had informed its recipient that Mrs Plackett was beginning to mend, and feeling much better now. Kitty thought this advisable, so that Mrs Plackett's sudden appearance at tomorrow's strawberry social would not attract too much unwelcome comment.

A postman met them in passing as they left the post office, and tipped his hat.

"Morning, young ladies," he said. "So sorry to hear about Mrs Plackett's nephew ailing."

They curtseyed in mute surprise, but the street all around them was too crowded now to discuss. They made their way to High Street. Over the rooftops of the Market Street lodgings and shops loomed grand Ely Cathedral – a friendly silhouette from a distance but almost terrifying in its ponderous bulk up close. Saint Etheldreda was its patron saint and founder, and their own school, as with so many other institutions in the city of Ely, was named for her.

"The Cathedral of the Maiden Saint," Pocked Louise murmured.

Dear Roberta bowed her head. "May she deliver us maidens from our present troubles."

Stout Alice patted Roberta's back. "We need all the help we can get."

"Young ladies," said a voice from behind them. They turned to see a woman dressed in a stately mauve jacket and skirt, with a peacock-green blouse, nodding graciously towards them. "Will you be so kind, my dear young ladies, as to convey to your headmistress Mrs Groutley-Ball's best wishes and concerns regarding her brother and nephew?"

They nodded mutely. Mrs Groutley-Ball did likewise and moved on down the street.

"What in heaven's name is going on?" whispered Disgraceful Mary Jane.

"Miss Fringle, I think," Stout Alice replied. "She wouldn't miss a chance to tell a living soul about the calamities at Constance Plackett's house."

Smooth Kitty's mouth was set in a grim line. "I don't like it," she said. "It does our cause no favours. The less people mindful of our affairs, the better."

"Then we should move to London," Pocked Louise said, "for there's no escaping everyone knowing your affairs in Ely."

Their next errand was far from pleasant. They made their way down High Street to St. Mary's Street, where they passed their own parish church. Reverend Rumsey waved good morning to them from the rectory window by raising his glass in the air. From St. Mary's Street they turned onto Cromwell Avenue, where the lord protector himself once lived. In a little row of dwellings, they found the number that marked where Amanda Barnes lived with her mother.

Smooth Kitty jingled the bell. Nothing happened.

A little boy rolling a hoop watched them from some distance up the street. He looked like a youth with a high opinion of no one.

They waited, and were just about to leave, when Kitty thought she heard something from within. It was a slow, shuffling, scraping sound.

The door creaked open, and there stood a very elderly woman indeed. Her white hair was pulled back off her face into a wispy bun. Her face drooped in folds of wrinkled skin, and her tired, careworn eyes took in the sight of the young ladies without any show of welcome.

"Mrs Barnes?" Smooth Kitty began. "Does Amanda Barnes live here?"

Mrs Barnes nodded once.

141

Smooth Kitty held out an envelope. "Then may we leave this for her?" The old lady made no move to take it. "It contains her letter of reference, and her upcoming month's pay."

Still the old woman stared blearily at them, without any gesture towards accepting the envelope.

"It's got *money* in it," Disgraceful Mary Jane added loudly.

Stout Alice elbowed Mary Jane. Slowly, the woman took the envelope.

Kitty curtseyed, and the other young ladies followed suit. Then they hurried back down Cromwell Street towards St. Mary's. The surly youth sent his hoop flying along the road after them. Pocked Louise heard it rattle, turned, and caught it before it struck Dour Elinor.

"I say!" she cried, glaring at the young miscreant. "What do you mean by this?"

The boy sauntered over and plucked the hoop from Pocked Louise. "Stuck up prigs, sacking my aunt," he said. "My brother Jimmy told me all about it. He's what delivers your groceries. Every week she fusses over the order. Makes Jimmy bring it to her so she can check if the foodstuffs is fine enough for you lot. There's nothing she hain't done for that school. Mam said so. And this is the thanks she gets." He scrunched up his freckled nose in a scowl laced with all the malice his eight-year-old face could hold, and stuck out his tongue.

"Stick your tongue out and somebody'll chop it off," snapped Disgraceful Mary Jane.

"Stop," Stout Alice murmured. "Let him be." To the youth she said, "Good morning, young lad," then turned and walked away.

Once clear of Cromwell Street, everyone breathed easier. They headed back to Market Street, prepared to fill their baskets with groceries.

"Let's not go to our usual shop," Pocked Louise suggested. "I don't think I'm ready to meet the wrath of another of Barnes's nephews just yet."

"You don't think it was the grocer, or his butcher man, who poisoned the veal, do you?" Dull Martha inquired. Poison and veal were subjects the poor girl still could not shake from her troubled mind.

"I considered that," Pocked Louise replied. "But if the poison had originated with the grocer's butcher, there'd be corpses all over town, and we've heard no death-knells ring."

"Was Mrs Plackett behind in her food bill?" Dour Elinor asked.

They found a grocer where no Barneses were employed. The proprietor, a smiling man with a shiny bald dome and red suspenders, asked to be remembered to Mrs Plackett, and wished her a speedy recovery.

"Good Lord," Kitty gasped, when finally they left the store laden with cans, boxes, and paper packages, including dogs' meat. "Did somebody advertise our troubles in the newspaper?"

"It's Miss Fringle, I tell you," Stout Alice repeated. "Sprained ankle or no, she'd canvass the town with any gossip."

"Next, my friend the chemist," said Pocked Louise. "Elinor needs better cosmetics for . . . you-know-what."

"Is he really your friend?" Dull Martha inquired.

Pocked Louise smiled. "No. He just operates my favourite store in town."

They entered the chemist's shop and set down their baskets. Kitty's eyes roved aimlessly over the rows upon straight rows of shining bottles, each with their neatly pasted labels. Odours of potent and heady chemicals, mingled with perfumes and caramel sweets, struck her nostrils.

Elinor, Louise, and Alice shopped for cosmetic supplies together, but it was Elinor who led the purchases. "These grease paints will do nicely," she said. "We need cold cream and stage putty."

"Putting on a drama pageant, ladies?" Mr Buckley, the chemist, greeted them.

Elinor ignored his question. "Do you have any Vaseline?"

Mr Buckley looked pleased to be asked. "As a matter of fact, I do," he said, reaching for a small grey bottle. "Been hearing all sorts of marvellous claims about this in the journals. Cures a multitude of skin problems, they say."

Disgraceful Mary Jane, Dear Roberta, and Dull Martha wandered off to explore a display of perfumes and face creams, leaving Kitty standing by the counter. Her mind was too preoccupied to notice a customer enter the shop and stand beside her.

Mr Buckley left the young ladies to greet the newcomer. "Can I help you, sir?"

"Bicarbonate of soda, please," the stranger said.

"A tin, or packets?"

Kitty glanced at the customer. He was a young man dressed in a tan linen coat and a grey John Bull top hat, with a shocking bow-tie of violet silk. His face and hands were unusually browned by the sun, and he spoke with an accent she couldn't place.

"Packets, I suppose," the young man said. He caught sight of Kitty watching him, and tipped the brim of his hat in her direction. Kitty quickly looked away.

Mr Buckley handed the customer his packets of powder and collected payment. "Rather young to suffer indigestion, aren't you?" he observed with a smile.

The customer returned the smile. "They're for my mother." He jingled his change in his palm then placed two half-pennies back on the counter. "Ha'penny caramels, if I may."

Mr Buckley fished two caramels out of a tall glass jar and handed them to the customer. He unwrapped the wax paper off of one and popped it into his mouth. Then, with a wink and another tip of his hat, he dropped the other into Smooth Kitty's grocery basket, and left the shop.

The bell on the door had stopped jingling long before Kitty stopped staring after him. "Aren't you going to eat it?" Mr Buckley polished his glass countertop. His eyes twinkled at Kitty. "Mrs Buckley made that batch fresh this morning."

Kitty fished the sweet from her basket and eyed it suspiciously. It felt wrong, somehow, to eat the candy. As though eating it would sanction the stranger's forward behaviour.

But he was gone, and the caramel felt soft and pliant between her fingers.

And anyway, the young man was much too well-mannered and well-dressed to be a scoundrel. It was only a spontaneous burst of generosity, she decided, not flirtation.

She slipped the caramel into her mouth. Rich, buttery sweetness oozed across her tongue.

"Next time Mamma sends me my allowance I'm coming back for this cologne." Disgraceful Mary Jane reappeared at Kitty's side, nearly causing her to choke on her candy. "By the by, who was that young man you were talking with? What did he want with you?"

Kitty struggled to conceal her chewing and keep her face blank. "Nufink."

Elinor, Alice, and Louise returned to the counter with their final items.

"Will this be all?" the chemist asked. He tallied up their purchases, and Smooth Kitty, who held the purse, stepped forward to pay. Mr Buckley counted out her change. "You're the young ladies from the school out on Prickwillow, aren't you?"

Kitty swallowed her caramel. "That's right." Now for the condolences for Mrs Plackett.

"How's your carpet beetle problem?"

Kitty blinked. "I beg your pardon?"

"Your carpet beetle problem."

Kitty turned to Pocked Louise for help. That girl nodded thoughtfully. "Now you mention it, I do believe Barnes mentioned carpet beetles vexing her. I haven't noticed them."

"Must be the preparation I made her did its job. You ladies have a good day, now. Oughtn't you to be at your studies?"

The girls looked to Kitty to answer this awkward question.

"Mrs Plackett believes it's useful for us to take field trips

146

from time to time to practice our, er, arithmetic in the shops," she said.

Mr Buckley nodded. "There's sense in that. Good day to you."

As they walked along Nutholt Lane towards Prickwillow Road, Kitty sucked caramel from her teeth and puzzled over the peculiar young man. Why her? Why would he single her out like that? Most likely it was not a particular compliment for her. He probably bought sweets for young ladies every day of the week.

Pocked Louise also occupied herself with thoughts of the stranger. What an odd coincidence that the very same person who had come looking for the school the day before should appear in the apothecary shop. Was he following them? Should she tell the others? She bit her lip. She would need to confess to withholding his appearance yesterday. No need, she decided. But she didn't trust him. He had just the sort of good looks a dangerous scoundrel *would* have. Maybe even a poisoner. They met him in a chemist's shop, after all . . . Louise wrote "strange young man" in her list of suspects in the notebook she'd begun to carry.

The girls were nearly to the junction of Nutholt Lane and Prickwillow Road when their attention was captured by a loud, insistent tapping. They looked about and saw the stooped figure of Admiral Lockwood, with his shoulders draped in a shawl, rapping at his windowpane and gesturing urgently at them.

"What on earth?" Dour Elinor asked. "Does he think we're trespassing?"

They waited uncertainly on the street outside Admiral Lockwood's tall, dark Gothic house. The other windows were shuttered and still. The man himself had withdrawn from his window, and the girls began to feel rather silly standing there for no purpose.

Finally the front door creaked open, and an ancient servant in a dignified black suit that hung off his gaunt bones stood in the doorway.

"Young ladies," he croaked, "Admiral Lockwood requests you do him the honour of stopping into his parlour for a moment, for some lemonade."

The girls looked at one another.

"Hadn't we ought to decline?" whispered Dear Roberta. "Young ladies venturing unchaperoned into a man's house?" She shuddered. "And such a frightful-looking house!"

"Rubbish," Disgraceful Mary Jane whispered. "He's as old as Methuselah. He can't harm us. Rich as Croesus, too. *I'll* drink his lemonade. Let's go."

"Besides," Pocked Louise said, "we may learn something. Admiral Lockwood is on my Possible Suspects list."

Dear Roberta squeaked. "Isn't that all the more reason *not* to go?" she cried. "What if he poisons our lemonade?"

Disgraceful Mary Jane laughed. "And what, exactly, would he do with seven girl's corpses? There's safety in numbers, girls. Let's go."

Mary Jane led the way up the steps and into the dark house. The others followed, clutching their grocery baskets as though they might offer some protection.

The house was cool and dark, panelled everywhere with black walnut. The servant bid them leave their baskets in the entryway, then showed them into a study where Admiral Lockwood stood with one gnarled hand gripping the head of a carved cane. The study was filled to bursting with grotesque statues from foreign lands, including, Elinor noted, several made from ebony. They saw curios and coins under dusty domes of glass. Ships in bottles lined the mantelpiece, and a massive anchor hung on the wall. A globe by Admiral Lockwood's side, and sextants, maps, and compasses scattered about on tables gave the impression that the admiral was planning an imminent voyage. A lifeboat with oars even hung from the high-beamed ceiling, right over the chair where Dull Martha sat, which made her very anxious. Pocked Louise took in the navigational volumes and the scientific instruments with great interest, yet for all this nautical atmosphere, the room had the dolorous grimness of a mausoleum.

"What a lovely room," Dour Elinor said. She, at least, felt right at home.

Disgraceful Mary Jane curtseyed for the admiral, and the others followed.

"Won't you sit down?" the admiral said. "Young ladies enjoy sweets, don't they?" He reached for a silver box on a table with a hand tremulous with age. "These are chocolate candies from Switzerland." He held out the box towards Stout Alice.

Alice hesitated, then dismissed her worries. She took a chocolate and bit into it. It was soft and waxy-smooth. Then it melted on her tongue. Sweet ambrosia! Bonbons of the gods!

"I've had chocolate candies before," Disgraceful Mary Jane said. "At my cousin's coming-out party. They're divine." She helped herself to a piece. "Mmm. Thank you, Admiral."

He nodded, obviously pleased. "Take more. My lads at the shipping office keep me supplied with all the chocolate I could desire." He leaned forward and whispered, conspiratorially, "Your headmistress is exceptionally fond of chocolate."

Dear Roberta felt her face blush hot. So it was true! The old admiral was linked somehow to Mrs Plackett. She shivered. She would never understand old people.

Smooth Kitty polished off her chocolate square. "It's delicious! Absolutely marvellous!"

The admiral turned to face her. "Right you are, young lady. Tell me, what is your name?"

"Katherine Heaton," Kitty replied.

"Well, Miss Katherine," he said, "the world is full of delicious foods and fruits and wines; flowers and perfumes and incense; spices and ointments and medicines; jewels and ores and wonders, as would boggle the mind. I've seen it all. Sunsets over the Caribbean, moonrise in the Congo, the Northern Lights in the Arctic Sea. I've seen tribes shoot tiny poison darts no bigger than a dragonfly and deadly enough to kill an elephant."

Pocked Louise jolted upright at the word *poison*. Kitty reacted more to *elephant*.

"I've seen the rice fields of China, ankle deep in water, and prettier than springtime. I've seen silk factories, temples, and treasure palaces studded with rubies and sapphires. Greater riches than England's banks can hold. But don't think I haven't brought some back with me!"

Alice decided she liked Admiral Lockwood very much. Her own grandmamma was a widow. If she could have chosen a grandfather, she would choose this one.

The admiral thumped his cane. "And why should a man not be permitted to share his treasures with a companion, a woman of mature sense, who likes to hear his tales, someone to pass the long hours with, and eat his chocolate, I'd like to know?"

"May *I* eat some more chocolate?" Dull Martha asked.

The admiral looked extremely pleased. "Help yourself."

He sat and gazed at each of the girls in turn, leaving them feeling somewhat self-conscious, but not altogether awkward. The servant appeared in the doorway, staggering a bit under the weight of a tray bearing eight tall glasses of lemonade. Chunks of ice bobbed in each glass. Ice in May! Admiral Lockwood was rich indeed.

"Come in, Jeffers," the admiral called, and the servant tottered in and served them. The lemonade seemed tart after the chocolate, but it was so wonderfully cold, none of the girls cared. He returned soon after with biscuits and crackers with cheese. The admiral, whose girth suggested he availed himself often of these midmorning repasts, urged the girls to eat their fill, and beamed at them as they did so.

"Now, Miss Katherine," he asked Kitty, while she still had a mouthful of chocolate and butter biscuit – an exquisite combination, as she was just then discovering – "tell me how your headmistress fares today. Is she recovering from Sunday's shock?"

Kitty struggled to chew and swallow so that she could answer politely. Admiral Lockwood's eager gaze showed her the horror of what she must now do. Here was someone who was truly fond of Mrs Plackett. Romantically attached to her, even. Heaven only knew why. What had he seen in her that Kitty and the others didn't? Kitty never for a moment had mourned her loss, but here was someone who would. And now she must lie to this surprisingly dear old man, and mislead his hopes.

"I say it's a fine thing that her young brother went off to India to be of some assistance," the admiral said. "About time he made himself useful to his family. In the navy, my dears, we value men of industry and purpose! Not gadabouts and wastrels like Aldous Godding." He gripped his cane as though imagining how he'd use it to teach Mr Godding a lesson, were that unworthy man on board one of his ships, and he, the admiral, a much younger man.

"Admiral Lockwood," Smooth Kitty said. "Tell us about the elephant."

The old man's eyes widened. "She showed it to you, did she?"

The girls exchanged glances. His reaction was informative in itself.

"She didn't mean to," Kitty said truthfully. "We . . . happened upon it. The fault is ours."

"I see." The admiral nodded. "Bound to happen in a house full of curious young ladies."

Pocked Louise spoke up. "It's good for young ladies to be curious, don't you think?"

The old man pursed his lips, as if he'd never before considered such a question. "Well, my dear . . . how old are you?"

152

"Twelve," answered Pocked Louise with a touch of defiance.

The admiral nodded. "Twelve. That's a grand age. Young ladies, curious? Why not? Why shouldn't they be? I always said a sailor needed to be curious, or he'd lose heart at sea. I suppose a curious mind won't do young ladies any harm, provided it doesn't leave them discontented with their lot in life." He surveyed the girls, and seemed to arrive at a satisfactory resolution of this thorny dilemma. "We live in an age of discovery, young ladies. New books come out by the hundreds each year. Even you can keep your minds stimulated by *reading* about the world."

"We don't merely want to read about it," Pocked Louise said. "We want the kinds of adventures you've had."

The admiral smiled indulgently. "And who can blame you for that? Here, have a chocolate." He took one himself, and bit into it thoughtfully. "The elephant is something I picked up in East Africa, years ago. Just a little curio that caught my eye. I thought your headmistress might enjoy it."

"Oh, she does," Kitty said. "But what does it do?"

The admiral shifted in his chair. "Do?"

Kitty realised she may have said too much. "Do. I thought . . . it looked like it might have some use . . . beyond ornamentation."

The admiral shook his head. "It's just a pretty knickknack." He thumped his cane on the floor for good measure. "But you were about to tell me how your headmistress is getting along."

He's like a young man in love, Kitty thought. "Mrs Plackett is recovering," she said. "Rest has done her good.

She plans to accompany us tomorrow evening to the strawberry social."

"Does she now?" He leaned forward in his chair. "Does she now indeed?"

Stout Alice began to wonder what additional horrors the following night might bring.

"She doesn't, by any chance . . ." The admiral coughed. "She wouldn't, I suppose, ever make a mention of me to you young ladies?"

A mortifying silence fell over the room. The girls didn't dare look at one another. The admiral became suddenly fascinated by a mole on the back of his hand.

"Frequently, as a matter of fact." Disgraceful Mary Jane jumped in to fill the void. "She often says, 'Now, girls, if every man could be such a perfect gentleman as Admiral Lockwood, I would have no worries for your future prospects.'"

Mary Jane's performance was so nonchalant, so convincing, that Smooth Kitty nearly believed it herself. Dull Martha and Dear Roberta gaped at her. The admiral, fortunately, was too tickled to notice their hanging jaws.

"I don't know as I'd go that far," he protested, beaming. "Plenty of my lads on board ship weren't fond of my manners. Not when they'd gotten into the rum, ho ho! I could be a terror then." He stroked his chin. "But I'm gratified by the compliment."

Disgraceful Mary Jane drained the last drops of lemonade from her glass and set it down on the table. "That was delicious, Admiral," she said. "Thank you so much for inviting us."

"My pleasure, my pleasure," he said, waving it away. "Please, come by any time you are in the village. It's a treat to entertain a group of such lovely young ladies as yourselves. I see your headmistress does a fine job with your education."

Jeffers showed them out and bid them come again. "The admiral always has plenty of chocolate ready for visitors," he whispered in a gravelly voice as they left.

They walked up the road to where it turned into Prickwillow.

"Admiral Lockwood seems to be a very nice man," Dull Martha observed.

"A besotted old duffer," Disgraceful Mary Jane said, "but an adorable one."

"Such language, Mary Jane!" scolded Stout Alice.

"Doesn't it strike you as odd that he should care so much for Mrs Plackett?" Mary Jane ignored the lecture. "Oh, come. You know you're all wondering, too."

"Sometimes different personalities complement one another," ventured Dear Roberta.

"I am beginning to wonder," said Smooth Kitty, "if we knew Mrs Plackett as well as we thought we did."

"If she was all the admiral thinks her to be," Stout Alice said slowly, "then we have misjudged her gravely."

Elinor snickered. "*Gravely*."

Dear Roberta's voice began to squeak. "I knew it was wicked of us to make her grave in the vegetable garden!"

"Hush, Roberta!" Smooth Kitty scanned the horizon for eavesdropping passersby. Then she sighed. "What's done is done. We'll make more prayers. Perhaps, Roberta, dear, you can help us think of some good deeds we might do as a private penance."

Dear Roberta nodded and sniffled. They trudged along Prickwillow Road, lost in thought.

"Anyway, I think the admiral's a dear," Stout Alice said, to break the silence.

Disgraceful Mary Jane laughed. "Lucky for you, then, he's your beau tomorrow night."

"A dear he may be," Smooth Kitty said, "but he didn't tell all he knew about the elephant."

"And why should he? A private gift for his lady is his own affair," Disgraceful Mary Jane declared. "Perhaps I'll marry the old sailor myself. I'll listen to his stories and eat his chocolates and spend his money. And before long, I'd be a wealthy widow with the world at my feet."

Dull Martha stopped in her tracks. "Don't say that you'd stoop to poisoning too!"

Disgraceful Mary Jane felt too cheerful to be offended. "No, goosey. Time would take care of it for me soon enough. He's an old, old man. It's really a wonder he's lived as long as he has." She winked at Kitty. "Don't worry, I'm not ready to abandon our little Saint Etheldreda's Maidens Club just yet. But I'll warn you, Alice. Tomorrow night I shall flirt with your escort shamelessly."

Stout Alice shrugged. "Is there any other way for you to flirt?"

Chapter Fourteen

That afternoon the young ladies gathered in the drawing room to work on their embroidered tablecloth while Dull Martha accompanied and coached Stout Alice in her efforts to learn the song she was intended to perform, as Mrs Plackett, at the strawberry social.

"This is absurd," Stout Alice protested. "I should beg out of singing, given my grief over dear Aldous and darling Julius."

"That would only attract more attention," Smooth Kitty said. "The sooner the people in Ely forget about Aldous and Julius, the better. You must appear to go on with life as usual."

"But think for a moment, Kitty!" Alice protested. "So far I've fooled people by sitting mainly in dimly lit rooms and talking like Mrs Plackett. How shall it be when I'm standing before a large room filled with people watching me in bright lamplight? What then?"

"People will see exactly what they expect to see," Pocked Louise said. "Magicians and stage performers rely upon it. It's how they do their tricks."

"What do you mean, 'their tricks'?" Dull Martha asked.

"I saw a magician once, and it was astonishing!"

Pocked Louise bent over to closely study the strawberry leaf she was fanning with dark green veins of silk.

Stout Alice was wholly unconvinced. "Perhaps with Elinor's cosmetic arts they may *see* what they expect to see, but they won't *hear* what they expect to hear," she said. "I can imitate Mrs Plackett's spoken voice passably well, but I don't sing. The whole game will be ruined by this spectacle."

Smooth Kitty was in no humor to indulge Stout Alice. "Don't forget it was you who insisted we must go in the first place." She knotted a thread and snipped it. "You made this bed; you'll have to sleep in it."

"Give me no more talk of beds!" Alice flung up her hands. "I've spent far too much time in the wrong beds these last two days."

"Come on, Alice, let's try again." Dull Martha tried to cajole her reluctant pupil. She played the sprightly introduction and sang the opening words herself.

A peacock came, with his plumage gay,
Strutting in regal pride one day,
Where a small bird hung in a gilded cage,
Whose song might a seraph's ear engage.

Her note trailed off on the last note. She watched Alice hopefully. "Now you try."

A peacock came . . .

158

Stout Alice only scowled at her. "*You* should sing, Martha," she said. "You can make anything sound lovely. This song is atrocious. "'Tis Not Fine Feathers Make Fine Birds.' I ask you! What nonsense!"

Disgraceful Mary Jane snatched the music. "Here's my favourite bit:

Then prithee take warning, maidens fair,
And still of the peacock's fate beware;
Beauty and wealth won't win your way . . .

Oh, won't they, then! Give me wealth and watch me. We'll see if I can't win my way."

"It goes without saying, you've already got the beauty," Stout Alice observed archly.

Mary Jane smiled. "Sweet of you to say so, dear."

Dull Martha repeated the pianoforte introduction and pleaded with her student. "Come along, Alice, you can sing it."

A peacock came with his plumage gay . . .

"I'm with Alice." Dour Elinor stitched sharp thorns spiking from her strawberry vines. (Perhaps she confused them with roses.) "This chirpy song isn't worth the paper it's printed on."

"Then why must I sing it?"

"You're Mrs Plackett, and Mrs Plackett misses no chance to perform," said Kitty.

Alice took a deep breath and glared at her music. Martha took that as a hopeful sign and began to play once more. "Why not sing the second verse?" she suggested.

"Indeed," Alice said. "Its second stanza is prophetic. Listen." And joining with the music, Alice sang, to the best of her limited ability:

> *"Alas! The bird of the rainbow wing*
> *He wasn't contented – he tried to sing!*
> *And they who gazed on his beauty bright,*
> *Scared by his screaming, soon took flight;*
> *While the small bird sung in his own sweet words,*
> *"Tis not fine feathers make fine birds!"'"*

Dull Martha paused her playing to applaud Stout Alice. The other girls looked at one another, unsure of how to respond.

"I wouldn't call your singing *screaming*, per se," Pocked Louise said cautiously. "I'm sure no one will actually take flight."

Stout Alice flung her music down upon the sofa and flopped beside it. "It's no use. We must find another plan." Aldous sprang up onto the sofa and began chewing the sheet music.

"No you don't!" Smooth Kitty cried. She was already vexed with him for shredding a sofa cushion during their morning walk to town. She thought he should be tied outside as punishment, which made Pocked Louise extremely piqued with her. Saint Etheldreda's School had witnessed much loud scolding and threatening of the little rascal when the girls returned home, which didn't bother the criminal in the slightest.

Aldous halted, sniffed the air, then bolted out the drawing room door, barking excitedly. Seconds later they heard the twirl of the door ringer striking the bell. Kitty set aside her stitching, but Dour Elinor, for once, was quicker. "I'll go," she said.

Kitty nodded her thanks. "We've had more visitors here in the last two days than all the months since we returned from Christmas holidays combined."

"Shall I go change?" Stout Alice asked.

"No, don't," Kitty said. "You deserve a rest. We'll make something up."

Smooth Kitty's gaze flitted to the curio cabinet, where the ebony elephant stood, trumpeting its brass trunk high. It had taken all her self-restraint not to gloat to Alice that it was still there, safe and sound. She saw Alice's eyes locate the elephant just then, and that was all the vindication Kitty needed. It was perfectly safe. Just as she knew it would be.

When Dour Elinor ushered their visitor into the drawing room, Disgraceful Mary Jane's needle fell from her fingers. Standing straight as a rail next to Elinor, who slumped rather more than not, was the new constable on the Ely police force with the handsome shoulders, looking resplendent in his navy blue suit, conical helmet, and shiny brass buttons. He smiled at the young ladies, flashing the gap between his front teeth and singling out, as he did so, Disgraceful Mary Jane, as young men were so prone to do.

"Good afternoon, ladies," he said, in an extremely pleasing baritone. "I apologise for inconveniencing you here in your pleasant pastimes."

"Not at all!" cried Disgraceful Mary Jane, who curtseyed long and deeply for the constable's benefit. "We're all bored with needlework and happy for some diversion."

The constable chuckled. "Most people don't consider a visiting policeman a diversion."

Neither, to be frank, did Smooth Kitty or any of the other girls, save Mary Jane. The sight of a policeman struck terror to Kitty's heart. She could think of no good reason – and at least two very bad ones – for him to appear. But Disgraceful Mary Jane was in such raptures of infatuation that these thoughts apparently had not occurred to her.

"I'm Constable Quill," he said, "and I'm here to ask a few questions of the lady of the house," here he consulted a card in his hand, "Mrs Constance Plackett. May I speak with her?"

"Please do sit down," purred Mary Jane. "May I relieve you of your hat?"

Constable Quill smiled slightly. "Er, no. We need to keep those on. It's no bother."

Smooth Kitty felt someone must prevent Disgraceful Mary Jane from monopolizing this conversation to disastrous effects. One never knew what she might say in the heat of a moment where broad shoulders and crisp uniforms were concerned.

"Mrs Plackett is not here at present." Kitty rose and offered the constable her hand. "My name is Katherine. I'm head girl at this school." She felt twelve eyes shoot daggers at her. They had no such hierarchy among the students, and Kitty knew there'd be a price to pay later among the girls for assuming such airs in public. It was for the cause, she told herself. "Is there something I can help you with while she's away?"

"Or I?" added Disgraceful Mary Jane.

Smooth Kitty would have liked to yank her roommate's hair at that moment, but she forbore.

"Perhaps you young ladies can help me," Constable Quill said. "Do you by chance know if Mrs Plackett's brother, a Mr Aldous Godding, stopped here at all this past Sunday?"

Even Mary Jane didn't rush to answer this time.

"He did visit here," Kitty said evenly. "He comes by custom for Sunday dinner."

Constable Quill pulled a small notebook from his pocket and began writing in it.

"And did he leave at the usual time, and in the usual way?"

Kitty wished she could retract her 'head girl' comment. This was spiralling fast. She thought of her namesake, Aunt Katherine. *She* wouldn't be intimidated by some young bobby boasting new-grown sideburns, not if she'd buried a dozen corpses in the vegetable beds.

"May I ask, Constable, towards what these questions tend?"

Constable Quill flashed a disarming smile, and lowered his notebook. "Of course. A Mrs Lally, of Witchford, keeps a boarder, and lately Mr Aldous Godding has been her tenant. She had occasion to drive into Ely today for some marketing she needed done, and while she was in town she stopped at the police office to ask us to inquire into the whereabouts of Mr Godding. She said he hasn't been home as expected these last two nights, and she felt this was an occasion for worry. Nothing he'd said gave her reason to expect he'd be away."

Stout Alice watched this scene unfold like one might a dramatic play. *You'll do well, Kitty,* she thought, hoping somehow her confidence might travel to Kitty's mind. Disgraceful Mary Jane was glad not to be called upon to speak, yet felt an absurd tinge of jealousy that Kitty should take control of Constable Quill at this moment, and not she.

"That's easily explained, Constable," Kitty said. She made a mental effort to speak slowly. This wasn't anywhere near as bad as it might have been. But why did she never consider Mr Godding's lodgings, and the others who would notice his absence? Foolish, foolish. "During their Sunday visit, our headmistress and Mr Godding received distressing news about a young relative of theirs in India. His health is poor. Mr Godding left immediately for London to board a ship bound for India, so he could be with his nephew."

The constable was back to smiling and scribbling. "Ah, there, see, there's always a reasonable explanation, isn't there? I told Mrs Lally it'd all come to nothing." He scribbled some more, then paused. "Did he say he would stop at home for some clothes and personal effects before leaving on his journey?"

Smooth Kitty began to despise the gap in the teeth which Mary Jane found so bewitching. "I was not aware of his plans in detail," she replied. "I only know he left straightaway."

"'Course. Makes sense." He closed his notebook with a snap. "It's a pleasure to meet you young ladies. I hope it's a pleasure I'll have again." He nodded, chiefly in Mary Jane's direction. She favoured him with a beguiling smile.

Constable Quill turned to leave, then paused in the doorway. "I forgot. Mrs Lally wants to know if he's likely to be back soon, or if she should pack up his things. My understanding is that he's already a good deal behind in his rents, so she's in no mood to extend more credit to someone who'll be gone a while." A slightly anxious look crossed the Constable's face. "That's something I ought to discuss with your mistress, when she returns. When will she be back?"

Kitty waved away this concern. "I'm sure I can speak for Mrs Plackett when I say that there is plenty of room here to store Mr Godding's personal belongings indefinitely. Mrs Lally is welcome to send his things here."

"Excellent. May I ask a favour?"

No, Kitty thought. *You can do us a favour and leave.* "Of course, Constable. How can we assist you?"

The six-foot-tall policeman somehow managed to look like a young boy asking for a sweet. "Might I borrow a photograph of Mr Godding? You have one, I presume?"

All of Kitty's senses flared up in warning at this suggestion. "Well, I don't know if I ought to loan Mrs Plackett's pictures without her permission."

The constable nodded. "Of course. I'll just come back when she's here."

Stout Alice, seeing Smooth Kitty's look of alarm, snatched a small framed photograph off a side table. "Here you are, Constable," she said. "Our headmistress won't even notice this absent for a few days. You will return it straightaway when you're done with it, won't you?"

"'Course." Constable Quill grinned and tipped the brim of his hat, then turned to leave. Disgraceful Mary Jane followed him towards the door.

"Should one of us accompany her?" Dear Roberta asked.

Smooth Kitty sank into a chair. "Let her go," she said. "She might as well have her fun. We couldn't stop her if we tried."

Pocked Louise fanned Kitty's face and neck with Dull Martha's piano music. All her former pique over the scolding of young Aldous was forgotten. "Well done, Kitty, well *done*," she whispered. "You were superb."

Smooth Kitty held up her hand before her face and examined her fingers. "Does my shaking show?" she asked. "I'm trembling all over."

"I don't see it," Dull Martha said loyally.

"Why did he have to be so nosy?" Kitty fumed. "Can't a man leave home for two nights without attracting police attention?"

"He's just a young pup, eager to prove himself on the police force," Stout Alice declared. "One of these overzealous types. You handled him in just the right way."

Kitty laughed weakly. "More likely, that's what Mary Jane thinks she's doing right now."

Chapter Fifteen

Wednesday morning dawned clear and bright, and Smooth Kitty announced over tea and toast that they would do laundry and housecleaning that morning.

"What would Mama say to see me operating a mangle?" Disgraceful Mary Jane muttered. "This independent living scheme has definite drawbacks."

"I've mangled laundry before," Dull Martha said. "It's fun. I used to help our washwoman do it when Mama wasn't watching. You crank the wheel as hard as you can, and watch all the water drip out."

Disgraceful Mary Jane groaned, then patted Martha's head. "Since you love it so much, I nominate you to mangle. I'll iron our skirts and bodices for the strawberry social tonight."

Their strawberry tablecloth lay draped in state over the dining room table. They'd all taken their toast and tea at the sideboard to keep crumbs off the embroidered linen.

"It came together so well," Stout Alice said. "I never thought we could finish it in time."

"All the credit's due to our dear Roberta," said Smooth Kitty. "She did two thirds of the stitching herself. What a lovely hand you have, dear."

Roberta blushed. "Oh, it was nothing, really. You all made such dainty strawberries and leaves. I just joined them together."

"And sewed half of them yourself." Pocked Louise fingered the border. "Elinor's vines look more like Briar Rose's forest of thorns."

"Strawberries are too cheerful," Dour Elinor said. "I can't stomach them plain."

"Thorns add interest," Roberta said generously. "We should stitch more throughout."

Smooth Kitty kissed Roberta's cheek. "You're so good and kind, Roberta, you make us all better creatures than we would otherwise be."

The doorbell rang.

Pocked Louise groaned. "*Now* what? Who can want to vex us this morning?"

"Come along, Elinor," Stout Alice said with a sigh. "Let's get ready, in case we must spring into gear and apply my costume."

"Maybe it's Constable Quill," Disgraceful Mary Jane said. "How do I look?"

"Let *me* answer the door," Kitty said. "I'll get rid of them quickly. The rest of you, put on old frocks for housework, and meet me in the kitchen."

Kitty opened the door to see an enormously tall, broad-shouldered man in a bowler hat and a violet waistcoat standing there, with a canary silk kerchief poking from his jacket pocket, and rather startling checkered pants. His thick blond moustache was oiled to a fine point, and pale sideburns curled around his cheekbones underneath his hat.

"Good morning, *mademoiselle*." The word was French, but his accent was as English as treacle tart. He took a step inside. "I'm Gideon Rigby," another large step, "and I represent the Order of Hilarion, patron saint of basket makers. By trade, I'm in the antique furniture business."

"Oh?" Smooth Kitty was speechless in the face of his flamboyance. He took another step, which afforded him a peep into the dining room. He looked about appreciatively.

"My fellow order members and I are taking a charitable collection on behalf of the retired basket weavers of the fens." He cupped his huge hands together in a gesture of deep concern and ventured down the hall. "Basket weaving is a proud tradition in Ely, but when old weavers grow crippled, and can no longer weave, the community must rally to their support."

He had a melodious voice that Kitty felt powerless to interrupt.

"A worthy cause, I'm sure," she said, "but we . . ."

"Is your headmistress home?" Mr Rigby asked. "I understood this to be a finishing school for young ladies. You, I presume, are one of the lovely young ladies?"

Kitty faltered. "Yes . . . well, not lovely, I mean, though perhaps . . . I am one of the . . ."

"Of course you are." The charitable collector flashed a warm smile at her. "I'll only require a moment of

Mrs Plackett's time. Ah! This must be your schoolroom."
He pushed its door aside. Kitty noticed a gold ring gleam
on his finger.

"Mrs Plackett is not at home," she said firmly.

Mr Rigby tsked. "I heard she was poorly. But if she's
out and about, she must be improving. I will come back
another time. Ah, what a handsome parlour! A modest
contribution is all we hope for, just the most nominal sum;
every bit helps, you know."

All the way to the parlour already! Kitty needed to get
him *out*.

"I'm sure every bit does help," Kitty said, "but we haven't
a single bit to spare. I must ask you to take your petitions
elsewhere. I am not at liberty to admit you to the house."

He clapped his hands together. "*Such* a delicate drawing
room pianoforte! Mahogany. Exquisite! Your headmistress
is a genteel woman of refined tastes, that's plain. I'm sure
she'll have a bit tucked away, out of the goodness of her
heart . . ."

"*Mr* Rigby!"

Both of them were surprised by the edge to her voice.

She took a deep breath. "I ask you, please, to take your
leave of us," she said, in the sternest voice she could produce.
"Consider our situation! You can scarcely think we pupils of
Saint Etheldreda's School would admit a man to the house
when our headmistress is . . . out?"

He nodded, wide-eyed with remorse. "My dear young lady,
a thousand apologies for distressing you. It is always this
way with me, I mean no harm, but I'm drawn to furniture

170

like a fly to honey, can't resist a nip and a peep. But what of that? I will take my leave this instant . . ."

"Please do." Kitty spoke through gritted teeth. He'd made no movement towards the door.

"This hutch, what a treasure, and so well preserved . . . you're certain your headmistress is in no position to remember the poor crippled basket weavers? Just so, just so. A pleasant day to you, *mademoiselle*. Gideon Rigby, Rare Antiques, at your service!" And, bowing, he backed down the gravel walk and hastened towards Ely with long, energetic strides.

At last, he was gone! But Kitty's relief was short-lived. A rider passed by just then on a speckled horse, walking at a leisurely pace. Kitty caught sight of a tan coat and a grey John Bull hat and froze in her step. The rider paused to examine the house, then caught sight of Kitty, and Mr Rigby taking his leave of her. It was the young man from the chemist's shop.

Kitty's senses flared into high alert. She felt both mortified to be seen by him in this faded old housecleaning frock, and furious with herself for such pointless vanity. And what might he surmise from the departing presence of the garish Mr Rigby?

The young man reined in his horse. Did he recognise her? Should she approach the road and greet him? Propriety demanded otherwise, yet Kitty felt drawn to speak to him, if only to better understand his mysterious behaviour.

He doffed his hat to Kitty, this time revealing more plainly a head of thick dark curls. She hesitated, then made a small curtsey in reply. Politeness demanded some reply, did it not? He had, after all, bought her a caramel. But with the greatest of cheek! And here she was, no better than Mary Jane, curtseying to strangers by the roadside like a common strumpet!

She turned and fled indoors, then darted into the schoolroom where she could peep outdoors unseen through the window blinds.

The young man lingered, peering at the house for many slow seconds. Then he scratched his chin, pressed his boots against the palomino's flanks, and trotted towards Ely.

Oh, he was a perplexing case. Kitty admitted, only to herself, that he would be far less perplexing if his features were not, coincidentally, so pleasing. No matter; she had embarrassed herself utterly this time, and could only pray (without full conviction, it must be said) that she might never be so unfortunate as to encounter this strange young man again.

Kitty shook herself. First Mr Rigby, and then the young stranger. What a morning! She wandered down the hall and down the stairs to the kitchen like a sleepwalker.

"Who was that?" asked Pocked Louise.

"Hm? Oh. A charitable solicitor."

Dour Elinor tied an apron around herself as cheerfully as if it were a hangman's noose. "It took you plenty long enough to get rid of him."

Kitty's thoughts were full of the young man's enigmatic colouring and voice. "Hm?"

Elinor's eyebrows arched. "It took you long enough," she repeated, "to get rid of him."

Kitty ignored Elinor's jibe. "I wonder if there really is a patron saint of basket weavers."

Elinor shrugged. "There's a patron saint for everything."

Stout Alice brought a load of dishes from the dining room into the kitchen. "Is he gone? We've got a lot to do. Let's get started. I'll light the fire, and then strip my bed and Mrs Plackett's."

"I'll dust the parlour and drawing room, after I've stripped my bed," Elinor said.

"I'll take dishes and kitchen cleaning," offered Dear Roberta.

"Silver. Brasses," announced Mary Jane, waving a polishing cloth.

Pocked Louise took a sip of tea. "Martha and I can wash and mangle."

Smooth Kitty, still preoccupied, realised she should have paid attention. With an effort, she banished the image of the curly-haired stranger from her mind, and made a face. "I should have spoken sooner," she said. "This leaves the ash pail to me. The stoves and the fireplace are getting frightfully clogged. Alice, let me clean out the stove before you light the scullery fire."

Alice helped herself to another wedge of toast. "As you please, Cinderella."

The girls dispersed to their chores. Smooth Kitty shovelled out the ashes in the scullery stove, and Stout Alice built a fire to get the wash water heating. Kitty went from room to room and from fireplace to fireplace to finish her grim, grey task. On her many trips outdoors to the ash pile, she couldn't help noticing the twiggy-looking cherry tree sapling poking up like a finger of accusation from the hidden graves of Mr Godding and Mrs Plackett.

"What a heap of trouble you've caused us," she told their buried bodies. "Now we're full of toil and trouble while you lie there, peaceful as sleeping kittens."

This, she considered upon some reflection, might not be wholly just.

When she finished dumping all the ashes for the house, Kitty filled her pail with water from the outside pump and poured it over the roots of the cherry tree. It wouldn't do for the sapling to die. They needed the tree as cover for their crimes. No, not theirs – someone else's. She refilled her bucket and was sousing the ground again, thinking rather gruesome thoughts of water and mud and manure sopping all over Mrs Plackett and Mr Godding, when Stout Alice approached carrying a letter in her hands. She looked worried.

"Kitty, look at this," she said, unfolding the paper. "I found it under Mrs Plackett's pillow when I stripped the bedding."

Kitty wiped her hands on her apron and took the offered paper. Ten pounds in notes were tucked inside the fold. She recognised her headmistress's even hand immediately, though not the ornate stationery, with scalloped edges and embossed roses around the border.

"My dear brother Aldous," she read aloud. "Many happy returns of your birthday to you. By now my little surprise party is complete. I hope you will see the party, and this enclosure, as an olive-branch. Pray do not remain angry.

It is already done; I have spoken with Mr Wilson, the matter is now settled, so let us have no more discussion. It is for your good, and for dear young Julius's sake. I will continue to do what I can for you, but I cannot allow my house nor my husband's legacy to be consumed by your dissolute ways. You have accused me of being unfeeling, but if I have turned what appears to be a heart of stone to your demands, it is not for lack of concern for you. Rather, in my great concern for you, I must take the high road and refuse to support your overindulgences. Check yourself, dear brother, and let me be as proud of you as I was in your early years. You may yet make much of yourself. Self-mastery is the key. Look to our father, and to our departed brother Geoffrey, as models of rectitude and moderation. Please accept this small gift to relieve your present awkwardness. I remain as ever, your sister, Constance."

Pocked Louise appeared, lugging a wicker laundry basket. Little Aldous followed at her heels, tugging ferociously on her skirt. She pulled wet sheets from her basket and pinned them to the clothesline, then noticed Kitty and Alice. They showed her the letter. She read it slowly.

"What does it mean?"

Kitty took the pound notes and folded them into her pocket. "This comes in handy," she said. "We need to pay Doctor Snelling's bill. Mr Godding can't enjoy his birthday present now."

Stout Alice scanned the lines of the letter once more. "What does she mean? '. . . it is already done . . . the matter is now settled.' *What* matter? What is now settled?"

"I suppose we'll never know." Kitty shook ashes out from her skirts. "It must have been some private family matter. Let's hope it died with them."

Pocked Louise took the letter back from Stout Alice. "I'm surprised at you, Kitty," she said. "Where is your curiosity? Surely this is important. Mrs Plackett and Mr Godding have some disagreement, Mrs Plackett does . . . something, and within a day, both are dead. There must be some connection. It's a clue!"

Stout Alice nodded. "Louise is right. She mentioned Mr Wilkins, the lawyer. Monday morning, Mr Wilkin's clerk, Mr Murphy, brought us a newly signed copy of Mrs Plackett's will. It must be that the *something* she did involved her will."

Pocked Louise's eyes grew wide. "She must have changed it. And that change must have affected Mr Godding."

They both turned to Kitty. "Did she leave any money to Mr Godding in the will?" Alice asked. "How much?"

Kitty frowned. She still felt miffed at Louise's rebuke, and irked with Alice for figuring out that the letter referenced the will first. This troublesome business of day-to-day survival was muddling her wits. With finances to pinch, and shopping and groceries and laundering, who could remember the details of obscure wills?

But Kitty wasn't about to abdicate her role as chief problem solver at Saint Etheldreda's.

"Let's go find the will and see," she said.

They hurried inside. Kitty washed her sooty hands and Louise abandoned her wet laundry. They went straight to

Mrs Plackett's private desk in her bedroom, where Kitty continued to store her ledger and lists of the invoices sent to their parents.

The will wasn't there.

"Are you sure you left it there?" Pocked Louise inquired.

Smooth Kitty felt her pulse race. "Positive," she said. "I always know what I've done with papers." She scrabbled through the desk's contents, searching every scrap and envelope.

"What about you, Alice, did you do anything with it?" Louise asked. "You first received it from Mr Wilkins's clerk."

Stout Alice crawled along the floor, searching through stripped bed pillows and blankets, in the nightstand, even under bedsprings. "Not a thing. I made sure to leave it with Kitty."

"The will's not the only thing missing," Smooth Kitty said. "I had eight pounds, a half crown, two shillings and sixpence in this drawer. It's gone."

"Girls!" Pocked Louise cried down the corridor. "Emergency conference!"

"Come down here," Martha bellowed from the scullery. "We're in the middle of a wash."

They gathered there in the steamy washing room, aprons and feather dusters and all. Dull Martha loaded more coal into the stove, clanged its door shut, and heaved another bucket of water into the copper kettle on top. Her hair clung to her forehead in soggy wisps.

She and the other girls piled onto heaping baskets of laundry while Pocked Louise quickly explained the situation.

"Do any of you know where the will might be?" she asked. "Have you come across any papers in your dusting and cleaning?"

They all shook their heads.

"I've gone over the entire parlour, and under every couch and cushion. Nothing there," said Dour Elinor. "And the drawing room. Clean as a pin, and no papers in sight."

Dear Roberta nodded. "The kitchen has no papers," she said, "but I can search again."

"We all can, if we must," Disgraceful Mary Jane said, "but first, let's think. If Kitty's sure she left the will and the money here, then she did. If they're now missing, someone stole them."

"Aha!" Pocked Louise whipped her notebook and pencil out of her pocket and began scribbling. "Our murderer strikes again!"

Dull Martha blinked. "Has someone else died?"

"No," Louise explained, "but it stands to reason that the person who murdered Mrs Plackett and Mr Godding is the same person who stole the will and the money. It's a clue. A second crime. It may help me eliminate some potential suspects." She frowned at her notebook in deep concentration.

"Say, who have you included in that list, just out of curiosity?" Disgraceful Mary Jane peered over her shoulder. She began to laugh. "Admiral Lockwood? Reverend Rumsey? *Letitia Fringle*? What a lark! Amanda Barnes, even?" Her laughter froze. "Why, you little sneak! You've written all of *our* names on the list!"

178

Smooth Kitty snatched the notebook away from Louise and perused it quickly.

"All of our names except her own," she observed.

Pocked Louise's face flamed red. She seized her notebook back and closed the cover. "Why on earth should I write my name there?" she demanded. "I *know* I didn't murder them."

Stout Alice folded her arms across her chest. "But you think the rest of us might have?"

Pocked Louise clutched her notebook to her body. The accusing eyes of her classmates seemed to surround her, leaving no escape.

"You put me in charge of investigations," Louise said hotly. "I can't overlook the *possibility* that one of the students here might have done it. That doesn't mean I think you *did*." She reopened her notebook and waved it in their faces. "See? I put you low down on the list. That means you're all highly improbable suspects. But suspects nonetheless."

There was a horrible moment of staring. Then Disgraceful Mary Jane wrecked it, as she did so many things, by laughing out loud.

She rumpled Louise's braids. "Never mind, turtledove," she said. "You did well to write us all down. I don't mind; I'm flattered to be thought suspicious enough to make your list."

"I'm not flattered," Stout Alice protested. "If I'd known I would be stuck impersonating Mrs Plackett forevermore, I'd have poisoned the poisoner before he could poison her."

Dour Elinor smirked. Dull Martha began counting on her fingers: "'Poison the poisoner who . . .' How was that again?"

Pocked Louise closed her notebook once more and slipped the pencil into her pocket. "There's no point conducting an investigation if you're not methodical about it."

"Right you are," Kitty said, and she flashed a smile at Louise. "We're sorry we got vexed. You can interrogate us all, if you like, and we'll cooperate."

"*I* don't want to be interrogated," Dull Martha said. "I didn't murder them, and I find the whole topic of poison and murder quite terribly distressing."

"Forgive me, Martha," said Dour Elinor, "but you're just not *interesting* enough to have wanted to kill them."

Martha peeked out from over the hem of her apron. "Thank you, Elinor," she said. "I take that as a compliment." She looked at the other girls. "You can search my room for the money and the will," she said bravely. "You can even search *my person*."

"Heavens, no." Smooth Kitty decided it was time for someone of sense to reassert authority. "I hardly think searching your person will be necessary, Martha, dear. We all trust you. You need to trust *us* when we tell you so."

Dull Martha nodded penitently.

"There. That's settled then." Smooth Kitty eyed the other girls sternly, as though any one of them might be next to burst into unruly hysterics. "We must return to the original question. We shall search the house, but even if we mislaid the will somehow, I couldn't have mislaid the money. This is my cash drawer. It points strongly to a thief. So we all must think. Who might the thief be? And why would a thief come and take a will, and money, but nothing else? There's no silver or china missing, is there?"

Disgraceful Mary Jane shook her head. "I've just dusted and polished it all."

"What about the jewelled elephant?" asked Stout Alice.

"Right where Kitty left it in the parlour cabinet," Mary Jane replied. "Everything valuable in the house is where it belongs, except the cash. Our thief makes no sense."

"Yes, he does," Pocked Louise said, pacing the floor and tapping her forehead, "if the thief only came looking for the will, then helped himself to the money while he was at it."

"But this begs the critical question," said Stout Alice. "Why would someone come to steal Mrs Plackett's will? Who even knew it was here?"

"That loathsome law clerk knew," Disgraceful Mary Jane said. Pocked Louise's eyebrows rose, and she reached for her notebook.

Stout Alice turned her back on her. "You're awfully precious, Mary Jane," she said. "Apparently only tall constables can please you. Mr Murphy isn't loathsome, and Louise, there's no need to write *him* down. Why on earth should he steal it?"

"Why should anyone?"

Dear Roberta cleared her throat timidly. "Ahem. Someone might steal the will if it was in their interest to conceal it from ever being found. Such as, for example, when the prior will is more favourable to their interests. I've heard my uncle speak of such cases."

Alice, Mary Jane, Louise, and Kitty all turned to Dear Roberta. She leaned backwards as if pushed by the weight of their combined gaze. Kitty marvelled yet again at how dear, innocent Roberta's remarks contained more sense than she'd ever expect from her.

Pocked Louise had caught hold of the same thought. "You mean, someone would steal a new will if the old one served them better," she said. "And the letter Alice found seems to suggest Mrs Plackett had only just updated her will. That leaves the question: who is left out of Mrs Plackett's new will?"

"Everyone," Dear Roberta said, looking puzzled. "Don't you remember? She left everything to dear Julius."

Smooth Kitty nodded. "Bless your memory, Roberta. You should be a lawyer someday."

Dear Roberta laughed. "Impossible!"

"Then marry one," Mary Jane suggested.

Martha handed Louise a wooden paddle from which a sopping bedsheet draped. Louise fed the sheet into the mangle and began to crank. "The stolen will," she said firmly, as if to rein in unruly matchmaking impulses, "changes the game. Before, we were looking for the person who benefited most from the new will. Now," she heaved the crank with great effort, "we want to know who benefits least."

Smooth Kitty attacked a muddy frock dangling from a wash pail with a bar of soap.

"Mr Godding would be the obvious choice," she reasoned. "Mrs Plackett's letter suggests she changed her will in a way that Mr Godding would find upsetting. But he died when she did, so he can't be our murderer. It must be that someone else was a beneficiary of the old will."

Pocked Louise wrenched the squeezed sheet from her mangle and dropped it into a basket. "This means that our murderer knew the will was about to change. He – or she, I suppose – tried to stop Mrs Plackett from changing her will by killing her. Oh!" Her eyes lit up. "Perhaps the murderer also disposed of Mr Godding so as to not share the inheritance with him. Then the murderer learned the will had been changed anyway, so he came here and stole it!"

Dour Elinor stirred the clothes in the washpail with the long paddle. "An all-too-common story," she said ominously.

"Really?" Disgraceful Mary Jane laughed. "I should hope not. Perhaps you find stories like these in the dreadful Russian novels you read."

Elinor ignored Mary Jane. "This could mean 'darling' Julius is in danger," she said. "If the murderer doesn't want to share the inheritance, young Julius would become a prime target. And Mr Wilkins, too, if he keeps another copy of the will at his office. I wonder if he does. The murderer won't want to share a penny with a child nephew."

"Merciful heavens!" Dear Roberta cried. "We must warn them both!"

Smooth Kitty took a deep breath, and tried to think how to be diplomatic. "We can't, dear," she said. "Not without giving away everything. This is all speculation. And Mr Wilkins keeps the wills of hundreds of clients. Surely he has made provisions for his safety. As for Julius, the child is far, far away. We're best doing nothing, except keeping a careful watch, and trying to solve the mystery ourselves." She smiled. "If anyone can, it's our Louise."

Disgraceful Mary Jane tossed a pair of soiled stockings into the wash pail. "I'm hungry," she said. "And we still need to bathe and dress for the strawberry social. It'll take hours to set my hair. I have a special style I want to try. Freddie Quill said he would be there . . ."

"*Freddie*! Pff!" Pocked Louise snorted. "Never mind your hair. We must find out who else suffered when Mrs Plackett redid her will."

"And we shall, Louise," Kitty said. "We shall pore over Mrs Plackett's documents with a magnifying glass and search for hints. There must be some. But not right now. The social is hours away, and each of us – even you, dear – must pretty up for it."

Chapter Sixteen

Dull Martha walked slowly down Prickwillow Road towards the Butts farm. Her errand was a brief one, and really she ought to hurry home to wash and dress for the strawberry social, but it was such a beautiful May afternoon, and she couldn't make herself rush. Spring bulbs bloomed in Mrs Butts's flowerbeds, and wildflowers filled the gully alongside the road. Hairy ferns uncurled their tender green spines among last year's black raspberry branches, and bees were hard at work sniffing and tasting. Such a fine day could only melt into a fine evening for a strawberry social.

Dull Martha had the task of walking to the Butts farm to ask Henry Butts if he'd hitch the Saint Etheldreda pony to his shiny cart and escort them to the parish social. Martha couldn't believe she had asserted herself and secured this task alone. It was the sort of thing Disgraceful Mary Jane usually would finagle a way to do. And it was nearly impossible to dissuade Mary Jane from doing anything she wanted to. For all her superior talk about Henry Butts and his farmer's boots, Mary Jane liked to be wherever young men were – any young men – and Henry Butts was young, male, and close at hand. Mary Jane liked watching her charms work their magic and didn't care much who the victims were. Was it wicked of Martha to think so? She was secretly thrilled that Mary Jane's attention was currently distracted by Constable Quill. Henry Butts was the first kind boy Dull Martha had ever met, and she hoped, secretly, to get to know him better.

She reached the gardens surrounding the farmhouse. Mrs Butts's superb husbandry was in evidence everywhere – in smart red geraniums blooming in gleaming white pots, in fat speckled chickens roaming and pecking, in smooth white gravel lining the walks up to the bright green door, in the fragrance of rhubarb pie wafting from the kitchen windows. Martha felt a pang of terror, of inadequacy, and quailed at the thought of approaching the farmer's house, never mind the farmer's son. Who was she, Martha called Dull, still so young, and no prettier than the spectacles pressing down upon her nose, to dare to strike up an acquaintance with Henry? She turned her steps towards the barns instead, and wondered if she could pretend she'd only come to visit Merry, their pony.

She found the gentle creature leaning out of his stall, apparently in some conversation with a pair of sheep, who wandered off to the far corner of their pen when Martha approached. Merry was a sociable pony, and he whickered at the sight of Martha. She stroked his long face and pressed her palms into his cheeks. He sniffed suggestively at the bouquet of wildflowers she'd tucked into her apron pocket.

"They're too pretty to eat, Merry, lad," she said. "Let's braid them into your mane instead." She found a brush and comb hanging on a nail and set to work grooming Merry's mane, weaving in delicate strands of wildflowers along with his own thick dark hair.

"You've got a good hand with him."

Martha was so immersed in her work that the voice shocked her, and she jumped.

"I'm sorry. I've startled you."

She turned to see Henry Butts in the doorway, still gripping the handles of a wheelbarrow full of straw. She ducked behind Merry and sank her fingers deep into his mane. How, exactly, did one respond to compliments from boys? Mrs Plackett's comportment lessons had never said. For Martha, this was a first. It felt nice, but it left her unsure of what to do with herself.

"I'm sorry to have come without asking," she said.

Henry set the wheelbarrow down and approached the pony. He ran his fingers along the braided portion of Merry's mane. "Merry belongs to the school," he said. "You can visit him anytime you like. He'd like more company, wouldn't you, you old flirt?"

"Flirt" made Dull Martha think of Disgraceful Mary Jane, and then of her own plainness, and her spectacles, and how she always managed to say the wrong thing, or miss the crucial point of important conversations. And here she'd felt, just a moment ago, so happy.

"Did you come to see Mother?" Henry asked. "Some message from Mrs Plackett about the milk?"

The thought of an interview with Mrs Butts made Dull Martha quail. Her temper was as famous as her cottage cheese. "No," she said. "No message about the milk."

187

"Just as well," Henry said. "Mother says there isn't room in all of Ely, much less on Prickwillow Road, for her and Mrs Plackett. Whenever she complains about the milk, Mother's banging pans and swearing bloody vengeance for days."

Dull Martha's fingers froze. "Bl-bloody vengeance, did you say?"

Henry nodded. "And milk's only the half of it. They've been fighting over the fence that divides your property and ours these past five years at least."

"Gracious." Dull Martha tried to process her spinning thoughts. "I didn't know."

Was it possible? Should she mention it to Louise? Could anyone in the world begin to believe that Mrs Butts, the supremely efficient farmer's wife, could have efficiently poisoned her widow neighbour and her bachelor brother, all of a Sunday evening?

Henry's voice jolted Dull Martha's thoughts once more. "That's some fine fancywork you've done, Miss Martha."

He remembered her name. Among so many girls, he remembered. Her face began to feel warm, and she realised she was starting to blush. This wouldn't do. She'd best get her errand over with and fly home. Why, oh, why didn't she leave this task to Disgraceful Mary Jane, or any of the girls?

"Henry, will you take me to the strawberry social?"

Henry Butts's mouth opened slightly, like a carp's. He looked like a schoolboy who can't guess the answer to a teacher's question, and the teacher wields a strap.

He seemed to need help, so Martha supplied it. "In your cart? With Merry?"

188

She waited in agony for his answer. Would he, or would he not take them?

Then she realised something had gone wrong. She knew the feeling well – a sort of buzzing in her ears that meant her dull brain and her wayward tongue had said the worst possible thing yet again. She groped desperately through her memory for the words that had passed her lips, still hanging suspended in the air between them.

Will you take . . . *me* . . .

She clapped her hands over her mouth, turned, and ran from Mr Butts's barn.

"Poison is a woman's weapon," Pocked Louise told Dour Elinor. They'd been sitting in the drawing room for an hour, as ready for the strawberry social as they saw any need to be, while the other girls still attended to their toilettes.

"You sound proud of it," Elinor observed.

"Why shouldn't I be?" Louise flipped through the pages of her notebook. "I don't condone killing, but if killing happens anyway, then I think women go about it much more sensibly. Leave it to men to be loud and violent and messy about the business. It's egotistical of them. It's not enough to eliminate their enemy. No. They must conquer them face to face and watch them plead for mercy, whereas women dispatch victims quickly and silently."

Elinor picked up a sketchbook and began to draw. "Men might say poison isn't sporting."

"Yes, and men think that organizing parties of dozens of riders and hounds to chase down one poor fox *is* sporting."

Louise snorted. "Men's opinions are irrelevant."

Dour Elinor shaded her paper briskly with a charcoal. "Tell that to Parliament."

"You're in an odd mood."

Dour Elinor shrugged. "I don't much fancy a strawberry social. I have a queer feeling about it. Something ill will come of our going."

Pocked Louise, who placed no stock in queer feelings, harrumphed. "You're a prognosticator now, are you?"

"I have instincts," Dour Elinor replied, quite unperturbed, "where death is concerned. Sunday morning, before Mrs Plackett and Mr Godding died, I had no appetite for breakfast, and I couldn't focus on Reverend Rumsey's sermon for persistent thoughts of the grave."

The tall, tight collar of Pocked Louise's dress chafed at her neck. "I dread the social, too," she said, "but not for any instinct other than avoiding tiresome spectacles intended to make us meet young men and parade us on display for older ones. Your instincts are pure piffle; no one concentrates on Reverend Rumsey's sermons, and you never think of anything *but* death."

Dour Elinor cocked her head and examined her sketch from another angle. "Say what you will. Something bad will happen tonight."

"Yes." Pocked Louise flexed her feet. "My toes will atrophy in these wretched slippers."

Disgraceful Mary Jane entered the room clutching a necklace. She skidded to a stop at the sight of Elinor and Louise on the sofa.

"You're wearing *those* frocks tonight?"

Louise and Elinor exchanged commiserating looks.

"And why shouldn't we?" Pocked Louise asked. "They're clean enough."

"Help me fasten this clasp." Mary Jane swooped onto Pocked Louise's lap so she could assist with the necklace. "Nobody wears dark grey drab to a springtime strawberry social."

"Mercy me, we forgot to wear our red dresses with yellow dots, and our matching green hats." Louise finished buckling the necklace clasp. "Then we'd *be* strawberries for the social."

"Don't be pert with me," Mary Jane said loftily. "I'm only trying to help you be seen to best advantage tonight."

Pocked Louise sniffed. "My best advantage would be to avoid being seen entirely."

"Come, that's no way to think," scolded Disgraceful Mary Jane. "Just because your face is pocked, that doesn't mean you must hide your candle under a bushel."

Louise sat, if possible, a little straighter. "I wasn't worried about my pocks, thank you very much," she said. "And don't go misquoting scripture to me. Candle under a bushel, indeed!"

Stout Alice wandered into the drawing room and sank onto a sofa. She clutched her forehead and moaned. "*Ohhhh* . . . don't make me go through with this."

Disgraceful Mary Jane, admiring and adjusting her curls in the mantelpiece mirror, shot her a disapproving look. "That's not the spirit we want to see in our stalwart headmistress."

191

"Something awful's going to happen," said Stout Alice.

"See? What did I tell you, Louise?" Dour Elinor looked extremely self-satisfied.

"My song will be a dismal failure," Alice went on.

Pocked Louise wrinkled her nose at Dour Elinor. "It takes no powers of divination to know that Alice's song will go badly, for heaven's sake."

"Thanks much, Louise." Stout Alice was too morose to take real offence. "Martha will have to play her pianoforte terribly loudly whilst I croak out my song. *'Tis not fine feathers make fine birds,*'" she warbled, badly. "'Tis a singing voice, which I lack, and that will ruin all. Everyone will see through my disguise, and we'll all be arrested for murder."

"Let's not be so gloomy." Disgraceful Mary Jane turned her attentions to Stout Alice's hair, powdered to look like Mrs Plackett's. "Maybe only *you* will be arrested for murder, Alice, dear. Elinor, my lamb, run and fetch your paintbox. You need to get working on Alice's wrinkles. And, Alice, I definitely suggest you wear your veil tonight."

"A widow in mourning wouldn't go singing a peacock song at a social!"

"Nevertheless," Mary Jane insisted, "you'll have to. Say it's your anniversary, or your dear husband's birthday, or some such thing."

"Has anybody seen Martha?" Pocked Louise inquired. "She left long ago to ask Henry Butts if he'd drive us to the social."

"I saw her come back," said Dour Elinor. "She came into the house, but I don't know where she's gone."

"Oh, Lord, you don't suppose he's said no to her, do you?" Mary Jane cried. "Then we shall have to walk, and we'll arrive all dusty." Disgraceful Mary Jane went about calling for Martha, searching in and out of rooms, and the others followed. They found her curled in a stuffed chair in the parlour, clutching her knees.

"I won't go to the social," she declared. "I'll stay home with Aldous. Go without me."

"Hear, hear," cried Pocked Louise. "I'll stay and keep you company."

Mary Jane crouched beside Martha's chair and slipped an arm around her neck. "Now what's all this?" she said. "What's made you decide you can't go?"

Dull Martha was nearly swayed by Mary Jane's tenderness, but when she recalled that Mary Jane represented all that she, Martha, was not – confident, sophisticated, fascinating, clever – she bit her lip and hunched down low in her chair.

The doorbell rang, and Disgraceful Mary Jane heaved a sigh of vexation. "I'll get it," she said. "You stay here. Alice, you can't be seen. Elinor's not done your makeup yet." She glided out into the corridor, where Smooth Kitty, having heard the doorbell, joined her from upstairs.

In the parlour, Stout Alice sat opposite Dull Martha for a quiet moment. "If you stay, Martha, you can't play the pianoforte for me, which means I couldn't sing, and nothing in this world could make me happier. But I think you'd actually like to go tonight. So why so sad?"

Martha sighed. "I just made an idiot of myself in front of Henry Butts."

Pocked Louise laughed. "Is that all? He does that in front of us on a daily basis."

Martha couldn't forgive this slur. "He does not. Now he knows, and he must hate me."

Dour Elinor, who'd brought her paintbox with her, began rolling bits of actors' putty between her palms to soften it. "Now he knows what?"

Martha slid down lower in her chair and hid her face behind a plush velvet cushion. Her words were somehow both whisper and wail. "That I *fancy him*!"

Stout Alice, who knew how unsympathetic Pocked Louise could be in matters of the heart, shot her scientific roommate a daggered look. "Martha, dear," she said, "Henry Butts couldn't possibly hate you, even if he suspects you fancy him. I'm sure he would find it extremely flattering to be noticed by such a charming young lady as yourself."

Dull Martha peeked up over the rims of her spectacles to gaze hopefully at Stout Alice. "Do you really think so?"

"I'm sure Henry Butts is home right now," Alice said, "getting himself all combed, and spiffing up for the social, thinking about the chance to visit with you there." Alice smiled and swallowed the Leland Murphy-sized lump in her throat.

"Did Henry agree to drive us?" Dour Elinor asked.

Dull Martha paused. "I don't know. I fled before I could hear his answer."

Stout Alice waved this concern away. "Of course he will. He'll be over here like a puppy dog, well in advance of when we need to leave. So you'd best hurry with my makeup, Elinor."

"Speaking of puppy dogs," Pocked Louise said, "has anyone seen Aldous? He chewed up Kitty's slipper earlier, and she's frightfully cross with me. As if *I* was the one to eat her shoe!"

Her question was soon answered by a growl and a bark coming from the hallway, followed by a crash of something wooden, and a man's voice uttering loud expletives wholly unsuited to the ears of delicate young ladies. Louise and Elinor hurried to investigate, while Alice, who could not yet be seen in public, stayed behind with Martha.

Louise and Elinor came upon a confused scene in the front doorway. A stout woman with brassy grey hair and an unfortunate straw hat decorated with wax grapes was scolding a man in workman's clothes. Aldous had attached himself by the teeth to the trouser leg of the workman and was threatening to worry a chunk of fabric clean out of those trousers. The man, who had apparently dropped a wooden crate on the floor, kicked and shouted at Aldous, calling that exuberant little fellow all sorts of colourful names and attempting to extricate his pants from the dog's jaws. Smooth Kitty looked astonished; Disgraceful Mary Jane gazed on with amusement.

"Don't crush the wee dog, Jock," the woman declared. "However much he may vex you."

"He's a bloody devil!" shouted the workman whose name, apparently, was Jock. "A foul cur what ought to be dropped in the pond with a rock tied to its tail!"

Pocked Louise hurried forward and snatched him up.

"I beg your pardon," Smooth Kitty said coldly. "The dog is only doing his duty and protecting us from strangers."

"I aren't a stranger," the man said. "I've worked for Mrs Lally eleven years."

Mrs Lally – for Jock obviously referred to the woman in the grape-festooned hat – saw no reason to correct Jock's social graces at this moment. "Young misses," she said, curtseying towards the girls, "are you *sure* your headmistress ain't around for me to speak with? I hate leaving these belongings of her brother's here without at least speaking to her."

Smooth Kitty shook her head. "I do apologise, but Mrs Plackett stepped out for the afternoon."

Mrs Lally's grapes quivered. "Well, it's most inconvenient of her. Not that anyone ever minds *my* convenience. It's only because I'm a Christian woman that I bother bringing these things by, instead of selling them at top price to recoup my losses on that brother of hers." The landlady peered from side to side, as though to catch some eavesdropper. "Other landlords would do it in two shakes, and the magistrate'd let 'em. Three months behind, he was! He assured me, just the last night I saw him, he told me his sister in Ely would float him out of his troubles. And doesn't he up and vanish on me without a word or a farthing!"

Little Aldous bared his teeth and growled at Mrs Lally from the safety of Louise's grasp. Louise's mind churned with her own thoughts. From the look of it, Smooth Kitty had the same idea – this Mrs Lally clearly expected Mrs Plackett to pay up Mr Godding's rent, if only to preserve their family's reputation. But the girls couldn't spare money like that.

"Mind you, I'm not the only one he owes money to," Mrs Lally went on. "Certain men've been coming around

for weeks now, troubling the gentleman over his debts."
She leaned forward and whispered as though somehow they
wouldn't all hear. "He *gambles*!"

The revelation failed to produce the shocked effect Mrs
Lally evidently hoped for. But she had heavier ammunition.

"I for one am not so sure he went to India to help some
precious nephew."

Remain calm, Kitty, that young lady told herself. "And
why is that?"

Mrs Lally now found some of the satisfaction she'd come
looking for, albeit not the monetary kind. "I think he went
running from the debt collectors and the bookies."

Dour Elinor and Pocked Louise looked at each other for
enlightenment.

"I beg your pardon," Smooth Kitty said at length.
"I don't know what that term means."

Mrs Lally pursed her lips, evidently enjoying the
worldly-wise knowledge she possessed that these higher-
born, better educated young ladies did not. "Bookies.
Bookmakers. The chaps that hold the betting books.
At horseraces. Roulette. Brag tables. Gentlemen's clubs."

Smooth Kitty began to feel a bit dizzy.

"They're smooth enough at first," Mrs Lally went on,
"with their fancy gloves and nice moustaches. It's when you
don't pay up that they take a different turn."

Finally some insight. "And you think Mr Godding has fled
from these . . . bookies? To avoid paying gambling debts?"

The landlady shrugged. "Seems more in his nature than
going off to help a nephew. What do you think?"

Smooth Kitty began rapidly to lose patience with this woman. "I only know what my headmistress told me, and I have no reason to doubt her."

While this conversation took place, Pocked Louise balanced little Aldous on one hip, and fished in her pocket for her notebook and pencil. It wasn't easy to write with a dog in her arms, but she managed to scrawl "*bookies*" on her list of suspects. If only she could learn their names!

Smooth Kitty, meanwhile, had decided it was time to change the subject with these unwelcome guests. Money had she none, but hospitality must be observed.

"Can I offer you something to eat or drink, Mrs Lally? Mr, er, Jock?'

"What're you having?" Jock licked his lips.

Mrs Lally would have none of this distraction. "Know what else he does, Miss?"

Smooth Kitty's voice was as frosty and uninterested as she could possibly make it. "We scarcely knew – *know* our headmistress's brother, never mind his private pastimes."

Mrs Lally was undaunted. "He consorts with *women*!" Her glance fell upon Disgraceful Mary Jane. "Can you countenance such a thing, Miss?"

Disgraceful Mary Jane swallowed a laugh. "Indeed, I'm shocked," that young lady replied. "I can't countenance a woman who would stoop to keeping company with him."

Mrs Lally had begun to nod at what she expected Mary Jane would say. When she caught Mary Jane's flippancy, her eyes narrowed.

"And why is that, Miss?" she asked stiffly. "His habits

may want correction, but he's an agreeable gentleman. He makes quite a dashing figure."

Smooth Kitty began to realise why Mrs Lally had allowed Mr Godding to fall three months' delinquent in his payments. For his charms! How repulsive. "Mr Godding's appearance is a matter of personal taste," Kitty said, as though to chastise Mary Jane for the landlady's benefit.

Colour rose in Mrs Lally's cheeks. "I'm respectable, and I keep a decent house. Gentleman or no, I need none of that sort of thing about. Your headmistress, if she has any decency, should speak to her brother about his morals."

"*Jilted lovers,*" Pocked Louise wrote in her notebook. "*Romantic hopefuls of either deceased party.*"

Smooth Kitty advanced towards the door, leaving Mrs Lally no choice but to take a backwards step towards it also. "I am sure this will be Mrs Plackett's first topic of conversation with her brother when next she sees him," she said. For a moment she pictured this joyful sibling confrontation taking place before Saint Peter at the pearly gates. "Mrs Plackett would wish us to thank you for bringing Mr Godding's things here."

Mrs Lally looked far from finished speaking, but the sound of wheels and hoof beats on the gravel drive made her pause. It was only Henry Butts approaching in his freshly-waxed cart, pulled by Merry, but the landlady looked caught out somehow, by this unexpected arrival.

"Come on, Jock." She yanked on his canvas sleeve. "We've said our piece. The missus ain't home. No point in us waiting." With that, she turned and marched out the door.

After aiming a malevolent look in little Aldous's direction, Jock ambled after. The grapes on Mrs Lally's hat bobbed as she climbed stiffly into her wagon.

"A touch for money, if I ever saw one," Pocked Louise stroked Aldous between the ears. "There's our good little guard dog! She thought she could squeeze some rent out of Mrs Plackett, didn't she, Kitty?"

Smooth Kitty watched their wagon drive away. "Oh, she's owed it, I'm sure. But she's not going to get it. Mr Godding took his debts with him to . . . well, wherever he's gone." She smiled slyly. "Perhaps not to heaven, if his landlady's reports are true."

Disgraceful Mary Jane had already forgotten all about Mrs Lally. "Look at that silly Henry Butts," she said. "Red as an apple at the thought of squiring us all to the social. And look! He's gone and done up the pony's mane with flowers. If he thinks he's going to pin a flower in *my* hair, he has another thing coming."

Pocked Louise and Dour Elinor exchanged a silent look.

"Run and thank Henry for driving us," Smooth Kitty told Mary Jane. "Try not to break his heart in the process. But tell him he'll have to wait a while. We're nowhere near ready."

Chapter Seventeen

Soft twilight hung over Ely proper, and candles in village bedroom windows twinkled at the young ladies of Saint Etheldreda's School for Young Ladies ninety minutes later as they bounced towards the Saint Mary's Church parish hall. The church bells began to chime eight o'clock, and the great cathedral's deeper bells took up a competing *bong, bong, bong*.

Stout Alice, disguised with putty, makeup, dress, and veil as Mrs Plackett, sat swaying next to Henry Butts in the front seat of the cart, as her headmistress would have done. The night was cool, but Alice felt sweat dampening her underthings and pooling in her slippers. Just another misery to endure on this frightful night. Perspiration was her albatross. As her grandmamma often said, it came of overdoing it at meals and taking on too much flesh. But tonight, with performance anxiety flooding her with nausea, there was no danger of Stout Alice consuming even a morsel of strawberry tart. Not until she could get home, climb out of these dreadful clothes, and peel this ghastly putty off her face, would she even think of food.

Wretched though she was, Alice had to admit that Dour Elinor, armed with her new tools of the makeup artist's trade, had done wonders in transforming her into Mrs Plackett. With putty she had built up Alice's nose to precisely the headmistress's distinctive shape. Elinor's eye was unfailing, and her fingers nimble. Disgraceful Mary Jane declared the likeness so complete that Alice could dispense with the veil, at least during her vocal performance. Alice preferred to hide behind a sheet of lace regardless, but the other girls prevailed upon her to remove it for her song.

Henry Butts said blessedly little on the way to town, for which Stout Alice was grateful. Henry would hardly be expected to maintain conversation with Widow Plackett, but Alice suspected his silence was due more to the terror he felt at escorting six handsome young ladies into town, than from any fear of their crotchety headmistress. The girls were, indeed, all looking uncommonly rosy tonight. Even Dour Elinor and Pocked Louise were forced to submit reluctantly to Disgraceful Mary Jane, who made what she called mandatory adjustments to their coiffures and added some ornaments from her own jewellery box to their sombre clothes. Dear Roberta, Dull Martha, and Smooth Kitty were pretty as pie. All their bonnets were fetchingly done in pink and red ribbons. As for herself, nobody explained to Henry Butts that Alice was upstairs with a headache. Her presence wasn't missed, a fact which only added to Alice's gloom.

They reached the parish hall. Light streamed from its tall windows all the way down to the path where church deacons stood assisting elderly ladies from their conveyances into the social. Henry Butts sprang the brake in his cart and leaped to assist the girls one by one.

"Oh, don't mind me, Henry." Disgraceful Mary Jane hitched up the hem of her frock, revealing a pretty ankle as she stepped down from the cart.

"If you say so," Henry replied, and reached to assist a blushing Dull Martha.

Disgraceful Mary Jane, who clearly did not expect to be taken at her word, frowned. But she quickly brightened. "Look, there's Constable Quill, still in uniform!"

Dear Roberta sat straight and tall, holding the precious embroidered linen tablecloth on her lap, carefully wrapped in tissue paper. She entrusted it reluctantly to Dour Elinor as she herself disembarked from the cart.

The parish hall dazzled their eyes after the deepening dusk outdoors. Lamps and candles blazed from every table, spread with smooth white tablecloths, and decorated with paper strawberries and short bouquets of white daisies and red roses. A heaping mound of fresh strawberries graced the refreshment table, alongside platters of dainties and a huge glass urn gleaming with ruby-coloured punch. The food looked too pristine, and the party as yet too sparse, for any of the guests to begin eating. What people there were in the room huddled in corners, eyeing the food and the clothing of the new arrivals.

"Well, here we are," Smooth Kitty whispered. "Pray heaven for an uneventful night."

"Easy for you to say." Stout Alice rapped Kitty's arm with her Chinese fan – exactly the kind of thing Mrs Plackett would do. "You don't have to play an old lady, nor sing a humiliating song for the assembly."

"Watch where you go swatting people," Kitty said. "You have only yourself to thank for our presence here. Let's just hope the food is good."

Just then, Alice saw Mr Leland Murphy duck into the room. His face shone bright with the effort of scrubbing and shaving, as evidenced by fresh nicks to his chin. His eyes went immediately to the Saint Etheldreda party – to Alice, then away, then to Alice again. His eyebrows knitted together. He seemed confused. Someone was missing from their party. Poor Alice's heart didn't know whether to sing or weep.

Her thoughts were interrupted by tender concern from Dull Martha.

"Do try not to be murdered tonight, Alice," whispered that young lady. "I should cry from now till forever if you were."

Smooth Kitty's fingers itched to cover Dull Martha's mouth. "Let's not talk nonsense, please," she hissed. "And let's not use the name *Alice* tonight for any reason."

"It isn't nonsense." Dour Elinor looked darkly around the room. "Whoever struck Mrs Plackett down is likely to be here."

"Sssh!"

Pocked Louise nodded knowingly at Dour Elinor. "We shall keep a close watch."

Mrs Rumsey, the vicar's wife, greeted them. She was a compact woman, straight and slim in her bearing, and severe of expression. Her efforts had wrought this magical transformation upon the parish hall, yet it was hard to reconcile her stern demeanour with the room's bright pageant of colour.

"Constance." Mrs Rumsey nodded to Stout Alice, who forgot, for an instant, that she must respond to that name. She realised with horror that she didn't know Mrs Rumsey's first name, and should. She nodded back and tried to think of what to say.

Dear Roberta rescued her. "We've finished the tablecloth, Mrs Rumsey." She surrendered her precious package. "I hope you like it."

Mrs Rumsey peeled back the tissue paper and examined the needlework. "The table linens were supposed to arrive half an hour ago," she said. "I'll have to strip one of the tables now. But I suppose we cannot let your work go to waste. Be sure to observe the cloth submitted by the young ladies from Mrs Usher's school. It's an absolute tapestry of strawberries." She moved off in the direction of the food, gesturing for another woman on her Ladies' Committee to assist her. Together they removed the lamp and flowers from a table, and switched its plain white cloth for their embroidered one.

"May those Usher girls contract the plague," Disgraceful Mary Jane muttered. "With a wife like her, it's no wonder Reverend Rumsey drinks."

"He *what*?" Dull Martha was shocked.

"Nothing."

Reverend Rumsey swooped over to greet the party from Saint Etheldreda's. His cheeks and nose were as bright as strawberries themselves, and he beamed at the sight of them.

"Dear Mrs Plackett, how good of you to join us this evening." He pumped Stout Alice's hand up and down. "How fine your pupils look tonight, all dressed for spring!" His eyes passed quickly over Pocked Louise and Dour Elinor in their sombre greys. "It's wonderful to see young people gather for the wholesome entertainment we have in store for them tonight."

"Thank you, Reverend." Stout Alice responded in character. "It is good to see you. What a lovely event you have organised for us."

"Not I, not I." Reverend Rumsey shook his head solemnly. "It's Patricia who has organised it all." *Patricia*. Alice made a mental note. "She's so wonderfully efficient. An extraordinary woman. I couldn't ask for a more *capable* helpmeet and companion."

Disgraceful Mary Jane developed a fit of cough. Smooth Kitty slid her foot so as to give Mary Jane an unobserved kick.

Out of the corner of her eye Stout Alice saw Miss Fringle come limping into the parish hall. "Indeed," she said. "*Patricia's* talents are legend."

Disgraceful Mary Jane found this conversation dull in the extreme. She searched for a sign of Constable Quill, who hadn't come indoors. He was probably still talking with the men, who had remained outside to smoke. The only man she saw coming in just now was Dr Snelling. *Eugh*.

"Mrs Plackett, I wonder if I might impose on your kindness?" Reverend Rumsey's anxious face began to sweat. "As part of the programme, I'd like to acknowledge the generosity of parishioners like you who have made bequests to Saint Mary's in their wills."

A thunderbolt went through Smooth Kitty from the crown of her well-coiffed head to the soles of her suede slippers. The church! Why did no one think of the church? She glanced quickly at the other girls. Pocked Louise knew exactly what Kitty was thinking. She reached for her notebook, concealed in her handbag. Kitty's eyes flew wide open in alarm. She shook her head at Louise. *Not here!*

Mrs Rumsey joined her husband at that moment. "Your table is ready," she told the girls.

Reverend Rumsey persisted. "May I, then, Mrs Plackett? I want to recognise your generosity. It stimulates similar generosity in others, without which Saint Mary's might struggle."

A tall older gentleman was just coming into the room, aided by his valet. He began to wave at Alice. With a gulp, she recognised Admiral Paris Lockwood. She wrenched her gaze back onto Reverend Rumsey's expectant face.

"I . . . I'd rather not be singled out," she said. "It feels . . . prideful to me, somehow." She searched for a more convincing reason, and found one in her catechism. "Did not Christ say that when we give, our left hand ought not to know what the right hand is doing?"

Mrs Rumsey's mouth straightened into a hard line. No one, it seemed, should dare quote scripture to her husband, the vicar. Smooth Kitty had to cover her own mouth with her hand.

But Reverend Rumsey seized at the chance to use scripture to make his point. "Your modesty does you credit. Don't forget what Christ said about the widow casting her mites into the treasury. He acknowledged publicly the widows who give their all to the church. Please consider it. This event is our largest parish gala until Advent season."

"Excuse me," Mrs Rumsey said, with a look of distaste. "I must greet other guests."

"And I, too." He kissed Stout Alice's hand. "We'll speak later on in the evening."

Stout Alice worked hard not to shake off her hand, or wipe it on her skirts. They sat at their table, and she let out a slow breath. "This night can't end soon enough for me."

"We've learned something, though," said Pocked Louise. "The church was a beneficiary of your old will, Headmistress, dear."

"Ugh, don't call me that."

"Surely you are not suggesting that the Rumseys are . . ." Dear Roberta lowered her voice to a whisper. "Suspects?"

"If they were," Kitty whispered, "they wouldn't bring up the will."

"Not the vicar!" Roberta gasped.

"'Give their *all* to the church?'" repeated Pocked Louise. "We can't ignore that."

The hall was filling rapidly now. A woman began to play violin on the platform, but this, it was understood, was background music, not yet the evening's entertainment.

"Here come those girls from the Queen's School," said Pocked Louise. "I hate how they look down their noses at us. As if they're so superior, just because their school is bigger, and in the city. And because they have libraries, and laboratories, and real Latin instructors . . ."

"And because their papas are rich, and can pay such high tuition and send them new dresses every month," added Stout Alice.

Smooth Kitty studied the Queen's School girls' dresses, which were undoubtedly fine. "Why haven't they brought the boys from the school?"

"Rugby," said Pocked Louise. "Wednesday night. I think I should enjoy that sport."

Dull Martha gasped. "Such a rough and muddy game, Louise! I'll never understand you."

Miss Fringle hobbled over to them. She had always used a cane, but Smooth Kitty felt certain she'd begun to exaggerate her limp when her gaze fell upon the Saint Etheldreda party.

"Well, Constance," she hailed Stout Alice, "I'm surprised I haven't seen you these last few days. I received your note, but I should have thought you'd pay a personal call, after one of your own students sprained my ankle."

Alice looked to Kitty for help. What could she say?

"I suppose I must not be critical. After all, you've had distressing events of your own this week. I'm surprised to see you out socially tonight, to be frank. Is there any word from Aldous? Has he reached Julius in India by now?"

Alice looked once more to Kitty, who shook her head slightly.

"No," she said. "No word. I . . . assume he is still sailing at this point."

"If his ship hasn't sunk," said Miss Fringle.

This idea of a sunken ship appealed greatly to Stout Alice – it would dispose of one of their corpses tidily – but Disgraceful Mary Jane decided it was time to change the subject. "Miss Fringle," she said, "who are all those young men who have just come in the door?"

The choir mistress peered over her spectacles at a group in long black coats. "Those will be students from the theological college."

"Ah." Mary Jane was clearly less interested now. "Future parsons."

"Listen to that awful violin squeak," Miss Fringle exclaimed. "Why they allowed Beatrice Nimby on tonight's programme, I'll never know. I'll speak to Patricia Rumsey about it." She favoured Alice with a smile. "Your song will be a high point of the programme. I congratulate myself on choosing a perfect tune for your voice. Light, airy, cheerful, but with an important message for young people." She peered at the young ladies, as if to ascertain whether any of them were under the delusion that fine feathers did, in fact, make fine birds, then hobbled away.

"Whew," Stout Alice sighed. "Another person fooled. Thanks again, Elinor."

Elinor nodded. "Not at all."

Dull Martha hadn't ceased watching for Henry Butts from the moment they sat down, though whether her plan was to seek him out or to avoid him, she couldn't say. He entered the room, and her courage splashed into her stomach. She decided avoiding him would be the best policy. He took a step towards the table where the Saint Etheldreda girls sat, paused, turned around, paused, then turned back again. Martha felt dizzy trying to interpret his manoeuvres and finally determined to flee the next time his back was turned. This she did, and collided headlong with Dr Snelling, who was on his way to the refreshments.

"I say!" The doctor glared at her, and brushed his waistcoat and jacket vigorously, as if they might now be speckled with young lady crumbs.

"I'm sorry, Doctor Snelling," Martha cried. "Forgive me. I can be so clumsy at times."

He peered at her through his spectacles while she adjusted her own. "I remember you – you're the one who nearly knocked over Miss Fringle, aren't you?"

She hung her head in shame. "I am."

Dr Snelling held out an elbow for Martha's benefit. "Well, then, I'd better pour you a glass of punch," he said. "Letitia Fringle hasn't enjoyed herself more in years. She's had me to her house twice a day all week, tending her ankle, which isn't out of sorts at all, by this point."

To her surprise, Martha smiled. Dr Snelling was making a joke! She, who found almost all men frightening, and particularly the cross ones, placed her hand on the doctor's arm and allowed herself to be led towards the impressive punch.

Smooth Kitty felt restive tonight, anxious, a curious mixture of anticipation and worry. Under ordinary circumstances she would have welcomed an evening out such as this, for a chance to mingle with other young people her age and, truth be told, take a peek at the younger gentlemen. But tonight was too soon after the deaths for her to feel relaxed. Especially not with Constable Quill in the room, striding purposely towards them.

"Look sharp, girls," she whispered. "Here comes Mary Jane's beau."

Disgraceful Mary Jane tutted. "Not yet, he isn't, not yet," she corrected Kitty. "Only give me this evening, and that'll be mended."

From the corner of her eye, Kitty caught sight of Amanda Barnes, dressed in an apron and standing near the kitchen. Kitty felt an ache of pity and shame in the pit of her stomach. She'd rather not encounter Barnes tonight. Not after their recent unpleasantness.

"Mrs Plackett. Ladies. Good evening." Constable Quill stood at attention, then bowed once Alice acknowledged him. "It is a pleasure to make your acquaintance, ma'am."

"Yes. Likewise." Alice spoke in exactly the wan voice Mrs Plackett would have used for meeting an unwelcome policeman. Kitty suppressed a smile.

"I trust your students have apprised you of the purpose of my earlier visit to your home?"

Stout Alice groaned inwardly. There was that perspiration again. What to do?

"They did." She fixed Constable Quill with her sternest, most Placketty look. "I'm sorry, Constable. Are we here tonight for business, or for pleasure?"

Disgraceful Mary Jane stood quickly. "Who will escort me to the refreshment table for some punch?" Her eyes were on the constable, and for once Stout Alice didn't object to her flirting.

Constable Quill ignored Mary Jane – he was a man of steel nerves, apparently – and tipped the brim of his tall copper's hat deferentially. "Indeed, ma'am, I am sorry to trouble you. We are, as you say, here for pleasure. Only I just wanted to make a small inquiry, you understand, just a very trifling matter." He pulled his notebook and pencil from his pocket. "You did say, didn't you . . ." He surveyed the other girls until his gaze rested upon Smooth Kitty. "That's right. You're the head girl. You were the one who said that on Sunday afternoon Mr Godding had departed for India, by way of London?"

Mary Jane sat down. *This* tiresome business again.

For an instant, Smooth Kitty wished that Stout Alice actually was Mrs Plackett, and that she could surrender her responsibility for this whole affair to the resident adult in charge.

"Yes. It was I who told you that."

Constable Quill's eyes twinkled and his dimples deepened. Curse him. Mary Jane was practically panting. The policeman turned back to Stout Alice.

"And, ma'am, did Mr Godding travel to London by train?"

Alice glanced at Kitty for guidance, but the 'head girl' was too agitated to advise her. So be it. She would answer this bobby if she must, but he'd receive only minimal civility from her.

"Naturally he did."

The constable's pencil scribbled across the page. "Do you know which train he took?"

Around the room, music and people and strawberry punch swirled into a twinkling red blur, but this odious constable remained immovable as Gibraltar, and unwelcome as the Plague.

"I'm not in the habit of memorizing the train schedules."

Pocked Louise nodded slightly. *Good job, Alice.*

Constable Quill smiled. "Of course not. Only, the reason I ask is that Charlie Neff, the ticketmaster down at the station, has a mind like a trap. Famous for it – he remembers every person who got on or off the trains in Ely, if they're someone he knows."

Smooth Kitty had the sense the walls of the parish hall were crumbling before her eyes.

Stout Alice remembered to speak. "And?"

"He worked all day in the booth this Sunday, and he's quite certain that Mr Godding never got on the train."

Chapter Eighteen

"Your headmistress is looking well tonight."

Dull Martha nearly choked on a gulp of punch. It was fizzy, and she hadn't expected the tingles now burning her nose. Dr Snelling drank his down without difficulty. Men were accustomed to strong drinks. A startling thought occurred to Martha. Could this punch contain liquor? Surely the beverage at a parish social wouldn't. Would it?

She sipped from her cup again. She expected the fizz this time, and found it wasn't altogether unpleasant. It made her want to giggle. Dr Snelling downed another half-glassful.

"That can happen with patients," he said. "They rebound. Needs of the moment give them . . . how d'you say . . ." He quenched his parched memory with a swig of punch. "Vim. Vigour. A new lease on life. Maybe it's this business with her grandson. No. Nephew, isn't it?"

"Julius," Martha offered.

Dr Snelling waved this information away.

"I've seen patients at death's door rally when a youngster in the family caught a trifling cold. Feeling needed is remarkable

215

tonic. Course, there are other powerful reasons to live, too. Like burning through all your dough."

Dull Martha took another long draught of punch. How curious that she hadn't liked it at first. Like nectar of the gods! It was pagan to think about gods. They didn't wear enough clothes, for one thing. But if they drank punch like this, they couldn't be all bad.

"'Dough'?"

Dr Snelling grinned and adjusted his gold watch. "Money," he said. "Rich people live forever, more's the pity if you're next in line. Live long to hoard your gold for spite."

Words just spoken tickled Martha's memory.

"Death's door, you said?" She drained her last drops of punch. "Anyway, Mrs Plackett isn't rich."

"Here. Let me refill you." Martha held out her glass, which he filled, and his own into the bargain. "Ahh. Nothing makes a man thirsty like riding around all day, talking to sick people. As to who's rich, you never know." He leaned in a little closer. "Do you want to hear a secret?"

Martha nodded. She wanted to hear what he meant by 'death's door,' but she could wait.

"Sick people *smell terrible*!"

Dr Snelling's face contorted into a grimace of hilarious laughter. He wheezed and chuckled to himself so contagiously that Martha couldn't help giggling, too.

"Do they?"

The doctor had to wipe his eyes with his shirt cuffs. "That's my professional secret. One they don't exactly teach at university. I can tell whose days are numbered by how they smell."

Henry Butts came into view across the room just then, and Martha found her interest in the doctor's company begin to wane.

"Your headmistress, for instance. She's got a liverish smell. Positively ripe, she is."

Martha snickered at this. It was true. Mrs Plackett had a distinctive sourness to her that no amount of scented powder could fully overcome. Martha took another deep draught of punch.

"There she sits now, looking like a picture of health." The doctor licked his juice-stained lips and watched Stout Alice keenly. "But I submit to you that she isn't long for this world. Months at most. Could be weeks. Money can't buy a new liver, more's the pity."

Martha nearly choked on her punch. Its bubbles shot straight to her brain and left her feeling dizzy. She gulped down the last swallow and stared at Stout Alice, talking pleasantly to Disgraceful Mary Jane's police constable beau. Months to live? Weeks? Had she misunderstood something? Poor Alice! So wise, and always so patient and kind. Martha looked to Alice as a shield whenever Mary Jane's vanity or Smooth Kitty's bossiness got to be too much. To lose her now would be unbearable. She hoped she was wrong. For once it would be a comfort to be wrong.

The doctor scowled and muttered under his breath. He eyed his empty glass as though it were his enemy. Finally he nodded curtly in her direction. "Didn't mean to worry you. Evening, Miss." He strode away, leaving Dull Martha with a sticky mouth and a frightened heart.

And it was in this state that Henry Butts found her when he appeared at her side.

"Evening, Miss Martha." He made a halting smile.

"This . . . Charles . . . Niff, or whatever he calls himself," Stout Alice-as-Mrs Plackett haughtily informed Constable Quill, with an indifferent wave of her hand, "might well be mistaken. Or perhaps my brother found an opportunity to ride with an acquaintance to another nearby train station. I couldn't say. And now, young man, you haven't kept your promise to keep this brief. If we must have this conversation, a church social is no place for it."

The policeman tipped his hat deferentially. "Pardon me, ma'am," he said in a voice of meekness that Smooth Kitty didn't trust. "I assumed you would share my concern for your brother's safety."

"My brother is a grown man, quite capable of looking after himself," said the false Mrs Plackett. "Good *evening*."

Constable Quill bowed left the table. Smooth Kitty had the distinct feeling he went away feeling he'd won.

Stout Alice's breath came shakily. Disgraceful Mary Jane rose and followed after the constable, but Alice felt too rattled to try and stop her, though there was no telling what Mary Jane might let slip under the spell of handsome shoulders.

Back at their table, the remaining girls couldn't give vent to emotions in a place like this, so stunned looks passing across their embroidered tablecloth had to suffice.

Smooth Kitty was the first to whisper aloud.

"We must not let this development rattle us," she said. "It proves nothing and implies nothing. No foul play is even suspected."

"Ssshh." Stout Alice's hush was full of warning. "Not here."

The parish social now felt full, and the girls looked about themselves with horror. What other eyes were spying them and plotting their ruin? After this distasteful encounter with the police force, what else could go wrong?

Stout Alice looked across the hall to find Mary Jane. She and the constable flirted in a corner, partially shielded from view by the red velvet curtains which had been pulled aside in order that the pianoforte and the stage could be in full view of the guests seated at the tables. "We should go get Mary Jane." Stout Alice shook her head. "She'll make a spectacle of us all. Mrs Plackett wouldn't allow her to throw herself at police officers in public like this."

They were deterred from retrieving Mary Jane. Like moles popping up from their holes, two young men suddenly materialised at their table. Both were tall and thin, and made to seem even more so by their somewhat oversized and faded black coats. Dear Roberta sat up straighter, and gave her coiffure a little boost.

"Pardon us, Madam," said one of them, a youth with ginger hair pomaded flat upon his scalp, as he bowed deferentially to Stout Alice. "Do I apprehend correctly that your name is Mrs Plackett, proprietress of Saint Etheldreda's School for Young Ladies? May we be permitted to make the acquaintance of your charming pupils?"

Stout Alice shook herself slightly, reasserting the role of Mrs Plackett.

"And what is your name, young man?"

The speaker bowed. "My friend and I are students at Barton Theological College. My name is Albert Bly. I hail from Northumberland. This is my friend, Charles Bringhurst, from Cambridge. 'Funeral Charlie,' we call him."

"Do you indeed?" Stout Alice examined the young man from Cambridge. His dark hair was somewhat longer than fashion permitted, parted severely down the middle of his scalp. He was all angles, with a long Roman nose, protruding bones, and deep hollows in each cheek. "And why have you given your friend such a sobriquet?"

Mr Albert Bly, who seemed incapable of *not* smiling, beamed. "His sermons on the state of the soul after death defy all description, and his eulogies make strong men weep over their mothers-in-law. *We* suspect he's a little too fond of death, but it's bound to make his career."

"You joke about it," said Dour Elinor, "but it seems proper that a future clergyman have keen sensibilities where mortality is concerned."

Funeral Charlie gazed upon Dour Elinor, then bowed deeply. Stout Alice smiled behind her Chinese fan, and performed the necessary introductions.

"I'm more of a marriages-and-christenings man myself," Mr Bly told Dear Roberta.

Stout Alice felt herself warming to her sixty-something role. "I should say you were somewhat young to have much to offer to young couples by way of marital advice."

Mr Bly responded in a jovial spirit. "Ah, but a well-educated clergyman need never let a lack of experience stand in the way of preaching. Or else, what are all these divinity studies for?"

Their conversation fizzed along. Stout Alice welcomed the harmless distraction. Albert Bly, the smiler, was by all evidence quite taken with Dear Roberta, whose cheeks had never looked so bright. Her smile never shone to such perfection as it now did by parish hall lamplight. Mr Charles Bringhurst somehow contrived to pull up a chair and insinuate himself between Dear Roberta and Dour Elinor, and soon he and the latter were deep in conversation on topics of morbid interest to them alone. Pocked Louise rolled her eyes at the transformation that had overtaken her classmates in the presence of these young gentlemen. She sent her gaze searching the room for Dull Martha, and scowled to see her smiling bashfully at Henry Butts.

Smooth Kitty found the scene amusing, but these theological gentlemen were a meagre distraction from their present difficulties. Constable Quill *would* prove difficult. Not even Mary Jane's bewitching green eyes could deter his investigative bloodlust. Alice's vocal performance – where would it lead? To discovery and disaster? Somewhere in this room of friendly familiar Ely folk, a murderer might well be concealed – one still out to get Mrs Plackett. But there Alice sat, conversing gravely as Mrs Plackett with the two collegiate youths. It seemed she could manage her own affairs. For a brief hiatus, Kitty decided to let her.

"Excuse me, girls." Smooth Kitty rose and pushed her chair in. "I need to stretch my legs a bit. I'll be back presently." She left before anyone could query her intentions, hoping she could look purposeful even with no place to go. The washroom, perhaps? The kitchen, where she might offer some assistance? No, Amanda Barnes might come in with a tray of empty glasses. She looked about for Mary Jane and saw her whispering into the constable's ear. What could that shocking girl be saying?

Over the party's hubbub Kitty's ears caught the notes of a train's whistle, down the hill at the station. Oh, that snoop of a ticket master! Someday soon, she vowed, they'd purchase seven tickets for that train, and ride away from this overly-inquisitive little city, where everyone knew everyone else's face and business – where, ironically, the guilty could get away with murder, but the innocent couldn't get away with innocently covering it up. There was no justice in the world, or at least none in Ely.

The train whistle's siren song called Kitty to far off places, to ports where swaying ships could carry the Saint Etheldreda sisterhood to any place they wished to see – Paris, Calcutta, America even. She wandered over to a piece of artwork tacked to the wall and pretended to examine it. In addition to the musical performances featured for the evening, members of the parish had contributed needlework samplers, sketches, and watercolours of their own make to display at the evening's gala, for the cultural edification of all Ely. Mrs Rumsey held adamant feelings about Culture, and Ely's lack thereof. Kitty's mind was so preoccupied that she failed to take much notice of the charcoal drawing that occupied her field of vision, except to observe that their own Dour Elinor could have done much, much better. It was a skyline of the cathedral, from the vantage point of the pretty park that lay on its southern side.

She drifted along the wall to another artistic offering. This was the cathedral from another angle, rather lumpy looking, but drenched in morning sunlight. Kitty stifled a yawn and wished she could stretch her arms over her head. She turned back to see Dear Roberta rise and walk to the punch table with the cheerful Mr Bly. Then, of all things, Dour Elinor rose and accompanied Funeral Charlie to the heaped strawberry platters. This left Pocked Louise sitting ramrod-straight and looking vexed, and Stout Alice laughing into her fan.

Admiral Lockwood tottered across the room, cutting a slow-but-straight swath through the assembled guests for the table he believed belonged to Mrs Constance Plackett. He held a glass of punch in one hand, and Kitty thought it more than likely some would slosh on Patricia Rumsey's immaculate floors. But he reached Stout Alice's side, set down the glass, bowed, and took one of the vacated seats beside Alice.

Kitty watched Stout Alice greet her octogenarian suitor. She should fly to Alice's rescue, she felt, but she was tired. The weighty burden of safeguarding seven girls *and* a morbid secret hung like a millstone around her neck tonight. Her confidence frayed, unravelling slowly like one of Elinor's poorly-knitted stockings.

"Shame on you," she chided herself. "Brace up and carry on. Or go home to Father."

Alice seemed to be managing with old Admiral Lockwood well enough. The admiral gestured broadly as he spoke. Kitty suspected Alice was fond of the old sailor. Perhaps she could better help Alice by standing guard, here by the wall, and watching for anything that could threaten her safety. People moved in and out of her field of vision, obscuring her view of Alice's table, and it left Kitty feeling anxious. She moved along the wall in search of a better view.

Reverend and Mrs Rumsey took to the dais and were met by polite applause from the assembly. "Ladies and gentlemen," the vicar boomed. "Young people, and those young at heart, thank you for gracing our evening's social with your presence. We are pleased to inaugurate the evening's programme of musical entertainment, but first, a few words of thanks to those without whom this event would not be possible. My *dear* and *devoted* wife, Mrs Rumsey . . ."

Kitty turned back towards the wall and forced herself to look at the next painting, which seemed little more than a blur of watercolour. Brown columns rising against a field of blue . . . oh, no. Not another one.

"A startlingly original concept, is it not? Painting the cathedral?"

"Oh!" She jumped at the sound of a low voice so close to her ear.

It was the young man from the chemist's shop. The same one who had ridden by the house that very afternoon and caught her in a shabby housekeeping frock.

Kitty cringed to remember her cowardly behaviour earlier. Now she had no place to hide.

Tonight the young man wore a dark blue coat and tails, with a white cravat and waistcoat. His dark brown curls gleamed in the lamplight. A faint smile played upon his lips as he studied this latest dubious work of art.

Kitty lowered her voice to a whisper. "You startled me, sneaking up like that."

He pressed a finger over his lips, and whispered so that Kitty had to lean close to hear. "The good vicar is still making his speech. I'm only here to admire the masterpiece."

The young man fixed his gaze piously upon the painting before them both, but there was mischief in the corners of his eyes, Kitty was certain. And then, uncertain. Somehow he seemed to take in both Kitty and the painting simultaneously. Again she noticed his skin, more brown from the sun than anyone in Ely so early in the year, and the note in his pronunciation she could not quite place. But she could not let his last word pass.

"Masterpiece indeed!"

"Don't you think so?"

A pair of elderly ladies seated close by turned to frown at them. Kitty covered her mouth with her hand. In the background, Reverend Rumsey's voice droned on. ". . . and Mrs Livonia Butts, for her generous donation of her award-winning butter, so ingeniously sculpted into frolicking hams . . . I'm sorry, that's frolicking lambs . . ."

The young man leaned in closer to whisper, pointing at the painting as he did so. "Let us analyze this painting, and prove my theory. There's an airy lightness to the building that belies its solid bulk. The artist has defied stale notions of line and form, and branched out into bold new territory with curves. One almost feels the cathedral is a smoky apparition that will float away upon the next breeze."

Kitty tried not to snort. "What rubbish! It looks like it's made of gelatin."

He raised an eyebrow quizzically, and peered at the painting. Kitty began to doubt herself. Was he serious? He sounded so well-trained in the language of art. Gelatin! Had her inane comments painted her to be a fool?

And why should she care if they had?

She watched his face anxiously for some sign, and saw his gaze move quickly to the placard naming the artist, T. Richardson. He looked back at the painting, and then at her.

A new and dreadful thought gripped Kitty. Was *he* T. Richardson? Had she just insulted *his* painting? Even if it was a gelatinous mess, Kitty would never dream of saying so to its creator. And especially when its creator had such a pleasant forehead. Well, dark curls, rather. Or was it the line of the nose? The thoughtful expression, surely. The brown Adam's apple might distract one's gaze, but that was only a comment upon the pure whiteness of its surrounding white collar. And *that* was a simple matter of good laundering.

Kitty began to feel a bit dizzy. The room around her ruptured into applause, for apparently the vicar had concluded his litany of gratitude. The young man began to clap as well, and as he did so he leaned in close to speak in Kitty's ear.

"I take issue with your assessment of the painting. You are too harsh a critic. I would more likely call it a mousse."

Kitty was too mortified to listen. "Oh, Mr Richardson, I do apologise. My knowledge of art is so . . ." The abrupt end to the applause drew up her short. She whispered. "So limited. I've no right to judge." She collected her wits. "Wait. Did you just say *mousse*?"

The young man's eyes twinkled. "Mr Richardson, am I? You cut me to the quick!"

A weedy-looking youth took the dais and began to play a breathy air upon his flute.

"*Aren't* you Mr Richardson?"

He shook his head. "Not this evening, at any rate."

Kitty began to feel unsure of who *she* was that evening. "You're better versed at art, anyway," she said, recognizing this for the feeble statement it was.

"At pretending, you mean," he said. "I've seen more cathedral drawings since I walked through these doors than I'll wish to see in a lifetime. I only came over here to see why a young lady such as yourself should be standing here alone, staring at sketches and muttering to herself."

Kitty, who felt anything but smooth tonight, would have traded her inheritance to know exactly what this person meant by, "a young lady *such as yourself*." But not even a queen's ransom would induce her to ask.

Kitty's attention was brought up short by the sudden appearance of Mr Leland Murphy, bowing to her. "I beg your pardon," he whispered. "Forgive my interruption. Is your friend, Miss Alice, here this evening?"

Without thinking, Kitty gestured towards the table where Stout Alice sat, then caught her error. "No. I'm

sorry. She felt unwell tonight, and remained at home."
She saw disappointment pass across Leland Murphy's
unprepossessing face and made a flash discovery. Leland
Murphy? Was he the reason why Alice was so reluctant
to come to the social as Mrs Plackett? Leland Murphy!
How could it be possible? Mary Jane called him odious,
and though Kitty would not have been so harsh, even she
could agree he was, at best, unfortunate in his endowment
of personal charms. But over his shoulder she saw Stout
Alice watch Kitty speak with him, with an expression that
betrayed all. Alice's other beau, Admiral Lockwood, unaware
of his young rival, had taken her hand in his while with the
other he urged her to drink her punch.

Leland Murphy regained control of his expression and
bowed abruptly. "Will you convey to her my best wishes
for her health?" Without waiting for an answer, he turned
and left.

"Poor fellow," observed her companion, who had watched
this exchange with interest.

Kitty noticed again the strange note in his accent. "You're
not from Ely, are you?"

"Originally," he said. "Christened right here at Saint
Mary's. But I've grown up in the colonies. My mother and
I are here visiting after many years away."

That explained his sunbaked colour. "How do you find
England after such an absence?"

He paused to consider. "Pleasant," he said. "But smoky,
and grey, and wet. We were in London two weeks before
coming here. I think my mother hoped I'd be dazzled by its

228

society. But I prefer the wildlife at home to London." He smiled at Kitty, and she found the effect entirely unsettling. "I suspect I shall prefer both the climate and the society right here in Ely."

Kitty felt warmth rising in her cheeks and hoped her flush didn't show. If she were as bronzed as he, her feelings would not be so easily advertised. She caught sight of Stout Alice turning to look at her, with a perplexed expression. What a spectacle she must seem! She should hurry back to the table. But she couldn't tear herself away just yet.

"Besides," the young man said, with a playful glance at the cathedral painting. "London's galleries can't compete with Ely's art."

Kitty suppressed a laugh. "Stop! You're too cruel."

"Cruel? You're the one calling every work of art a gelatin." He steered her a pace down the wall. "Look. Speaking of gelatin, here's a sketch of a fisherman with his basket full of eels. Lifelike, yes? An eel jelly of a painting. One feels as slimy and wet as the piece's subject."

Kitty couldn't help giggling. The young man's laughter didn't help matters. Mercifully, the flautist's song ended, and applause filled the chamber, covering their crimes. They added their own guilty applause to the noise. Over in the corner Kitty caught a glimpse of Mary Jane pulling away teasingly from the curtain in the far end of the room. The constable seized hold of her hand and kissed it for an eternity and Mary Jane made no protest at being thus pulled back. Such behaviour, and in public! Kitty would flay Mary Jane alive for it. Then she realised she'd clapped a beat or two longer than the rest of the room, and blushed to find her gentleman stranger watching her with an amused look. Flaying Mary Jane could wait.

"I saw you today," the young man said. "I was out riding."

Kitty had no wish to remember *how* he'd seen her. "Are you fond of strolling our English country lanes on horseback?"

"I could be, with good company to pass the time," he said. "Today I went in search of someone's home. Directions led me to where I saw you – and you ought to have at least waved to an old friend—"

"Old friend!" Kitty protested.

"Yes, an old friend. As I say, directions led me there, but I have it on good authority that my address was wrong. Did I have the pleasure of meeting your sister, two days ago?"

Kitty shook her head. Who could he mean? "I have no sister."

He cocked his head. "Curiouser and curiouser."

Kitty recognised the allusion. "A reader of Mr Carroll's book, are you?" The young man smiled. "I must ask you, sir," whispered Kitty, "whether you are in the habit of buying caramels and flinging them at every young lady you meet."

He regarded her with a look of wounded surprise. "Surely not," he said. "I discriminate carefully, and save my *flinging*, as you so callously call it, for only those young ladies whom I can tell favour caramels."

"You'd be hard pressed to find half a dozen young ladies in all of England who *don't* favour caramels."

The young man was undaunted by this rebuke. "But I," he said, "can spot the difference between a workaday taste for sweets, and the palate of a true connoisseur. I knew at a glance that your sensibilities in the matter of caramels would be as astute as they are in the matter of cathedral paintings and eel jellies."

Kitty could only shake her head and try hard not to laugh. "You are a bold one, sir."

"So much so," he bowed politely, "that I now make bold to ask your name."

There would be no telling this person no, and truth to tell, she had no wish to try. "Kitty. Katherine!" Oh, foolish slip, to use her pet name! "Katherine Heaton."

"Well, Kitty Katherine Heaton, it is entirely my privilege to meet you." He bowed once more. "I hope we shall again have the pleasure of discussing art and other subjects in their turn."

"It's Katherine," she said firmly. She gave up trying to hide her pleasure. "Our chances of discussing art again, or any other subject, will be materially improved if I, also, learn your name. 'The Young Man from the Parish Social' will scarcely suffice for an introduction."

As she spoke, Kitty's attention was fractured by hearing a familiar name announced as the evening's next performer. ". . . the pleasure of hearing Mrs Constance Plackett, of Saint Etheldreda's School, who will sing, ''Tis Not Fine Feathers Make Fine Birds,' by Masters Carpenter and Spoble." Alice's song! Oh, no. She should hurry back to her table. But must she? *Good luck, Alice*, she thought. *I . . . I will listen and support you. From over here.*

Her companion was unaware of Kitty's dilemma, but he noticed Reverend Rumsey's introduction. He seemed to grow excited. "At last! I must pause to hear this particular number," he said, "for sentimental reasons. But first, permit me to introduce myself to you. Julius Godding, lately of Bombay, India, at your service."

Chapter Nineteen

The words fell soft on Kitty's ears. Soft as the folds of a snow-white cravat.

Bombay, India. Darling Julius Godding. Not a child, not lying in a sickbed, and certainly not in India anymore. Her flights of fancy, her musings over coats and caramels, her flattery, even, and all the while this person was *Darling Julius Godding*.

"Excuse me." Kitty pushed past him and all but ran to her table. She must warn the others. They would flee from this party and make a new plan, and quickly. Once Constable Quill got wind of who this newcomer was, he wouldn't rest until he'd combed over Saint Etheldreda's School with his magnifying glass and notebook.

Kitty slipped into Alice's vacant chair, dabbed her forehead with her handkerchief, and willed her pulse to resume its normal smooth drumbeat.

Pocked Louise's eyes met hers, and she leaned in close. "What's the matter, Kitty?"

Kitty didn't trust herself yet to speak. Her mouth felt dry.

She reached for a drink then remembered it wasn't hers. *Julius Godding is here tonight.* If she had kept a level head she might have asked him useful questions. She might even have found a way to intervene, to forestall the inevitable disaster if she'd kept her wits – if, in fact, she hadn't parted with her wits when she first noticed Mr Godding's Indian suntan.

Oh, the cruel mischance that he should arrive *now*, of all times, and ruin everything!

Now.

Of all times.

Two weeks in London. A few days at least in Ely.

Mrs Plackett, poisoned. Her brother, a likely heir, eliminated. And here, out of nowhere, was the chief heir, poised to inherit. She shook the bitter thought from her mind. Could those smiling eyes belong to a *murderer*?

The air in the crowded hall wavered with heat, but Kitty felt chilled.

Stout Alice climbed the dais, nodded once to her hosts, and then to Martha at the spinet. Martha received the cue and began playing the lively introduction.

"It's always a treat to hear your headmistress sing." Admiral Lockwood nodded congenially to Kitty. Her smile made a weak reply. The admiral held up a glass of punch towards the dais as if toasting Mrs Plackett, and drank.

Finally the introduction ended – Martha had been obliged to play it twice – and Stout Alice took a brave deep breath and began to sing:

A peacock came, with his plumage gay.
Strutting in regal pride one day,
where a small bird hung in a gilded cage,
whose song might a seraph's ear engage.

Kitty rather doubted that Alice's song might engage a
seraph's ear, or that of any other heavenly creature. Alice's
expression was a mask of stoic misery. She would sing this
song if it killed her. Kitty looked around the room to see if
any earthly ears had detected a false note in their performer's
voice. But the only face her eyes found in the sea of people
was Julius Godding's, listening with that same thoughtful
attention he'd given to the sham cathedral painting. He
caught Kitty looking at him, and smiled. Kitty turned away.

As soon as this song was over, she vowed to herself, they'd
leave. She'd pry Mary Jane away from her policeman and
shake off those eager theological students, and Henry Butts
would drive them home. No question, he'd leave the party
early for their sakes. He'd wrestle a score of hungry eels
for Mary Jane's sake. Then Kitty noticed the farmer's son
leaning against the wall, watching Martha play the piano.
Something in his look made Kitty pause. Could it be someone
else at Saint Etheldreda's upon whom Henry's attention
rested? This discovery sent her thoughts spinning back to
the painting gallery, where Mr Godding still stood, joined
now by a handsome woman of middle age who could only
be his mother. *For shame, Kitty! Quit gawking!* Then Kitty's
roving gaze singled out Miss Fringle, staring at Stout Alice.
The choir mistress's face was livid. She clearly wasn't fooled

by Alice's voice. Oh, they couldn't leave here fast enough.

Admiral Lockwood began to cough. Kitty and the other girls politely looked away to spare him any embarrassment. His coughing persisted, as old people's little fits often will, and Kitty rather welcomed the public distraction from Alice's singing.

> *But the small bird sung in his own sweet words,*
> *"Tis not fine feathers make fine birds!'*

Clink.

Admiral Lockwood's glass tipped over, spilling a scarlet tide of punch onto the snowy tablecloth. The stain spread till it looked like a giant strawberry in the center of the table. The four seated girls all saw the stain, then looked away discreetly. Dear Roberta closed her eyes in pain. Her precious tablecloth.

Clunk.

Kitty jumped. Louise turned. Elinor's eyes opened wide.

Admiral Lockwood's large head jolted the table where it hit.

Chapter Twenty

Kitty felt a twinge of irritation. Must he make a spectacle of himself? And at their table, no less? He must have added liquor to his punch. People who couldn't handle drink should restrain themselves in public.

Then Dear Roberta began to whimper. It rose and swelled to a shrill squeak. Dull Martha's fingers fumbled on the keys. Stout Alice paused, mid-note.

Smooth Kitty pushed her chair back and hurried to hush Dear Roberta. A fine time this would be for one of her faints. Pocked Louise scooted to the admiral's side and jostled his shoulder. He made no response. She listened for his breath, and pressed her fingertips into his neck. No one else in the room moved, except Mr Julius Godding and his mother, who hurried through the stunned crowd to their table. Mrs Godding, if that was her name, assessed the situation instantly and joined Louise in her examination by checking the admiral's wrist.

"Let me, love," she told Louise. "Julius, locate a doctor quickly."

Julius turned and addressed the room. "Is there a doctor

present?" he called out. "Any physician within close distance? If you'll point me in the right direction . . ."

Henry Butts bolted for the outside door. Admiral Lockwood's elderly servant, Jeffers, approached, trembling. His footsteps faltered. Julius caught him and eased him into a chair. In no time Henry returned with Dr Snelling, who had joined other less musically inclined men outdoors for cigars. He hurried to the admiral.

Constable Quill emerged from his curtained corner and jammed his helmet onto his head. "What's happening here?"

By now men and women had risen and gathered round the table, a ring of curious eyes hemming the girls in by the admiral's still form. Louise felt she couldn't breathe. Then Stout Alice broke through the throng, with Dull Martha at her heels. "Are you all right, girls?"

Dr Snelling ministered to the admiral for some moments, thumping his back, listening to his heart, feeling his wrist. At length he laid the admiral's limp hand down on the table and stood. He shook his head.

The room absorbed this information in thick silence, slowly, like the inhale and release of a painful breath. A small sound escaped from Jeffers's throat. Comforting hands gripped his shoulders, while tactful eyes looked away.

Kitty gripped her arms tight to her body. The room was beginning to spin before her eyes, and she feared she might unravel and join the whirlwind. More death. Why did it stalk them? And why, when she didn't feel any remorse at the death of her headmistress and her brother, did she feel so woeful now? She caught sight of Disgraceful Mary Jane slipping discreetly through the crowd. Her cheeks were flushed. No doubt her little tête-à- tête with Officer Quill had taken a fascinating turn. Kitty couldn't feel any real vexation for her disgraceful roommate's shocking behaviour. Admiral Lockwood had fallen down dead beside her. What difference did propriety make now?

Mary Jane halted at the sight of Admiral Lockwood. The bright blush faded from her cheeks.

Dear Roberta's sweet voice penetrated the stillness. "Was it poison?"

"Poison!" a woman cried.

"Poison?" a man demanded.

"Now, now." Dr Snelling held up his hands. "The admiral had lived to a good old age. It was most likely his tired heart giving way."

Dour Elinor spoke. "He sat here with us for some time," she said. "All he had was punch. We all drank punch."

"Is this his glass?" Constable Quill pointed to an empty glass on the table.

"No," Pocked Louise said, thinking fast. "The glass he drank from was . . ."

"Mine." Stout Alice found a chair and sat down.

Constable Quill and Dr Snelling sniffed the glasses and reexamined the admiral's face and lips. No words passed between them.

"It *was* poison," Miss Fringle declared aloud. "Poison in the punch!"

Mrs Rumsey's words were clipped. "I made that punch myself, Letitia."

"I was at the piano!" Martha wailed. "I was nowhere near the glasses of punch."

Everyone turned to stare at Dull Martha.

"Of course you weren't, dear." Julius Godding's mother was the one who spoke. She had a capable, calm presence. Her grey eyes conveyed reassurance. Kitty felt she would have liked to know her, if she weren't the mother of their undoing. She cringed at Martha's inane remark. She *must* get them home before anyone else did something stupid. Thanks to Mrs Godding's tone, others looked upon Martha with pity, and didn't question her bizarre statement.

Disgraceful Mary Jane made her way to Stout Alice and whispered briefly in her ear. A look of revulsion passed over Alice's face, but she nodded, and fished for her handkerchief.

"The poor, poor admiral." Alice spoke in a tremulous voice. She dabbed her eyes and nose. "He was always such a kind and thoughtful gentleman." She sniffed, and allowed herself to be faintly overcome with emotion. Mary Jane nodded her approval. Leave it to her to remember the romantic angle. How would it look for Mrs Plackett to feel nothing at the death of her gentleman friend?

Reverend Rumsey, who had watched these proceedings from some distance with alarm writ large upon his long face, now asserted himself. "Ladies and gentlemen," he said. "I pray, let us not succumb to speculation and fear. We are all grieved at the departure of our eminent retired admiral, though I must say, to leave this life while listening to such, er, lovely music was no doubt a mercy. But, I'm afraid this sad event must cut our evening short."

"Ronald." Mrs Rumsey's expression was severe. "We haven't served the strawberry trifle yet."

Reverend Rumsey held up a hand in a rare show of firmness. "Please, let us all disperse to our homes now, to allow the poor admiral's body to be tended to with proper respect."

The crowd began to thin slowly, with whispers and stares. Stout Alice obliged them with a tragic sniffle.

A scream emerged from the kitchen. A serving volunteer came running out, leaving the door swinging wide. "Another one!" the young woman cried. "It *is* poison! Amanda Barnes 'as fallen down dead in the kitchen!"

Chapter Twenty-one

Mrs Godding ran for the kitchen. She was halfway there before anyone else had time to think. "Stay with the gentleman, Julius," she called, and disappeared through the swinging door.

Dr Snelling, Constable Quill, and Reverend and Mrs Rumsey followed after her. Stout Alice rose to do the same, but Pocked Louise restrained her. "Stay," she said. "Please, Mrs Plackett, stay here away from the commotion. So we can tend to you."

Kitty found Julius standing close by her. "Your mother is a marvel," she said.

"She was a nurse before she married," he said. "Now she volunteers at a clinic, and acts as midwife to local women."

"Julius?" It was Miss Fringle speaking. "Your name is Julius?"

Kitty's stomach sank. Here it came.

"It is," Julius said. "Does anyone know where we might find a bedsheet?"

Miss Fringle opened her mouth, and Kitty felt sure she

would probe for a surname. The choir mistress paused, and closed her mouth. "I'll ask Patricia for one," she said, and limped off to find Mrs Rumsey.

The students from Saint Etheldreda's School held a silent meeting. Dull Martha and Dear Roberta held each other's arms tightly. Pocked Louise, Dour Elinor, and Disgraceful Mary Jane stood in a protective ring around Stout Alice's chair. Mr Albert Bly stood at Roberta's side, ready to offer help, and Charles Bringhurst knelt down by Jeffers's chair, speaking to him in a low voice, and offering him a handkerchief. Good old Funeral Charlie. Perhaps his nickname wasn't such a joke after all. But it was time for them to leave. And yet, Amanda Barnes? What was happening? Would they all begin to fall like dominoes?

"Good news, everyone!" Reverend Rumsey appeared from the kitchen door, followed by his wife, the doctor, and the constable. The vicar spoke. "Miss Barnes is well. She merely fainted. Shock weakened her momentarily. So I think we can dispel this notion of poison."

Dr Snelling and Constable Quill exchanged glances, but said nothing.

"I must go inquire after Barnes." Stout Alice rose decisively. "She's been in my employ these many years. I must know for myself that she is well."

Kitty could not stop Alice, so they trouped along after her and watched the scene from the kitchen door. They found Amanda Barnes lying upon the floor with a cushion propped under her head. Mrs Godding, kneeling beside her, fanned her face with a dessert plate. Amanda's skin was deathly pale. Her breath came in short, shallow pants. When she saw Alice, she covered her face with a trembling hand.

"There, there," said Mrs Godding. "Everything will be all right. I'll tend you until you're feeling better."

Barnes spoke feebly. "Will the admiral be all right?"

Mrs Godding rocked back on her heels and gave the girls a look filled with caution. "Never mind the admiral," she said. "He's a tough old oak. Is he family?"

Amanda Barnes shook her head. "I just felt so badly for him. I was in here spooning up trifle, and when I heard the word poison, I . . ."

"Of course." Mrs Godding brushed Barnes's damp blond hair off her forehead. "Now, you just worry about yourself. You need rest."

Barnes drew a deep breath. "You're all kindness, ma'am." She lowered her protective hand. "I don't believe I know your name, begging your pardon."

Mrs Godding handed her patient a cup of water. "No pardon needed," she said. "You haven't met me. I'm newly arrived from Bombay. My name is Elaine. Mrs Geoffrey Godding."

Amanda Barnes blinked. She swallowed hard and struggled to sit up. Kitty felt Louise and Alice stiffen with shock.

"No, not yet, dearie." Mrs Godding was cheerfully determined to keep her flat. "Too soon to be getting up just yet. Let's let the place clear out first."

Kitty looked away. She couldn't bring herself to face Barnes, or her classmates. She saw Dull Martha beckon to them from the parish hall, so she tugged Louise and Alice along after her.

"Henry's ready to take us home," Martha said.

Chapter Twenty-two

Damp clouds obscured the stars, leaving the night sky black as ink as Henry Butts helped the girls down from his cart in front of Saint Etheldreda's School for Young Ladies. Stout Alice thanked him for the ride, then Dull Martha thanked him half a dozen more times, until Pocked Louise dragged her indoors.

Once inside, Kitty dropped her shawl and bonnet on the flagstone floor and shook her clenched fists before her face.

"*How could this have happened?*" she cried aloud. "We *never* should have gone!"

Kitty's words echoed through the dark corridor. The girls filtered into the parlour, and Dour Elinor struck a match and lit a pair of candles. The noise, the sulphur smell, the jittering flame jarred Kitty. She gnawed on a knuckle and tried not to think.

"What are you saying, Kitty?" Elinor inquired. "Are you saying Admiral Lockwood wouldn't have died if we hadn't gone tonight?"

"Yes . . . no . . . yes!" Kitty groaned. "I mean, that part's obvious, isn't it? The attempt that was made on Mrs Plackett killed *him* by mistake."

"You're not saying *we* killed him, are you?" pressed Elinor.

Kitty fumed. "Don't be absurd."

"By mistake . . ." Pocked Louise repeated.

"Yes, what about it?" Mary Jane snapped, but Louise didn't answer.

"Where are the brass candlesticks?" Elinor asked.

"It feels drafty in here," Dear Roberta ventured. "Let's light a fire."

"I don't simply mean the admiral, though that's the worst of it," Kitty said. "He's gone, God rest his soul. I mean, everything else, too." She sank down into a chair. Her body felt limp, utterly drained. "The song. Miss Fringle. Mary Jane's snooping constable, and the wretched man at the train station. Alice in danger, God help us. Julius Godding showing up!"

"Ah yes," Mary Jane said. "*Darling* Julius." She tossed her coat upon a chair. "After all these years away, he must pick tonight to appear. Would somebody *please* start at the beginning and tell me everything that happened?"

"If you hadn't been chasing after your policeman, and doing who-knows-what with him behind the curtain, you wouldn't need to ask," Pocked Louise said.

"Aren't *you* the saucy one tonight," Mary Jane said indifferently.

Her smugness rankled Pocked Louise. "I'm not saucy," she cried. "I'm right. I don't care how much older you are. I've got enough sense not to make a shameful spectacle of myself, and enough to know when my friends need me to stay close by and help, unlike *some* people."

246

"Pooh, pooh," sneered Disgraceful Mary Jane with her nose high in the air. "I won't be lectured by you. Mind your business, little girl."

Pocked Louise opened her mouth to blast Mary Jane with a retort, then felt her eyes sting. She hated, above all else, to be called "little". She turned away quickly so Mary Jane couldn't see her barb hit its mark.

Kitty watched in dismay. After such a dreadful night, must they make matters worse with pointless bickering?

A small, muffled sound reached her ears. She looked up to see Stout Alice bending over the fire, attempting to kindle a blaze. Her shoulders shook.

Dull Martha noticed her too, and knelt beside her. "Let me start the fire, Alice, dear," she said. "You've had a trying evening. But don't cry. Your song wasn't *that* bad."

"*Oh*." The sound escaped Alice's lips as a sob and a sigh, together. "I'm not upset about the song." She sat on a divan and plied her handkerchief to her eyes.

Kitty rose and sat down next to Alice. "Aren't you?" she asked.

Alice wiped her nose. "Maybe I am," she said. "It was mortifying. But that isn't the point." They waited while her kerchief did its absorbent work. "Someone tried to kill me tonight. To *kill* me! And here you all are, squabbling like chickens." She blew her nose. "Mercifully, I managed to survive, but a dear old man died in my place. I threw away my one and only chance to . . ."

"To what?" inquired Disgraceful Mary Jane.

Alice struggled to suppress another sob. "Never mind."

She shook her head. "None of it matters now." She began to laugh bitterly through her tears.

Poor Alice, thought Pocked Louise. *Strain has made her lose her mind.*

"Do you want to know something?" Stout Alice asked the room. "I received a proposal of marriage tonight."

Smooth Kitty spoke without thinking. "From Leland Murphy?"

Stout Alice shot her a withering look. Even in the dark room, Kitty felt its sting. Alice gestured towards her grey-powdered hair and makeup, and Kitty realised her horrible mistake.

"Don't be daft, Kitty!" cried Disgraceful Mary Jane. "Look how poor Alice has suffered! Don't torment her with thoughts of Leland Murphy." She patted Alice on the shoulder.

"The proposal was from Admiral Lockwood." Dour Elinor spoke up.

"Oh, you heard?" Alice said. "I thought you were too busy talking to Funeral Charlie."

"Funeral Charlie!" Mary Jane threw her hands up in the air. "Someone, enlighten me quickly, before I pop."

"His name is Charles Bringhurst." Dear Roberta said. "He is the particular friend of Mr Albert Bly. They're students at the Barton Theological College."

"Oh hang the young men from the theological college!" Kitty flung down her gloves. "They could be cardinals for all we care. Young men are the last things we should be thinking about. Don't you see the predicament we're all in?"

"You're a fine one to talk." Stout Alice glared at Smooth Kitty. "You spent plenty of time over in the picture gallery, chatting with your young stranger."

Kitty felt sick. Alice was right, and Kitty felt painfully just how much so. She had abandoned Alice to her dreadful masquerade, to that galling musical performance, and to dangers that were only now too apparent, while Kitty flitted and flirted – yes, flirted! – with a young man. That he turned out to be Darling Julius now seemed a fitting punishment for her crimes.

Kitty found it hard to swallow, but she managed to do so, and spoke. "Alice," she said. "I'm sorry. I'm sorry you had to sing tonight. I'm sorry you had to go as Mrs Plackett and not as yourself." A look passed between them, and Kitty knew that Alice knew she understood why. "Your friend . . . Lucy . . . Lucy Morris inquired after your health and sent you . . . her best regards for a speedy recovery from your headache."

Alice nodded. Kitty could see she was mollified, partly. "Thank you for letting me know. That was very kind . . . of her." She sighed.

Kitty took a deep breath. "More than anything," she continued, "a thousand times more, I'm sorry you came within range of . . ." Kitty tasted bitterly her hollow assurance to the girls that they would all keep Alice safe, "within range of the poison."

Alice shuddered, then bit her lip. "It's not your fault, Kitty. You were right. We never should have gone. I was a fool to say we would."

Kitty embraced Alice. "No, no, don't say that," she said. "No one could have foreseen this. Whether we'd walked into the trouble or not, trouble was on its way here. And," she turned, "for shame, Mary Jane. Don't vex Louise so." Kitty was starting to feel rather like Mrs Plackett herself. "You *did* pick a most unfortunate evening to misbehave."

Disgraceful Mary Jane shrugged. "How was I to know everyone was guzzling poison?"

The other girls stared pointedly at her.

"Oh all right," Mary Jane sighed. She put on her dazzling smile for her youngest classmate. "Pax, Louise?"

Pocked Louise stuck out her chin. "Pax," she said, with a forgivable touch of stiff superiority, "though what you see in that oily constable, I'll never know."

"Give it time, turtledove," said Mary Jane. She seized Louise by the hand and pulled her onto the couch beside her to plaster a kiss on her cheek.

"Ugh!" Pocked Louise cried, and wiped it off.

Dull Martha's questions could not wait for this tomfoolery to pass. "Does no one else find it peculiar," she said, "that another Julius Godding should show up tonight at the social, when we've all been so interested in the one in India?"

Kitty swallowed a groan. "Martha. Dear heart. It's not *another* Julius Godding. He is *the* Julius Godding from India. It's Mrs Plackett's nephew, come unexpectedly for a visit."

Dear Roberta took Martha's hand. "So he isn't a child."

"Only, perhaps," Alice said, "in comparison with Miss Fringle. She's the one who led us to picture him as young."

"He told me he hasn't been in Ely in ages," Kitty said.

Pocked Louise rose and paced the floor. "He isn't a child," she repeated. "He stands to inherit all that Mrs Plackett owns. And," she said triumphantly, "he's been here a few days."

Kitty watched her curiously. "What makes you say that, Louise?"

Too late did Pocked Louise realise her mistake. She had no desire to confess to lying to the young man out by the road. "Well," she said, "didn't we see him yesterday in the chemist's shop?"

Kitty tapped her chin thoughtfully. Mr Godding had said he'd ventured by Prickwillow Road a day earlier and spoken to another girl, one who told him it wasn't a school. Could that have been Louise? "My sister . . ." she mused aloud.

"That's *right*, he *was* the fellow in the shop!" Disgraceful Mary Jane said. "I thought his face looked familiar." She whacked Kitty with a sofa cushion. "You shameless thing. Always carrying on about *me*, while *you're* setting up covert rendezvous with strange men you meet in shops!"

"I did no such thing!" Kitty exclaimed. "Meeting him was pure chance."

Mary Jane winked at the others. "If you say so."

"Never mind that," Louise cried. "Don't you see? We don't know exactly when he arrived in town, but almost certainly," she swallowed, "it wasn't yesterday."

"So?" inquired Alice. "What of it?"

Louise waved her notebook triumphantly. "Until we can prove he wasn't near Ely on Sunday, we must place Julius Godding at the top of our list of suspects."

"Oh!" Dear Roberta cried. "He's so very young. With *such* nice tailoring, too."

Kitty felt as though she might be physically ill. Louise was right, and she knew it. But in that moment she hated her for saying it.

"What do you think, Kitty?" Mary Jane inquired. "You spoke with him. Does he seem the murderous type?"

"And what, exactly, is the murderous type?" Kitty attacked the ebony buttons lacing up her collar. "I didn't see an axe in his back pocket, if that's what you mean. But don't you see? Murderer or no, he's here now in Ely with his mother. Even if he's the soul of charity, he's here. He exposes our lie, and this will ruin all. It's the worst thing that could possibly have happened tonight."

Dour Elinor shook her head. "Not the worst thing. We've been spared the worst thing."

Dear Roberta leaned her head against Stout Alice's shoulder. "Admiral Lockwood wasn't so fortunate."

Alice began to feel that looking as old and tired as Mrs Plackett required no effort at all. She turned to Pocked Louise. "It was poison, wasn't it, Louise? And only in my glass of punch?"

Dull Martha's lower lip quivered. Kitty gave her a stern look, lest she commence her poison hysterics again.

Louise opened her handbag and pulled out a folded-up cloth napkin. She unfolded it to reveal a large red punch stain. "I'm not sure if this will be a large enough specimen to test, but I'll try."

Kitty put her arm around Louise's shoulder. "Good

girl, Louise," she said. "Quicker thinking than doctors or policemen any day."

"Oh, I don't know about that," Louise said. "I'm fairly certain it is poison, and I think Doctor Snelling knows it, too. He can probably recognise symptoms. Admiral Lockwood had the same blotchy pinkness to his skin that Mrs Plackett and Mr Godding did. The spilled glass of punch had an almond smell, which would indicate cyanide."

Smooth Kitty suppressed an inner quivering that had come over her limbs. "I nearly drank that glass of punch," she said, "when I sat in your empty chair, Alice."

Stout Alice dabbed gingerly at the makeup on her face. "Admiral Lockwood urged me to drink that punch," she said, "right after I accepted his marriage proposal."

"What a mercy you didn't drink it," said Disgraceful Mary Jane. "Wait. *You accepted him?*"

Alice looked up in surprise. "How could I not? He's a wealthy man. I'd have to be a fool to refuse him."

Pocked Louise looked visibly wounded. "Are you that ready to leave us?"

Smooth Kitty found she was no less stunned. "What about, er, Lucy Morris?"

Dull Martha sat up. "What, is she engaged to Admiral Lockwood, too?"

Stout Alice began to laugh. "You gooses. *I* didn't accept his proposal. Mrs Plackett did. She did because she would. Don't you see? Of course she would. She'd take his money and send us packing back to our parents before you could say 'Italian villa.' So I had to say yes."

"At least he died happy," said Dear Roberta.

Stout Alice smiled a bit. "More than happy. I won't tell you *what* he said to me after I said yes. It's not decent to repeat. The wicked old salt."

Disgraceful Mary Jane giggled. "Tell me later on, won't you, love?"

They sat together in the dark, each occupied by their own private worries. Red flickers from the fire danced with dark shadows across their faces. Despite the growing blaze, the room felt dank and chill.

Dear Roberta shivered. "Brr! Stir the coals, please, Elinor? I just can't seem to get warm."

Pocked Louise suddenly sat up straight. "Where's Aldous?"

The girls looked at each other in alarm. How could they have failed to notice? Usually the scamp would greet them barking at the door when they returned home. Louise began calling his name, while they all fanned out across the dark house to search for him.

Each creak of the floorboards sounded ghostly in Roberta's ears. She held onto the chair rail in the hallway for reassurance and made her way to the schoolroom. They'd stowed Mr Godding's crates of belongings in here. Now the tops were open, and Mr Godding's effects were strewn everywhere.

"Kitty?" Dear Roberta's voice quavered. She wished they'd gone two-by-two to search. "Did you open up Mr Godding's things?"

She backed out of the schoolroom and crept towards the dining room. Bare shelves in the china cabinet greeted her. Its doors were left wide open.

"Mary Jane?" she called. "Did you remove the dishes from the cabinet when you dusted in here?"

But her calls went unanswered. Louise's echoing calls to Aldous drowned out other voices. Roberta heard one of the girls – she wasn't sure who – let out a frightened cry.

She ran for the parlour with its protective fire. But the other girls weren't gathering there. They were in Mrs Plackett's bedroom. Roberta groped along the hallway to join them.

The window to the back garden was smashed. Cold air blew in and waved the sheer curtains like fronds of seaweed. By candlelight, shards of glass glittered on the floor like diamonds in new snow.

There on the floor, by the foot of the bed, lay the still form of little Aldous.

Chapter Twenty-three

Pocked Louise sank to her knees. She reached out to touch Aldous. Her hands shook.

Dour Elinor knelt beside her and wrapped her arms around her. By the light of her little candle, the others saw a teardrop fall into Louise's lap.

Stout Alice took a pillowcase from Mrs Plackett's bed and draped it over Aldous, then gently lifted him and laid him on the bed. She pressed her palms against his side and frowned.

"Louise," she said. "I think he's alive."

Pocked Louise wiped her eyes furiously and hurried to the bed. The other girls gathered round.

"What's happened to him?" Dull Martha's voice trembled. "Who could have done this?"

A chill breeze blew in from the open window.

Louise's scientific mind regained mastery of her emotions. "No blood," she said. She palpated his head and side. "No sign of trauma." She looked at the others. "Perhaps he was drugged."

Kitty watched Louise with the little dog; she took in the flapping curtain and the shards of glass. She looked at each of the girls, their drawn faces flickering between candlelight and shadow. How dear to her they *all* were. How sweet it would have been, just the seven of them there, forever! And then, Julius Godding. Admiral Lockwood. Miss Fringle. Their prospects had shattered like this window. This thief put an end to all their hopes by robbing them, not of dishes and candlesticks, but of safety. It was so cruel and so arbitrary that greed should have such power, and all for a sack of silver and china.

But was it the thief who had stolen their safety? Or was it the murderer?

What if they were one and the same?

What should she do? What would Aunt Katherine do?

History books never say so, Kitty thought, but sometimes surrender is the bravest choice.

"Martha, Mary Jane," she said. "Run quickly together to the Butts home, and tell them what's happened. We've had a burglar, and they've hurt our dog. Ask Henry to hurry into town and notify the police. Ask him to find Doctor Snelling if he can, and beg him to come along."

Mary Jane nodded. "Will you be safe here?" she asked.

Stout Alice seized the poker by Mrs Plackett's fireplace, and Dour Elinor surprised them by gripping the coal shovel. They nodded grimly. Martha and Mary Jane disappeared down the hall. In seconds the others heard the front door slam.

"Let's bring him in by the parlour fire." Alice gathered up Aldous and carried him out.

"Roberta, dear, help me tack up a blanket to cover this window," Kitty said. "We can sweep the glass while we're at it."

Elinor shovelled coal onto the parlour fire, then brought in a teakettle from the kitchen and hung it over the flames. It would heat slowly that way, but they had time to burn. Alice lit the parlour lamps and some extra candles she found in a drawer, which made the room feel more cosy and more safe.

Kitty and Roberta rejoined the others in the parlour and found Louise sitting in front of the fire, stroking Aldous in her lap.

"Come on, boy," she whispered. "Wake up and tell us who did this. Come on, Aldy. If you tell us, we'll let you bite his ankles."

They sat, waiting, watching, expecting, and trying not to expect.

"What was that?" Dear Roberta cried. She sat straight and tall, wavering, sniffing the air like a mongoose. "Didn't you just hear something, out in the garden?"

Stout Alice and Smooth Kitty looked at each other. Not another hysterical fit. Not now.

"It was just an animal, Roberta," said Pocked Louise. "Or maybe the wind in the trees."

"Alice," Kitty said, "come around with me, and let's make a list of all that's missing."

"It'll pass the time," Alice agreed.

They couldn't believe the devastation. Brass candlesticks, stolen from almost every room. Mr Godding's belongings, stowed in the schoolroom, were strewn everywhere, but there was no way to know what might be missing. China dishes and silverware had vanished from the dining room.

They entered the drawing room. The glass curio cabinet was smashed and ransacked, and the ebony elephant and every other valuable object inside were gone.

Alice wrote *elephant* on her inventory of stolen items.

"You're a brick not to say 'I told you so,' Alice," Kitty said. "You warned me not to leave the elephant here in plain sight."

"It doesn't matter," Stout Alice said. "Our thief has been a thorough one. Chances are if you'd put it anywhere else, he'd have found it."

Disgraceful Mary Jane and Dull Martha returned just then, shivering from the cold night air. They hurried to the parlour, where Kitty and Alice joined them.

"Henry and his father rode into town on horseback," Martha said. "They'll be back with the constables soon. And the doctor, if they can find him."

"Mrs Butts offered to come and sit with us until the police arrived," Mary Jane added, "but I told her that we were quite well here with Mrs Plackett."

"I've got matters well in hand," Stout Alice said wryly. "No fears for our safety, with Mrs Plackett here to guard us all."

There was a defiant set to Pocked Louise's chin. "*I'm* not afraid," she said. "Whoever did this to Aldous had better be afraid of *me*."

"Hear, hear!" cried Disgraceful Mary Jane. "That's the fighting spirit!"

"And me, too," Alice said, in Mrs Plackett's voice. "Whoever meddles with my girls will get a wallop they won't soon forget!"

"A toast," cried Kitty. "Hold a moment." She hurried to the kitchen and returned bearing a tray, cups, and bottles of foaming, just-opened ginger beer. She poured and passed a cup to Mary Jane. "To the Saint Etheldreda Maidens! Sisters forever, come what may tonight."

"Or tomorrow." Mary Jane smacked her lips, heedless of the moustache of foam left by her ginger beer. "Or whenever Julius Godding shows up to greet his aunt and claim his inheritance. Say! Suppose I marry him. Then you can all stay as my students-in-law. He was rather a good looking fellow, wasn't he, Kitty?"

"I don't know," Kitty snapped. "I had no chance to measure his shoulders."

Dear Roberta sipped her ginger beer delicately. "Would you really wallop someone, Alice?"

Alice laughed. "We never know what courage we might find in extreme moments, Roberta, dear."

Pocked Louise shook her head when Kitty offered her a drink, so Kitty rubbed her back and peered over her friend's shoulder. "How's our laddie getting on?"

"I may be wrong," Louise said, "but I think his heartbeat's growing a bit stronger."

Kitty was surprised at how much this lifted her spirits. "Good boy, Aldous."

They leaned against each other in chairs around the fire and watched Louise caress the dog. Every sound from

260

outdoors – and there were maddeningly many – made Martha run to the front door to peer out the window, only to trudge back with no news to report. But finally there could be no mistaking the sound of hoof beats and carriage wheels on the gravel drive.

Kitty flew to hurry the newcomers in. She was glad, for once, to behold Constable Quill on their doorstep. He brought two other constables with him, sturdy chaps whose eager expressions suggested they'd waited long, dull years at the Ely police station to face this one moment of bona fide crime. Henry Butts and his father were there, and Dr Snelling, mercifully, was with them also.

Less merciful, perhaps, or at any rate less welcome and less expected, were the arrivals of Reverend Rumsey, and Julius and Mrs Godding, climbing out of the police carriage. Kitty failed to suppress her astonishment at the sight of them.

"We were both at the police station," Julius explained, by way of greeting. "There were statements to make for the coroner's report. It appears there will be an inquest into the admiral's death."

Kitty nodded, still too shocked to speak.

"Naturally, when we heard that my sister-in-law's home had been burgled, and her dog savaged, we wanted to offer any aid we could," said Mrs Godding. "I had no chance to greet Constance properly this evening at the social, so we hurried along."

"And I am here," announced the vicar, "to offer what spiritual comfort I can at trying times like these. I, too, was at the station when the message came."

"Of course. How kind of you." Kitty hoped she had regained her composure. "Please come in."

They converged upon the parlour.

"Constance!" Mrs Elaine Godding cried. "How good to see you, after so many years, but under what sorry circumstances!"

Stout Alice returned her embrace without missing a beat. *Does she know her name?* Kitty wondered in a panic. She racked her brain to think of a way to supply it before disaster struck, but Alice showed her true mettle.

She gripped the woman with both hands and gazed meaningfully into her eyes. "Elaine," Alice said. "It was good of you to come. I don't know how to thank you."

Kitty sagged with relief.

"Doctor," Dull Martha cried, "will you please see to our dog? We found him in this state near the smashed window in Mrs Plackett's room."

"Come on, lads, let's start investigating there," Constable Quill said. "Mrs Plackett, ma'am, begging your pardon, but would you show us which one is your room?"

Stout Alice nodded. "Right this way." She left with the constables following after, while Dr Snelling, with some difficulty, knelt down beside Louise.

"They never said my patient was a dog," he muttered.

Dr Snelling opened his black bag and pulled out his stethoscope. Kitty remembered how she'd feared that device only a few nights ago. Now she held her breath as he slid the bell of the instrument around Aldous's ribs, searching for a suitable spot. Close by and leaning against the mantelpiece,

Dour Elinor watched over Aldous. Her black eyes seemed even larger and more inky-black than ever tonight. *As if she's watching for Aldous's spirit to fly away,* Kitty thought.

"We believe he was drugged by the thief," Pocked Louise told the doctor.

"The brute!" cried Mrs Godding.

"I can't believe someone from Ely would stoop to such an act," said an indignant Reverend Rumsey. "This miscreant must be from out of town."

Henry Butts sat in a chair by the door, clutching his hat in his lap and seeming all knees and elbows. He'd run out the door, Martha realised, having pulled trousers on over his night shirt, and the effort to tuck it into his pants had not produced a neat result. She was glad he was here, all the same. His father stood behind him, likewise gripping his hat.

"Come on, Son," the elder Butts said at length. "Let's help the officers look around."

Kitty edged away from the center of activity near the fire and leaned against a wall. Its papered surface felt cool against her flushed cheek. She closed her eyes. There was nothing to do but wait. Wait and see. She wondered what Dr Snelling's stethoscope would reveal if it amplified her own racing heart.

"Miss Heaton." A low voice beside her made her start. She opened her eyes to see Julius Godding close by. He took a step back. "I'm sorry. I didn't mean to frighten you."

"Not at all." She tried to smile.

"Miss Heaton. How can I be of help? After all you've been through tonight, is there anything I can do?"

Kitty wished, for a moment, that Julius Godding did not need to be her enemy. But matters had left her control.

"I scarcely know," she said. "Unless you can restore drugged dogs. I don't know what else it is we need. But I thank you."

He nodded, and turned to watch the doctor, but stayed by Kitty's side.

"I'm going to try something," Dr Snelling told Louise. "I don't know what effect it may have on a dog, but it can scarcely hurt to find out." He fished around in his bag, retrieved a small round jar, and unscrewed its cap.

"Camphor?" Louise asked.

The doctor nodded. He held the jar close to Aldous's nose.

Nothing happened. Then the dog snorted, sneezed, and pawed its top leg for a moment.

Pocked Louise laughed aloud and hugged Aldous to her.

"Ho, not yet," Dr Snelling said. "He's got a long way to go, sleeping that off. My guess is it's laudanum he's been given, and that will take time. Your dog is lucky to be alive, and in my professional opinion, it's too soon to celebrate his recovery."

"What's this?" Louise said, picking something up off her lap. "A bit of wet fabric."

"From between his teeth," the doctor said. He gathered it up with his handkerchief and tucked it into his pocket. "Puppies like to chew."

Stout Alice slipped into the parlour and joined Kitty in the rear of the room. "Julius, dear, how wonderful to see you, and your mother," she said, and Kitty marvelled once again at her presence of mind as an actress. "I wish our reunion had been more joyful than this one. But how well you both look."

"Thank you, Aunt Constance," Julius replied, and kissed her cheek. Alice blushed. She turned to Kitty. "Katherine, dear, the constables are exploring the grounds with their lanterns, looking for footprints and evidence. I thought you would like to know, since you've been so concerned about this whole affair."

Smooth Kitty curtseyed. "Thank you, ma'am," she said. "It is a comfort." It was anything *but* a comfort! Exploring the grounds . . . Kitty prayed the darkness would hide their buried crimes.

Over by the fire, Dr Snelling packed his gear back into his bag. With great effort, he shifted his weight so as to rise to his feet.

Just then, the kettle began to steam, and Kitty remembered she must play hostess. She moved towards the fireplace and stood next to Disgraceful Mary Jane.

"Doctor Snelling," she said. "Mrs Godding. May I fix you some tea? Reverend, if not tea, might I offer you a ginger beer?"

"Ahem." Reverend Rumsey made a small cough. "Any more of that Port? If, er, ginger beer is all you have, I'm sure it will be refreshing."

"So that's why he tagged along," Mary Jane muttered, for Kitty's ears alone.

"Ssh!"

"I'll come with you, Katherine," said Stout Alice. They started for the kitchen.

Then a shout from outside made them pause. Men's voices shouted in reply, and running steps converged from all sides of the house to the front.

The girls' eyes met.

"We've got him!"

They heard a shrill cry. Then the front door opened, and loud, scuffling footsteps echoed down the hall.

"We've caught our thief," Constable Quill announced.

Behind him came the other two officers, each pinning in their grips an arm belonging to Amanda Barnes.

Chapter Twenty-four

Kitty felt she'd better sit down.

"Miss Barnes!" cried Mrs Godding.

Amanda Barnes struggled against the iron grip of both her captors. But could it be Amanda Barnes? Dishevelled hair, soiled skirts, hands and face streaked with dirt. "Is this how you treat a woman, you vultures?" she cried. "I wasn't doing anything wrong. Let me be!"

"Oh, Barnes," Stout Alice said. "What is the meaning of this?"

Kitty's mind raced. *She couldn't have done it. There must be some mistake.*

"Amanda Barnes," barked Constable Quill. "You are hereby charged with breaking and entering, grand theft . . ."

"Dr Snelling?" said Dour Elinor.

Dear Roberta sniffled into her handkerchief. "It's not possible!"

"Now, ladies, let's calm ourselves," said one of the officers.

"Let me *go*!"

"What she means," said Disgraceful Mary Jane tartly, "is that it's *not possible*. What have you done to her?"

Mrs Godding rose from her seat. "Did you find stolen goods on her person? What evidence do you have to accuse her?"

"Doctor Snelling?" said Dour Elinor.

Reverend Rumsey raised both hands. "Now if *everyone* would settle down for just . . ."

"Look at her!" cried Mrs Godding. "The poor woman looks about to faint. Bring her over to this couch, and let her lie down, if you have any decency."

"She can rest later," said Constable Quill. "I have any number of questions to ask her."

"Thank you, ma'am," said Amanda Barnes. You're the only one here to treat me decent." She cast a venomous look at Stout Alice. "And I include you in that charge, *Mrs Plackett*."

The whole room quieted.

Alice met this verbal assault bravely. "Never mind, Barnes," she said. "I understand why you are upset with me."

"No you don't. Not a bit of it." Barnes struggled against the policemen's grip. "While you're arresting left and center," she cried, "go on and arrest *her*." She nodded fiercely towards Stout Alice.

Alice took a step back.

"On what charge?" said one of the bobbies grabbing her arm. "Sacking you from your post? We heard about that. It's a revenge case, this is."

Barnes ignored the officer. "Threatening your flesh and blood. Hoarding your gold. Not sharing your bread with a brother in his hour of need!"

She flung each accusation at Alice like daggers at a target. Alice turned to Kitty to silently plead for help.

"Barnes!" cried Kitty. "What can you possibly mean?"

"Cooking up a story about her brother going off to India, when I know for a fact he was here Tuesday. I heard her yelling at him. Threatening to punish him, to throw him out. And she's done it!"

The girls looked at each other in astonishment. Was the poor woman hallucinating?

"Tuesday?" inquired Dull Martha sweetly. "Do you mean a week ago Tuesday?"

Then Kitty remembered, and groaned. It was too, too absurd! "Constables," she said. "Miss Barnes has misunderstood. Mr Godding was long gone by Tuesday. The little dog, there, on my friend's lap – on a whim we nicknamed him Aldous. This is what Miss Barnes is referring to on Tuesday. We scolded him for chewing up couch cushions, and threatened to punish him for it, by *putting him out* in the garden." She paused. "Barnes, what were you doing here on Tuesday? Were you spying on us?"

"She *lies!*" Amanda Barnes cried. "Mr Godding never left England." She glared at Stout Alice. "Oh, and you did put him out in the garden, didn't you, soon after? Once and for all, you *witch*."

"Miss Barnes, please," begged Mrs Godding. "I beg of you, compose yourself."

"Serenity," began Reverend Rumsey, "that highest of virtues, requires we curb the tongue, that unruly member, and cultivate the ear . . ."

"Doctor Snelling," said Elinor.

Stout Alice took a deep breath. "I've told you before, Constable Quill," she said. "My brother is on his way to India."

"India!" cried Mrs Godding. "Why would Aldous have journeyed to India?"

"What I don't understand," Alice interrupted, rather desperately, "is why Miss Barnes is so interested in my brother's affairs. They scarcely knew each other."

Amanda Barnes's eyes glowed with hate. "The officer knows, and I know, Mr Godding never boarded that train. Isn't that right, Constable Quill?"

Constable Quill's brows furrowed. He took a thoughtful look at Amanda Barnes. "Now why would you say that?"

A gleam of triumph lit Amanda's eyes. "Because it's true," she said. "Charlie Neff talks to me and he talks to you. What's more, there was no telegram delivered here Sunday. I spoke to the boy at the office. And here's something else that's true. Aldous Godding's not on any train or boat. She put him out into the garden, all right. He's dead and buried there."

Chapter Twenty-five

Amanda Barnes surveyed the faces in the room like a gambler collecting her winnings. Her eyes were unnaturally bright, her face flushed. Her breath escaped her lips in intense, laboured pulses.

Kitty watched her but her mind, strangely, had floated elsewhere. Her fancies carried her home to her father's house, where she sat at breakfast with him in their grand dining room, with nothing to look forward to but buttering his toast and remaining still unless addressed. Life was dull – deadly dull – but oh, how much simpler then.

"Uncle Aldous?" Julius Godding said. "Buried in the garden?"

Amanda Barnes held her head erect. "With my own eyes I've seen it."

"That's a murder accusation, that is." Constable Quill addressed Henry's father. "Mr Butts. Would you relieve Constable Tweedy, here, and take hold of the prisoner, so he can go outdoors and investigate this outlandish story?"

Farmer Butts gulped dry air. He shuffled backwards

towards the door, inch by inch.

"Beg pardon, Constable," he managed to say, "but I'd rather not, if it's all the same." He shuddered like one swallowing medicine. "Her being a woman."

Constable Quill gestured towards one of the officers. "Out you go, Tweedy," he said. "Take a lantern, find a shovel, and look for a grave. Farmer Butts here will help you. You can keep Miss Barnes occupied by yourself, can't you, Harbottle?"

Constable Harbottle grunted in the affirmative, and Constable Tweedy and Farmer Butts left on their errand.

"I'll go, too," Julius Godding said. "I need to see for myself."

Don't, Kitty thought. She almost spoke the words aloud. Let the police find what they would, and let the consequences follow, but she dreaded the moment of Julius's discovery. She was ashamed now of her self-absorption and cowardice. This young man, whom she'd called their enemy, and even a suspect, was, in the first place, a nephew of the dead. What a painful shock to him this would be . . . unless he *was* their killer.

The door closed behind him with a hollow bang.

And that, Stout Alice thought, *is the end of that. I may as well scrub off this paint.* She suddenly felt old and weary. Mrs Plackett's sixty-two years, which she'd worn as a costume, had now become her own.

Disgraceful Mary Jane whispered in Smooth Kitty's ear. "Want me to do something to stop them, Kit?"

"No, lovey, don't bother," was Kitty's reply. "We've gone too far beyond that."

Mary Jane nodded defiantly. "So be it, then."

Over by the fire, Aldous the spaniel sneezed once more, and opened his eyes. Louise held him up in the air for the girls to admire.

Alice laughed aloud, and wiped her eyes before her laughter could become tears.

"Attaboy, Aldous!" Disgraceful Mary Jane cried.

"Doctor Snelling," said Dour Elinor.

Mrs Godding's grey eyes were full of worry. She approached Amanda Barnes and gazed thoughtfully into her face. "Why, Miss Barnes?" she whispered. "Can you tell me why you make these accusations? What could possibly make you think this of Mrs Plackett?"

Amanda's gaze back at Mrs Godding glowed with trust. "It was the money, ma'am," she said. "The money."

Reverend Rumsey sat bolt upright in his chair. "How *much* money?"

Others in the room turned to stare at him.

"Er . . ." He coughed. "That is to say, approximately?"

Mrs Godding ignored the vicar. "*What* money, Miss Barnes?"

Amanda Barnes fixed a malevolent gaze upon Stout Alice. "Her own money, which she wouldn't share with her own brother, who only asked her for some help. That's why Mrs Plackett killed him."

Pocked Louise shifted little Aldous off her lap. "How would you know all this, Barnes?" she asked. "And why would you care what happens between Mrs Plackett and her brother?"

Barnes scowled at Louise. "I don't work here anymore, Miss Nosey," she said. "I don't need to answer you, nor put up with any of your stuffed-up airs."

"But Miss Barnes," Mrs Godding asked, "Do you really mean to suggest that my sister-in-law would murder her brother *for her own money*?"

Barnes spoke through clenched teeth. "How else do you explain him disappearing, then showing up buried in her back garden?"

The Saint Etheldreda girls eyed each other.

"She hated him!" Amanda Barnes continued, with a venomous look in Alice's direction. "Didn't you? Deny it if you can! Miserly old crone, you were always haughty to me, and harsh to him, and to anyone who didn't lick your boots!" She elbowed Constable Harbottle, who still had her by the arm. "Don't take my word for it. When they come in from the garden, you'll be arresting her any moment now, and letting me go free."

Louise's mind raced. She felt split, torn between trying to follow what was being said, and trying desperately to *think*. Wayward thoughts popped to the surface like boiling bubbles in her chemist's beakers back home. *By mistake.* The admiral died by mistake. Poison meant for Alice – for Mrs Placket – killed him. What did it all mean? A drugged dog, a dead admiral, an ebony elephant, a coo in the garden. A stolen will, poisoned meat, an heir appearing out of nowhere, a grocery delivery boy, Spanish coins, an extra frying pan . . .

Dear Roberta began to cry. She seized Stout Alice by the arm. "They can't arrest her! They just can't!"

Mrs Godding took a thoughtful look at Stout Alice. "I'm quite certain *she* didn't kill Mr Godding," she said. "She's not Constance Plackett."

Amanda Barnes's face froze. "What's that?"

Constable Quill's mouth dropped open. He closed it with a snap, opened his notebook, and started flipping through the pages.

"That's right!" Dull Martha nearly wept with relief. "She's not! So you can't go arresting her. And you should stop saying hateful things about her, Barnes. I think it's horrid of you. Mrs Plackett – the real one – she's buried in the vegetable garden too. She and her brother both died after eating poisoned veal. But I didn't poison it at all. Not one single bit."

"Martha!" Mary Jane said through clenched, smiling teeth. "*Be still.*"

Mrs Godding turned slowly. She looked intently at Mary Jane, and then at Kitty. Kitty couldn't withstand her gaze, and had to look away.

When she spoke, Mrs Godding's voice could barely be heard. "My sister-in-law is dead?"

Kitty's tongue was salt. She nodded.

Mrs Godding turned her face away from the others.

Amanda Barnes stared at Stout Alice. Terror had taken hold of her. "What's she saying?" she whispered. "What does Miss Martha mean?"

Mrs Godding turned to Reverend Rumsey and Dr Snelling. "Could it be possible that the rest of you were unaware that this is not my sister-in-law?" She gave the sheepish men a disgusted look, then pivoted and examined Stout Alice. "I haven't seen my sister-in-law in eleven years, but I can spot an impostor when I see one. Did the rest of you just not *look*?"

She turned her disgust towards Constable Quill, who raised both hands in a show of innocence. "I'd never met the Widow Plackett before this week!" he protested.

Reverend Rumsey was a stammering mess. "I . . . She . . . How was I to . . ."

"What about you, Doctor?" cried Mrs Godding. "Can't *you* tell the difference between an old woman and a young one?"

Dr Snelling puffed out his chest. "My attention is on symptoms," he said. "I'm not . . . gazing into women's eyes and whatnot. Unless they've got glaucoma." He straightened his waistcoat savagely. "And even then, not for long. I refer them straight to a specialist."

"Miss Alice?" Amanda Barnes peered at the supposed Mrs Plackett. "Is that you?"

Alice rose and stood straight, ceasing her performance. "It is, Barnes."

"But how? Who?" She gulped. "Miss Martha." Barnes's voice was humble, weak, pleading. "What was that you said about the veal? Tell it to me slow, if you have any compassion in you."

Dull Martha, who'd stood biting her nails ever since her unfortunate revelation about Mrs Plackett, turned to Kitty for guidance.

Kitty could hear the men's voices outside. She couldn't stay vexed with Martha. It was only a matter of moments; the damage was done before the poor girl uttered a word.

"It's all right, Martha," she said. "Don't be afraid."

Dull Martha became conscious of the staring eyes of all the others in the room. She shrank back against the wall. Dear Roberta reached and took her hand.

"I cooked the veal." Martha spoke slowly and deliberately, step by step. "Mrs Plackett and Mr Godding ate the veal. Then they died. One after the other."

Amanda Barnes faltered. She placed a trembling hand over her mouth. A tear spilled down her cheek.

The sight of the daily woman's grief cut Alice to the quick. Remorse stuck like a stone in her throat. "Oh, Barnes," she said. "I'm so sorry." When her words brought no response, Alice went on. "I know Mrs Plackett could be harsh towards you, and perhaps she was a bit unfeeling, but of course, as her faithful domestic, you would take her passing painfully."

Amanda Barnes's knees buckled. She toppled to the floor, nearly dragging Constable Harbottle down with her. The two constables lifted her drooping form off the floor and carried her to the couch.

"Have you any smelling salts in your bag, Doctor?" Mrs Godding asked. "These heartless constables ignored this poor woman's distress until it was too late."

Dr Snelling lowered himself to his knees again, opened his bag, and searched for salts. He found the bottle and unscrewed it under Barnes's nostrils. She awoke with a gasp.

There was a loud crash. Dour Elinor had dropped a stack of dusty books onto the floor. *"Doc-tor Snelling!"*

The doctor jumped where he knelt. "In the name of Mike, what is it, young lady? You keep on saying my name!"

Mrs Godding placed a hand over her heart. "Are you trying to wake the dead, child?"

"No." Dour Elinor's black eyes were so wide, so piercing, they gave Alice chills. "I'm trying to ask a question. I want to know . . ." She reached into Dr Snelling's bag, pulled something out and held her prize high. "I want to know what Doctor Snelling is doing with Mrs Plackett's stolen ebony elephant."

Chapter Twenty-six

"An elephant?" asked a stunned Constable Quill.

"An elephant," declared Dour Elinor.

"Doctor Snelling, how could you?" Disgraceful Mary Jane hissed. "For shame!"

"He's the thief!" Stout Alice cried. "Arrest *him*!"

Constable Harbottle scratched his head under his helmet. "Didn't we switch to talking about murder? Or did I miss something? I got confused around the veal part."

Kitty jumped up from her chair. "Constable Quill," she said, "tonight this home was savagely invaded, ransacked, and searched. You've seen it. Windows were smashed and dishes, brass, and silver stolen. Our little dog was nearly drugged to death. And one thing we know for certain was taken was Mrs Plackett's ebony and gemstone elephant. Miss Elinor Siever just fished it out of his bag. He's the thief."

"Well, Doctor?" the constable said. "What say you to all of this?"

Dr Snelling rose to his feet. "Constable, you know exactly

what I was doing this evening. I smoked cigars outside the parish social, as half a dozen other men can attest," he said. "I followed you to the police station afterwards. Now, pray tell, exactly what are you accusing me of doing tonight?"

"Doctor Snelling." Pocked Louise stood cradling little Aldous close to her, but she spoke pointedly. "You tucked a scrap of fabric into your pocket this evening. May I see it?"

The doctor bent to fasten his bags. "I don't know what you're talking about. What scrap of fabric?"

Louise met his gaze defiantly. "The one the dog sneezed up as he revived. Won't you show it to us?"

He shouldered his bag and turned as if to leave. Constable Quill coughed suggestively. Dr Snelling paused, looking much put upon, then inverted the liners of his vest and jacket pockets. "See? No scrap of fabric. You must have imagined it, owing, no doubt, to a surplus of hysteric nerves."

"It was your right trouser pocket," said a relentless Louise. "You pushed the scrap all the way down in, with your handkerchief. It was damp from being in the dog's mouth."

Dr Snelling's upper lip twitched, as though words wanted desperately to escape his mouth that oughtn't to be said in ladies' company. He plunged his hand into his trouser pocket and pulled forth the small scrap of black-and-white checked fabric. The sight of it puzzled Smooth Kitty.

"Appears the girl's memory is correct," he said. "I'd forgotten. I was just getting it out of the way. Always shoving things in my pocket; my forceps just the other day. Couldn't find them when . . ."

That's when it hit Kitty. "Trousers!" she cried.

Constable Harbottle scratched his head. "How's that?"

"More hysteria," said Dr Snelling, diagnostician.

Kitty nodded vehemently. It was all becoming clear. "Gideon Rigby's trousers!"

Constable Quill snapped to attention. "Whose trousers?"

"Gideon Rigby's," Kitty said. "He came here collecting donations for retired basket weavers. He runs an antique furniture shop."

"Not in Ely, he doesn't," said Constable Harbottle.

Constable Quill flipped through his notebook so quickly, the pages might have caught fire. "Gideon Rigby," he said, "is another name for Gainsford Roper. He's a surgeon from Haddenham, out past Witchford, and if I'm not mistaken, one of Dr Snelling's friends from their university days."

"You're babbling," said Dr Snelling. "You've taken laudanum along with that dog. So I have a friend from Haddenham who wears trousers. What are you accusing me of? Murder?" He buckled his black bag shut. "A doctor won't stay in business long if he murders his patients."

"Right now I'm only accusing you of running an illegal betting parlour," said Officer Quill. "I'm arresting you for it, too."

Dr Snelling laughed aloud. "Betting parlour? You must be daft. I'm a man of medicine."

"And a rich man," said Pocked Louise, "though you said yourself that a country surgeon can never be wealthy."

Constable Quill took the ebony elephant from Elinor and examined it. "From the looks of things, you and your friend Roper used rather extreme means to collect unpaid gambling debts. Breaking and entering. Aggravated theft. And that's just for starters."

"On what evidence?" demanded the doctor. "How do you know I didn't come by that . . . rhinoceros in a perfectly reasonable way? Buy it in a shop?"

"Elephant," said Dour Elinor.

"Aldous bit the evidence right out of your friend's ghastly trouser leg," snapped Smooth Kitty. "Your doctor friend nearly drugged him to death for it."

Pocked Louise spoke before the officer could. "You yourself said you had no time. If you had no time to steal it, you had no time to buy it at a shop. It was here before we left for the social. The thief must have broken in, stolen it, then slipped it to you at some point during the strawberry social, perhaps when you were outside smoking cigars. I wonder what else is in that bag of yours."

"As for the betting parlour," said Constable Quill, "the force has been building their case against you for quite some time. Mrs Lally of Witchford has been extremely helpful. One of her tenants is one of your best clients. She became concerned when he went missing, and alerted us, thinking there could be some connection. She's seen Mr Roper come by to collect more than once, and even seen you together. That's why we pursued Mr Godding's disappearance so strongly." His chest puffed out rather larger than usual. "This burglary and this . . . elephant give us all the evidence we needed."

"Balderdash," declared Dr Snelling. "I'm heading home. I don't need to submit to such slander."

"Harbottle," said the Constable. "Take him into custody."

Dr Snelling made a show of refusing to cooperate, but Harbottle moved with a speed one might not expect from a person of his girth. The older man quickly surrendered to the handcuffs Harbottle slapped on his wrists.

As this bit of police bravado unfolded, Pocked Louise flipped frantically through her notebook, crossing out names and scribbling. It was here. It was all here, she was sure. If she could just make the pieces fit!

"Constable," said Mrs Godding. "I'm confused. Are you saying my sister-in-law, Constance Plackett, was a gambler? That she owed debts to this man? This is absolutely preposterous."

Constable Quill shook his head. "No. Her brother was. Aldous Godding."

Mrs Godding opened her mouth as if to contradict, then closed it once more and shook her head. From down the corridor they could hear footsteps on the stoop, and the sound of the front door opening. Pocked Louise watched the conversations closely, capturing every detail. She knelt and laid little Aldous gently down on the rug, then commenced a stream of steady scribbling in her notebook.

Amanda Barnes lifted her weary head off the couch, where she had lain in a daze ever since her faint. "He was just trying to get ahead in the world. Make something better of himself."

Mrs Godding frowned. "Gambling's a wicked, foolish way to do it."

Stout Alice turned towards the couch. "I still don't understand, Barnes," she said. "Why should you care what

Mr Godding was trying to do, or why? What made you look for him? Why are you so anxious to defend him?"

Pocked Louise snapped her notebook shut. "I suspect," she said, "they must have been a couple. It's the only reason I can think of for why she would murder Mrs Plackett for him."

Chapter Twenty-seven

"You take that back, Miss Pox," Amanda Barnes cried. "She lies! I'll not be spoken down to by a little slip of a girl like her."

The door opened, and Constable Tweedy, Farmer Butts, Henry, and Julius entered the parlour. Julius went to his mother and took her hand in his. Shock had made even his tanned skin pale and drawn. Smooth Kitty couldn't bear to see his downcast face, nor could she leave off watching it.

Constable Tweedy surveyed the scene and noticed Dr Snelling in handcuffs. "Ho!" he cried, and leaped to Constable Harbottle's side. He frowned at the sight of Amanda Barnes stretched upon the couch. "What about . . . Weren't we . . ." Constable Quill silenced him with a shake of the head.

"It's true," Henry Butts said. He seemed so stunned by what he'd seen, that he forgot to be tongue-tied. "The bodies are wrapped and lying in the back of Father's wagon. We found them both buried in the garden. Right where the young ladies planted their cherry tree."

Dull Martha covered her face and began to cry.

The adults in the room turned accusing eyes towards the students at Saint Etheldreda's School.

"Wrong time of year for planting trees," added Farmer Butts, as if that clinched the matter.

Dr Snelling sneered at the girls. "Looks like you've found your murderers, Constable," he said. "These little minxes! Do you have enough handcuffs to go around? Take mine. I haven't any need for them."

Amanda Barnes lay still upon the low couch, gazing at the ceiling, paying no attention to the conversation but speaking like one in a dream. "I told you he'd be there," she said. "I found him there tonight. I saw the grave yesterday, after teatime. Just earlier, I'd heard her threaten him. So she'd done it, I thought. Tonight, after the social, I dug him up." Her voice grew soft with weeping. "I knew he wouldn't go off and leave for India without telling me."

"'Course he would've," scoffed Dr Snelling. "In a minute, if it suited his purposes. He was a scoundrel and a wastrel. You're not the first woman . . ."

"Hush!" Mrs Godding hissed. "Have you no pity whatsoever?" She turned to Barnes. "Were you a couple, then?" inquired Mrs Godding in a low voice.

"We were going to be married," Barnes said in a faraway voice. "In a church, with my mother there, as soon as Mrs Plackett was . . . as soon as Mrs Plackett gave her blessing."

Pocked Louise knelt and stroked little Aldous.

"What you mean to say, Barnes," she said, "is that you and Mr Godding planned to marry as soon as Mrs Plackett was out of the way."

Constable Quill paused and studied Pocked Louise. "How old are you, exactly?"

Louise ignored this. "It's quite simple," she said. "Martha. Tell us how you cooked the veal, and why you did it that way."

"I fried it in two little pans." Martha's voice was small. "But first, I roasted both cutlets together in the oven with a little water. Cook, back home, taught me that trick, so I wouldn't undercook the pork chops and make Pappa sick again."

Constable Quill frowned. "I fail to see what undercooking veal has to do with murder, unless you think the deceased contracted food poisoning."

"It's hard to know with meat!" Dull Martha cried. "Pre-roasting it makes sure it's done. Pappa got ever so ill that one time, and I never wanted to make the mistake again!"

"And, now, Martha," Louise said reassuringly, "tell us who provided you with the recipe you used to cook the meat."

Martha's eyes were wide. "Why, Barnes, of course," she said. "She always leaves instructions for how to cook Sunday dinner."

Louise nodded. "And how did she tell you to prepare the veal?"

"By breading and frying it," answered Martha obediently. "Only, it was the strangest thing. Ordinarily we have at least three skillets that would serve to fry several cutlets. But they all went missing. The only things I could find were two tiny frypans, the kind you use to fry a single egg. Each barely large enough for one cutlet. One pan was ours, but the other I'd never seen before. That's the one Barnes came and collected on Monday evening."

"Don't you see, Freddie?" Mary Jane cried. "Barnes left the recipe, swiped the skillets, and left the little pan. She wanted the cutlets cooked separately, because she had poisoned one of them."

"Yes, don't you see, *Freddie*?" mimicked Dr Snelling, making the constable turn purple.

"But Miss Barnes left work on Saturday afternoon, I presume. Isn't that correct?" asked the constable.

"That's true," Kitty replied. "And the groceries didn't arrive until later, Louise."

Louise smiled. "It doesn't matter. The groceries were delivered to us by her nephew. His younger brother told us just the other day how he makes a point of bringing them to her so she can inspect them before he brings them to our house. She could poison one veal chop from her home in town and wrap it separately."

"Where would she get poison?" inquired the usually silent Officer Harbottle.

"Simple," said Louise. "Insect killer made from cyanide. The chemist asked us just the other day if Barnes has been successful in getting rid of our carpet beetles. To our knowledge, we've never had a bug problem."

"Cyanide," scoffed Constable Quill. "Now you're

inventing madcap ideas you've read about in mystery books. You'd have no way to recognise cyanide."

"Oh, wouldn't she, though?" cried Disgraceful Mary Jane. "Freddie, you're being a beast and showing your ignorance. Our Louise is the best scientist in all of Cambridgeshire, I'll wager! You march into the schoolroom and see for yourself all the equipment she's set up, with . . . acids and chemicals and things. She proved it was cyanide."

Constable Quill nodded towards Officer Tweedy then glanced towards the door. Tweedy lumbered off in search of the laboratory.

"I brought it out of suspension using potash, iron sulphate, and oil of vitriol," Louise said simply. Constable Quill looked quizzically at Dr Snelling, who hesitated, then nodded. "But you don't need to take my word for it. Dr Snelling, you know it was cyanide that killed the admiral tonight, don't you?"

Dr Snelling, still handcuffed, stuck out his lower lip. "I'll save my professional opinions for the inquest."

"You smelled the almonds, too, didn't you, Constable?" Louise asked.

Constable Freddie Quill seemed torn by some great inner struggle. "But it makes absolutely no sense!" he sputtered. "I never heard of a more reckless, foolish game. To poison one piece of veal, and not the other, and trust that the right one would be eaten by the right person . . . it's an outrageous gamble!"

"You've already told us," Stout Alice said, "that Aldous Godding was a gambler."

The constable's pencil flew across his notebook pages.

Miss Barnes struggled upright on the couch, peeping over its edge like a corpse rising from its coffin. Mrs Godding and Julius stood close to one another, listening mutely to all that unfolded.

"Mr Godding and Miss Barnes must have used some system of communicating about which cutlet to choose," said Kitty. "It doesn't really matter how."

Pocked Louise snapped her fingers. "Oh, but we know that, too," she said. "Roberta, dear, will you fetch for me the little urn on the sideboard in the dining room?"

Dear Roberta tiptoed across the parlour, shrinking at her awareness of all the people watching her. She returned in a moment with the rough stonework urn and handed it to Louise.

"This is where we placed all the items we found in Mr Godding's and Mrs Plackett's pockets, the night they died," Louise said. She retrieved a small scrap of paper from the bottom and held it up to the lamplight. "This. This bit of paper, with what we thought was a scribble or an inkblot on it. That scribble was your drawing, wasn't it, Barnes?" She held it closer to their former housekeeper, who kept her lips pressed tight. "The triangular shape. It's a piece of veal. The one Mr Godding was supposed to eat. The one that was free from poison?"

"Mr Godding took the largest piece, like he always did," said Stout Alice. She added, as an afterthought, "It always struck me as just the piggish sort of thing he would do."

"But *this* time," said Pocked Louise, "it wasn't greed – or I suppose I should say, it was greed on a much larger scale – that made his choice. He had Barnes's sketch to guide him. The veal that looked like that," here she indicated the paper Constable Quill had taken from her, "was the one she had not poisoned."

"Wrong." Amanda Barnes spat the word.

Constable Harbottle turned to face her. "What was it then?"

Constable Tweedy reentered the room. "There's some sort of laboratory in there, all right, though what it aims to do I couldn't begin to say."

"Never mind, Tweedy. Go on, please, Miss Barnes. You were about to tell Miss Dudley how wrong she was. What did the paper illustrate, if not the unpoisoned veal?"

"Nothing." Amanda Barnes sagged back onto her couch. "I don't know anything about that scrap of paper."

Pocked Louise let out a laugh. "Oh, I see," she said. "The picture indicated the *poisoned* piece, if we must split hairs."

Miss Barnes glared at her, but said nothing.

"Hm." Constable Quill appeared in genuine danger of running out of notebook. "Miss Dudley. If only one piece of veal was poisoned, how did they both die?"

Disgraceful Mary Jane, who now saw herself as a culinary expert, since baking her burnt Mansfield muffins, answered before Louise could. "Martha has already explained that," she said. "She roasted the cutlets together in the oven, in a pan with some water, before frying them. That's how the cyanide would have spread, through the water and juices in a shared pan."

291

"Foolish girl," said Barnes.

Dear Roberta's face lit up. "And remember, Louise, when I said that one veal specimen made your testing water more blue than the other?"

Pocked Louise grinned. "That's right, Roberta. The pieces were unequally poisoned. Mrs Plackett's piece got the full dose, then some of it seeped into the other cutlet."

Constable Tweedy was puzzled. "Blue?"

Dr Snelling sighed. This whole affair appeared to bore him. "Prussian blue," he explained. "Cyanide."

Smooth Kitty wondered aloud. "Perhaps that's why Mr Godding took longer to die."

Disgraceful Mary Jane would have none of this theory. "Perhaps it was because he was an evil rat, persuading his infatuated accomplice to poison his sister so he could inherit her money. And what money, at that? Other than this house and that elephant and a few dishes and trinkets, precious little." She tossed back her pretty head, and Kitty noted that Constable Quill seemed to momentarily forget his notebook. "You're a fool, Barnes, if you think he would actually have married you. You might have been next in line for a special veal dinner."

Amanda Barnes swung her legs off the couch and rose somewhat shakily to her feet. "You take that back, Miss Mary Jane," she said, pointing a finger at that young lady. "I won't be sassed around by you lot anymore! You take back what you said about Aldy Godding. And about me."

Disgraceful Mary Jane's eyes flashed. "I shall not! You *are* a fool to have trusted him. And he's fool enough to have died from his own poison. The wretch didn't deserve to live. Divine justice will prevail over fiends like him." She clapped her hands. "Oh! I see it now. Remember, girls, all that cooing we heard in the back garden that night?"

Constable Quill wiggled his finger in one ear. "Pardon me. Did you say 'cooing'?"

"That's right, Freddie. Coo! Coo! Like that."

"Coo, coo." Constable Quill looked, for a moment, like a man regretting his choice of profession, but he plowed onward. "And you say you heard someone cooing in your back garden on Sunday night?"

"Exactly. It was Barnes, hoping her precious Mr Godding would come outside and tell her all was clear, Mrs Plackett was dead, and we girls had been sent packing." Mary Jane folded her arms across her chest in triumph. "And to think, Henry, I was so certain it must have been *you,* cooing for me to come outside to see you!"

Farmer Butts's eyebrows knit together. "How's that again? *Henry?* Are you chasing after these girls? Do you have something to tell me?"

The farmer's son cringed. "No, sir. Not a bit of it." He sent a pitiable glance in Dull Martha's direction.

"He *would* have married me," Amanda Barnes cried. "He told me. Right here in this room, he promised me. I know in my heart, he meant it truly. I was going to be a lady, with a parasol, and live respectably, and boss my own servants around! I could take care of my little mother proper. Aldy was going to buy me a ring, a golden one, with a ruby in it, just as soon as . . ."

"As he'd paid off the fortune he owed me?" Dr Snelling sneered.

"As soon as, apparently, he'd gotten his hands on Mrs Plackett's money," said Constable Quill.

"Which," interrupted Reverend Rumsey, who rose eagerly to his feet, "is now bequeathed in large part to Saint Mary's, as her other heir, Mr Godding, is now dead."

"Not so," said Stout Alice. "Isn't that right, Barnes?"

The former daily woman shook with rage. She pointed at Alice as though she was still confusing her for Mrs Plackett.

"She threatened to take Aldy's name out of her will after they quarrelled," she cried. "Who knew the witch would up and do it before the weekend was over?"

Constable Quill sighed. In the lamplight he began to look like an older, wearier man. "Will? What's this about a will?"

Amanda Barnes drooped and collapsed back onto the couch. "She left her fortune all to Julius," she said. "She got to her solicitor before we could stop her."

Julius Godding's eyes grew wide, but he said nothing. Reverend Rumsey sat down with a thump.

Stout Alice nodded her head. "Barnes could only know that, Officer, if she stole the new will, which Mr Wilson's office delivered here on Monday morning. Tonight isn't the first time she's been prying and snooping about the house, searching, I suppose, for Mr Godding himself."

"Or for the money," said Dr Snelling.

"That's what I still don't understand!" cried Kitty. "What money? Doctor Snelling believes there's a fortune here, or he and Mr Rigby wouldn't have burgled the place. Barnes and Mr Godding believed there was a fortune, large enough to murder for. But I swear, I've been through every ledger, every file and drawer, every speck of paper in this house. There isn't a spare farthing, I assure you."

Constable Quill snapped his notebook shut. "Makes it all the more ironic, doesn't it? To murder for nothing?" He nodded towards Constable Tweedy, who unlatched the handcuffs from his belt and slipped them over Amanda Barnes's wrists.

Miss Barnes submitted to the handcuffs while her face streamed with tears. "Oh, Aldy, Aldy," she whispered. "We were so close."

Pocked Louise and Smooth Kitty exchanged a private glance. She'd actually loved him, then? Impossible though it was to conceive, there was a woman whose heart throbbed with affection for Mrs Plackett's greasy, odious rascal of a younger brother. She would spend the rest of her days knowing she'd poured the poison that had killed her love – even if, as both girls suspected, the entire nefarious plot had been his idea.

"What I don't understand, Miss Barnes," asked Mrs Godding, "is why you poisoned Admiral Lockwood's punch tonight."

Miss Barnes blinked. She gaped at Mrs Godding. "You said he was all right. You said not to worry. He was *tough as an old oak, you said*!"

Constable Quill replied with clipped words. "Admiral Lockwood died of poison."

Barnes's gaze at Mrs Godding dripped with betrayal.

"You were in shock," Julius's mother said. "I wanted to spare you further pain."

"You needn't have bothered," said Constable Quill. "Clearly, Miss Barnes volunteered in the kitchen tonight to poison the drink. Isn't that right?"

Miss Barnes set her jaw tightly.

All the fight went out of his captive. She nodded towards Stout Alice. "She killed my Aldous. She threatened to throw him out in the garden. Then, that's where a grave appeared." She began, quietly, to cry. "The stupid old admiral drank from her glass. The poison was meant for her."

Chapter Twenty-eight

The girls clustered together in a forlorn little knot and watched as the officers, with the help of the junior and senior Buttses, shackled Dr Snelling and brought him to the police wagon. The machinery of official business and transport had taken over, leaving the girls feeling like spectators in their own home. Though it would not, Kitty thought bitterly, be their home for much longer.

Kitty's gaze shifted to the forlorn figure of Amanda Barnes, small and shackled, seated on the couch. Fury and pity, horror and remorse, swirled together in Kitty's heart. Amanda Barnes had cooked their breakfast eggs, washed their beds, dusted their desks and shined their shoes. She'd been as much a part of the rhythm of their daily lives as afternoon toast with tea.

And now this.

Kitty wondered what, if anything, might have saved Barnes. She remembered the thousand ways in which she and the other girls had taken Barnes's service for granted. They hadn't been rude or beastly, not especially, but at times they'd treated her like she wasn't there. She was, after all, their domestic.

Could more kindness from them have prevented this?

Neither justice nor reason could ever suggest that their uneven kindness had *caused* this. But as for what might have happened differently, no one would ever know.

Kitty thought of Mrs Plackett in her abandoned grave. She was glad their garden burial would be undone. They'd worked so hard to hide it, but now she was glad Mrs Plackett would finally have a proper coffin and burial service. She deserved so much more than that. Kitty had never felt any warmth for her headmistress. Her dying, it must be said, had caused Kitty to see her with new eyes.

Pocked Louise's thoughts held much to occupy her as well. Her heart thrummed faster with the private thrill of victory. She had done it! She, youngest of them all, solved the puzzle. She doubted Disgraceful Mary Jane seriously thought she could, back when she nominated Louise to be their – what was the name again? Spurlock Jones? But victory, Louise noted, was bittersweet. True, she'd saved her friends from a cloud of suspicion, and justice would now be done. But their time together, she was certain, was at its end. It made her victory a hollow one. Losing the other girls broke her heart.

"What will happen now, Kitty?" whispered Dull Martha.

"I don't know, dear heart," Kitty replied. "The world's gone upside-down." She took Martha in her arms and kissed her forehead. The others followed suit, leaning on each other and linking elbows. Even Dour Elinor put her arm around Pocked Louise, whose eyes were red and brimming.

"Is this the end of our sisterhood?" Louise whispered.

"It mustn't be," Dull Martha said. "We can't allow it to be."

Smooth Kitty pressed her lips together. "I'm not sure we have the power to stop it."

"Poor Barnes," Alice whispered.

"Poor Mrs Plackett," said Dear Roberta.

"Louise," said Disgraceful Mary Jane, "I shall never torment you about your drab clothing again so long as I live. You were marvellous tonight. The youngest, smartest sleuth in all of Cambridgeshire!"

Louise tried not to smile, but her twitching lips betrayed her.

The police returned for their next prisoner after taking Dr Snelling to the wagon.

"Wait."

The voice was Mrs Godding's. Amanda Barnes looked up in some surprise.

Mrs Godding took a deep breath. "Miss Barnes. I believe you were very much prevailed upon by my brother-in-law. I will speak to the judge on your behalf and express these thoughts to him." She paused, and shook her head. "All the same, to take your mistress's life . . . Was she unkind to you?"

Amanda couldn't meet her gaze. "Yes, ma'am, but . . . That is to say, in the way any mistress sometimes is."

"And the poor admiral, tonight. Miss Barnes, I don't know what to hope for on your behalf, or for your immortal soul. But I will speak my mind, and I will pray for you."

"Come along, Miss Barnes," ordered Constable Tweedy. "It's time to leave."

The door closed behind them, and soon wagon wheels crunched over gravel. Mrs Godding sank into a chair and buried her face in her hands. Julius stood close by and rubbed her shoulder.

As he did so, he turned and looked searchingly at Smooth Kitty.

How you must despise me now, she thought. *What a terrible thing I've done to you. And I am the one to blame. This whole charade was my idea.*

She tried to console herself. After all, she'd only properly met him tonight, and she was sure never to see him again once this business was behind them. What difference did it make?

Constable Quill entered the room once more.

"Well, Freddie," said Disgraceful Mary Jane, "you've done splendidly tonight, haven't you? There'll be new stripes on your uniform soon, I'll be bound. A burglar, a bookie, and a murderer all in one night. They'll be promoting you to Scotland Yard in no time."

Constable Quill ignored Mary Jane.

"Mrs Godding, Mr Godding, we're ready to leave for town. The vicar will accompany us. Will you, also?"

"I shall remain here," said Mrs Godding. "Julius, I think, can hardly do so under the circumstances, so he will return with you and pass the night at the Lamb Hotel, where we have engaged rooms. Julius can return in the morning and bring me my things."

The constable nodded. "Just as I hoped," he said. "May I, then, leave these young ladies in your custody?"

A shock went through the group of girls. "Custody?" cried Disgraceful Mary Jane. "Exactly what do you mean, Freddie?"

The constable went on as though they weren't there. "Bodies buried in the backyard, impersonating the dead, conducting business transactions on her behalf . . . these are serious charges. I have a number of questions to ask these young ladies. But first I must attend to the more pressing charges, against the two prisoners. I will be back in the morning."

"'These young ladies!'" fumed Mary Jane. "Well, I like that! Suddenly we don't exist. Why, only a few hours ago . . ."

An anxious look passed over the constable's face. "Good evening, ma'am," he said hastily. "I will return in the morning." He turned heel and fled.

Julius Godding kissed his mother and followed the constable without a backward glance. Kitty watched him go, and swallowed hard.

"Come along, girls," she said. "Let's go to bed."

Chapter Twenty-nine

Smooth Kitty sat on the edge of her bed and buttoned her dress. It was five o'clock in the morning, and she'd been awake since three. Between retiring to bed and three, she wasn't sure what had happened. There may have been some fitful sleep. She couldn't quite remember.

The night before, the girls had huddled together in the room Kitty shared with Mary Jane, whispering absurd plans for how they might flee and escape prosecution, none of which would hold a drop of water. Finally Mrs Godding had poked her head in the door and, without a word, ordered them into their own beds, and silence.

Kitty felt physically ill. It was rather late now to wallow in regret for her choices. *I didn't kill anybody,* she told herself fiercely. *I didn't start any of this. All we wanted was to stick together. All I wanted,* she thought, and here the selfish truth became painful, *was to not go home.* Now going home looked like the best she could hope for. Even her father's icy indifference was far, far preferable to prison.

She brushed her hair and twisted it into a bun, which she fastened with pins. She clipped her stockings to their garters, then pulled on and laced her boots. What would today bring, she wondered vaguely. Should she pack her things?

It didn't seem to matter what she did, so she let the idea pass. She spied her schoolbooks, stacked in a windowsill, and felt nostalgia for the days when they actually did wallow through their studies each day, under Mrs Plackett's bored and lifeless tutelage.

She listened at the doorway but heard no signs of life. She opened her bedroom door and ventured out. Her steps led her down the stairs and through the long corridor.

She opened the front door and stood on the stoop, breathing in lungfuls of morning air. Over across the way towards Ely, the cathedral spires shone in morning light. Curls of fog shifting low over the grasses gradually gave way to the searching sunshine. Nature neither knew nor cared about what had happened here just the night before.

"Good morning, Miss Heaton," said a voice behind her.

She turned to see Mrs Godding standing behind her with a mug of tea in each hand.

"I didn't realise you knew my name," Kitty said.

Mrs Godding offered her a cup. "Someone mentioned it to me. It seems to be a fine morning. Will you join me outside in the garden?"

Kitty followed her through the damp grass towards a pair of chairs in the rear garden, facing away from the cavity in the ground where the graves had been. Aldous chased along after them, bounding after grasshoppers.

"He seems no worse off for his misadventures," Mrs Godding said, and sat down. "Here we are. Tell me about yourself, Katherine, or should I say Kitty?"

Kitty sat carefully in the garden chair. "Katherine, please," she said, then on an impulse added, "though you may use Kitty if you prefer."

The older woman took a sip of tea. "Well?"

Kitty hesitated. There seemed so little to say, and no good place to begin. "I am an only child," she said. "My mother died many years ago. I barely remember her."

Mrs Godding watched her closely. "I am sorry to hear it. I lost my own mother when I was a young bride. I think of her often."

Kitty thought about this. "I wish I thought of my mother more," she said. "There just isn't much there."

Mrs Godding nodded. She gazed thoughtfully at Kitty. "How does your mind work, Kitty?"

Kitty hid her confusion behind a sip of tea. "I don't know how to answer that question."

Mrs Godding looked out across Farmer Butts's fields. "The mind that chose to bury my brother- and sister-in-law in secret in the back garden was either a heartless and depraved one, with no proper respect for others, or it was . . . something else. I am not sure what."

Kitty's father filled her mind's eye. She pictured him at his desk in his office, marshaling clerks and secretaries and junior officers in the firm. How efficient he was. How effective. And how cold.

How much was she fashioned in his image?

"Mr Godding was an unpleasant man," Kitty said. "He was boorish and crude, and never treated us girls politely. We could sense, I think, the friction between him and his sister, though I don't think any of us knew the reasons why. But that friction never stopped him from coming over often enough to eat all her food and drink all her wine."

Mrs Godding nodded knowingly. "Some people never change," she said. "When my husband and I first moved to India, I wondered if half a globe was distance enough between us and my husband's younger brother."

"Mrs Plackett was a respectable woman," Kitty went on, "but there was never any warmth between her and any of us girls. She was harsh and cross much of the time, and preoccupied otherwise. I don't think she ever enjoyed running a girls' school." Kitty wrapped her fingers around her mug and savoured its warmth. "The strange part is, I feel we've gotten to know her better – at least her kinder qualities – now that she's gone."

"Did she have kinder qualities, then?"

Kitty looked at Mrs Godding in surprise. "Well, didn't she?"

Mrs Godding laughed a little. "I've often thought that the only thing that made my sister-in-law human was her inexplicable fondness for sailors," she said. "She had rather a forbidding nature, even when I first met her."

Kitty smiled. She wondered what Mrs Plackett would have been like twenty or more years ago when Mrs Godding first made her acquaintance.

"I think she tried to help her brother, even though she knew he was beyond help."

Mrs Godding nodded. "It is often that way within families."

"I don't say any of this to excuse myself," Kitty said, "but perhaps it illustrates why we never felt we owed them special kindness when they died. Their deaths were quite horrible, you know. So sudden and astonishing. But we never cared a fig for either of them. And then we all realised we would be sent home, and I couldn't bear the thought of going home. Nor of leaving my friends behind."

Mrs Godding waited for Kitty to continue. Mr Shambles strolled by, stalking through the tall grass and clucking to himself, until little Aldous caught sight of him and galloped off to bark at him.

"I only thought of Mrs Plackett as she related to me," Kitty went on. "In other words, as a nuisance. And then, in the instant, the nuisance vanished, but if we told anyone, we'd be sent home. If I went home to Father would send me off to some other horrid school. Or worse, keep me home. I couldn't bear being trapped there."

Kitty wondered how she could tell so much to this woman she'd met only yesterday.

Mrs Godding shifted in her seat and turned towards Kitty. "I comprehend," she said. "Some women are born for more independence than society offers them. Perhaps all are, but some have not yet learned to recognise it." She gazed off into the distance. "Before I married, I was a nurse, Kitty. I enjoyed four wonderful years of working in hospitals. In fact, my husband was one of my patients." She smiled.

"Yes, I knew you were a nurse," Kitty said. "I think that's wonderful. Julius told . . ." Her voice died away, and she felt her face flush with heat.

"Did he, now?" Mrs Godding seemed surprised and pleased. "Isn't that nice."

"I don't know what will happen to the other girls," Kitty said, and for a sickening moment she feared she might cry in front of Julius's mother. "They would all be so much better off if they hadn't listened to my scandalous, unforgivable plan."

From behind them, inside the house, they heard some stirrings and signs of life. Out front, cart wheels could be heard crunching over the gravel of Prickwillow Road. Not even hidden corpses would stop Henry Butts from bringing the morning milk.

"You give yourself rather a lot of importance, I think, Kitty," Mrs Godding chided gently. "To hear you talk, you deserve all the credit for the scheme, and your special reward is to enjoy all the blame."

Kitty gaped at her. What an enigmatic thing to say!

Mrs Godding watched Kitty thoughtfully then rose to her feet. "I've enjoyed our conversation, Kitty," she said. "You've told me all I needed to know."

Kitty followed her indoors, sipping her tea and wondering what on earth that meant.

Chapter Thirty

An hour later the girls sat around the dining room table, staring at their plates in penitent silence. Mrs Godding served up toast, eggs, mushrooms, bacon, and porridge. Stout Alice's mouth watered at the sight of the food, while Dear Roberta thought the aroma of the bacon might be reason enough to faint with happiness. If only everything around them weren't so terrible. Disgraceful Mary Jane willingly conceded that her own cooking might be traded in for better.

Mrs Godding joined them at the head of the table, and held out her hands. "Say grace, girls," she said. They joined hands, bowed their heads, and held their private, guilty devotions. Then Mrs Godding dumped a heaping spoon of brown sugar onto her porridge, and drizzled it with cream.

"There's nothing like breakfast," she declared, "for making one think fond thoughts of lunch."

Any other day, Smooth Kitty would have smiled.

The doorbell rang.

Mrs Godding pushed back her chair. "That will be Julius," she said. "I'll go." She closed the dining room door behind her.

The girls watched her leave, then turned to face each other.

"Don't sprain your ear listening to see if it's him, Kitty," said Disgraceful Mary Jane.

Smooth Kitty halved her toast with a vengeance. "I thought *you* were already picking out the lace for your wedding veil, Mary Jane."

"That's not Julius," said Pocked Louise. "It sounds like a pair of men."

"Policemen!" squeaked Dull Martha.

Kitty rose from her chair. "For heaven's sake, let's hear what's going on." She opened the door to find Mrs Godding guiding two deliverymen in through the front door, each carrying supporting beams bearing a large wooden crate. Aldous barked furiously at their boots.

"More of Mr Godding's things?" Stout Alice wondered.

"Present," gasped one of the men. "For Mrs Plackett."

Word had not yet gone far, Kitty realised, that Mrs Plackett no longer lived on Prickwillow Road, nor any other road, for that matter.

"Set it right down here, gentlemen, in the drawing room," ordered Mrs Godding. "I thank you."

The two men set to work prying the wooden top off the crate. The girls clustered around to watch. The top came off, followed by a spate of packing rags, to reveal . . .

"What is it?" inquired Dear Roberta.

They stared at the object.

"Well, that's that," said the deliveryman. "Here's a letter for you. We'll be off now."

And with that, he handed Mrs Godding a letter from his pocket, then he and his companion gathered up the pieces of the crate and left.

"But what is it?" Dear Roberta continued to press her question.

Pocked Louise examined the thing all around. "It's . . . wood."

It was indeed wood, a thick and heavy object carved intricately from solid wood, of a rich amber colour. It stood about as wide and deep as an ottoman on four wooden legs, and possibly twice as tall.

"Is it furniture?" inquired Dull Martha.

"I wouldn't care to sit on it. The top's too pointy." Pocked Louise had knelt down to examine it from all around. She traced her fingers along the grooves and protrusions, and followed the scrolling carved lines with her eyes.

"What do you think, Mrs Godding?" asked Smooth Kitty.

Mrs Godding folded her arms and frowned at the thing. "It's indigenous, at any rate," she said. "I would venture to guess African. Let's see what this letter tells us."

"It's a palace," declared Pocked Louise. "See? These are pillars. These represent windows, and this is the roof."

Mrs Godding unfolded the letter. "Dear Mrs Plackett," she read. "This is a gift the admiral had prepared specially for you. He had already made arrangements for this to be delivered to your home today. I saw no reason to interrupt his plans. I'm sure you are as grieved as I am at the loss of the admiral. I hope this gives you something by which to remember him." She folded the paper and tucked it into her pocket. "Well, well. So my sister-in-law was linked to the admiral. I wondered, when I saw him sitting next to her. Or next to you, I should say, Miss Brooks?'"

Stout Alice curtseyed. "Please. Call me Alice."

Pocked Louise had not ceased her probing of the wooden palace. "Here's our problem!" she cried. "It's backwards. The front is facing the wall. Help me turn it around, Kitty."

It was astonishingly heavy, and it took several girls to do the job, but together they heaved and hoisted the carving around until it faced the right way. Now it clearly represented a palace. Pocked Louise bent to examine the doors. Aldous licked her face helpfully.

"They're locked," she said. "There's a keyhole, but no key." She searched everywhere for a key's hiding place, then studied the door closely.

"This is nothing that can't keep until after breakfast," Mrs Godding announced. "If there's one thing I dislike, it's cold, clammy porridge. Come along, girls."

She had an air one did not quite dare disobey, but Pocked Louise didn't budge. "Elephants," she breathed, pointing to small carvings near the door.

Stout Alice shook her head. "What, Louise?"

"Elinor," Louise cried urgently, "fetch me the elephant!"

Dour Elinor slipped silent as a specter out of this room and into the next. She returned moments later bearing the ebony elephant. Louise fitted the brass end of the elephant's trunk into the figure-eight shaped keyhole.

"It has prongs that fit the nostrils," she cried.

"Disgusting," said Mary Jane.

She twisted the elephant slowly, rotating it on its trunk, and they heard the latch click. She pulled away the door. Out poured a cascade of gold coins, flowing like endless corn spilling from an opened silo.

Aldous barked and chased his bobbed tail at the commotion. Coins clinked and showered over Pocked Louise and rolled every which way, under the furniture and out into the hall.

"Mercy," cried Mrs Godding. "Fetch a basket! Something, quick."

The girls scrambled to chase and gather coins into their aprons.

"They're doubloons," Kitty whispered in wonder. "Just like the ones we found in Mrs Plackett and Mr Godding's pockets."

"Each one's worth twenty pounds, or more," said Pocked Louise. "Look! Here's another note!"

Louise fished a folded piece of paper from the opened palace door. She handed it to Smooth Kitty, who recognised the admiral's hand immediately. Mrs Godding was still scooping coins from her skirt into an empty vase.

"Dear Connie,'" Kitty read. "I told you I had a perfect way for you to store your husband's gold. Your fortune and your secrets are safe with me. Yours, P.L."

Disgraceful Mary Jane dabbed the corners of her eyes with a handkerchief. "He was just big Romeo, wasn't he?" she sniffed. "Even if he was horribly old. I wish he hadn't died. I would have married the old dear in a heartbeat."

"Hmph." Mrs Godding's eyebrows rose at this. "I thought you had your sights set elsewhere."

Mary Jane shrugged. "Oh, I'm flexible."

Mrs Godding bit her lip. Kitty could swear she was trying not to laugh. "There. That's the last of it. Lock that door back up, Miss Dudley, and I insist we return to breakfast." She wiped the smell of coins off her hands and onto her skirt. "So Constance really *was* hoarding a fortune."

"Lucky for Julius, she chose to hoard it at the home of her gentleman friend," said Mary Jane.

Mrs Godding's self-assured step faltered slightly, as if this thought had not occurred to her. "Yes," she said slowly. "Lucky for Julius. She wrote and told me that some of her late husband's associates had recently sent her some 'valuables' belonging to him. She suggested that with them, she might assist in Julius's university costs. She urged us to come for Julius's entrance exams, and we would discuss all the particulars. That is why we made the trip when we did." She sat back down at her place at the head of the table. "I confess I never imagined 'valuables' on such a scale as this."

"Don't forget the elephant," said Dour Elinor.

They sat at the table and picked at their plates. The butter on the toast had congealed, the eggs had turned to rubber and water, and the bacon fat had gone gruesome, but nobody said a word about it. They barely looked at their food.

"It all begins to fit," Pocked Louise said excitedly. "Mrs Plackett receives a fortune in Spanish gold. She writes to you and Julius about it. She gives the gold to Admiral Lockwood for safekeeping."

"She asks him to see what the doubloons are worth on the exchange market," added Kitty, remembering the admiral's note and the twenty pounds.

"Meanwhile," said Pocked Louise, "she keeps one in her pocket, and for some reason we'll never know – perhaps a whim, or a generous impulse – she gives one to her brother Aldous."

"Thereby alerting him," said Stout Alice, "to the fact that she's come into money."

"He asks for a large amount," said Smooth Kitty, "probably to pay his gambling debts."

Dear Roberta's eyes were wide. "But she says no."

"I think Mr Godding would have become angry then," ventured Dull Martha, "knowing him."

"They quarrel, and Mrs Plackett threatens to remove him from her will," said Pocked Louise. "Remember the letter you found, Alice, under Mrs Plackett's pillow?"

"And that," said Disgraceful Mary Jane, "was when Mr Godding persuaded his accomplice – or pawn, rather – that he'd marry her if she helped him put his deadly plan in motion, before Mrs Plackett could change her will."

"The old will must have favoured Mr Godding," said Pocked Louise. "It may have been written before Darling Julius was even born."

Mrs Godding blinked. She'd been observing this sudden volley of conversation like a spectator at Wimbledon. "Before *what* Julius was even born?"

Smooth Kitty froze. Her face went cherry-red.

Disgraceful Mary Jane snickered. "Oh, that's just Kitty's pet name for your handsome son."

Kitty dealt a kick under the table. The rest of the girls covered their mouths with their unused napkins.

The ever-tactful Stout Alice tried to come to her friend's rescue. "Pass the marmalade, would you, Kitty?"

"These eggs look delicious," added Dear Roberta bravely. In truth, they did not. It was a tribute to her loyalty that she would set aside truth in favour of kindness, but these last few days had tested Dear Roberta's mettle and shown her just how murky truth could be.

They listened to the muted tock of the glass-domed mantelpiece clock, and watched the dining room curtains billow in the morning breeze. Outside and across the way, the Butts farm and its sheep-speckled pastures gleamed in sunshine.

"I wonder," said Mrs Godding, "if I could teach a school."

Kitty glanced at Mary Jane, then over at Alice and Elinor.

The doorbell rang once more. Mrs Godding rose to answer it. The girls could hear the voice of Constable Quill.

"Your beau is here, Mary Jane," groaned Pocked Louise. "Save me from visits by more young men! I'm going upstairs to read a book."

Disgraceful Mary Jane came close to growling. "He's not *my* beau."

"Don't go, Louise," Kitty pleaded. "We may not have much more time together. Don't anybody leave."

The constable entered the dining room. Mrs Godding offered him a chair, which he accepted, and a cup of tea, which he declined.

"It isn't poisoned." Mary Jane's dark eyes shot flaming darts at the Constable.

He avoided her gaze.

"Mrs Godding, ma'am. I've been speaking with the sergeant about the case of these young ladies, and we both feel that due to the serious nature of their crimes . . ."

"Constable Quill."

The officer closed his mouth, and waited for Mrs Godding to speak.

"I've had a talk with these girls," she said. "I believe they're only guilty of high spirits and poor judgment."

Dull Martha looked very confused. "Talk? What talk?" she mouthed, which, fortunately, the police officer did not notice. Smooth Kitty placed a warning finger over her own lips.

Constable Quill pulled his notebook from his pocket. "But the law," he began. "Deceiving an officer of the law. Impersonating a dead person. Improper burial. These are serious offences."

Mrs Godding took a thoughtful bite of toast. "So they are, indeed. Now, with respect to the school, it now belongs to my son. With his permission I propose to remain here and run it. He will be enrolling at Oxford University this fall, and I would prefer to remain in England rather than return alone to India."

Constable Quill scratched his head. "That will be very nice for you, I'm sure, but I fail to see what . . ."

316

"Have a piece of toast." Mrs Godding spread marmalade on an extra slice and handed it to him before he could object. He took a bite of the toast without thinking, then paused, startled, as if having just woken up.

"Now, see here," he said loudly. "These young ladies can't just get away with what they've done! They must face consequences."

Mrs Godding continued to gaze at Constable Quill with the same unruffled expression she'd had since he arrived.

"They should most definitely face consequences," she said. "I am a firm believer in accountability. It is the only way to learn maturity."

"At the very least, I must write to their parents."

"Allow me to do that, if you don't mind," said Mrs Godding.

Constable Quill was not appeased by this. "I don't care how high-born they all are. They lied to an officer of the law . . . to me! And they tried to trick us all into thinking their headmistress wasn't dead. If I have my way, and the judge reads the law like I do, they'll spend time in a ladies' reformatory for what they've done."

"Would you like a slice of orange, Constable?" Mrs Godding asked.

"No, I would not."

Mrs Godding proceeded to slice herself an orange. "Time spent in a detention facility by these young ladies would no doubt place a damper on your upcoming marriage."

The officer's notebook and pencil clattered onto the table. "My what?"

"Your marriage." She beamed a congratulatory smile at him. "Why, Constable, with my own eyes I watched you last night. Your behaviour left no other conclusion in the mind of a decent observer but that you two were engaged, or very soon to be so."

The policeman pushed his chair back. "Now, hold a moment . . ."

"Of course I had not met either one of you, but who could fail to notice such an extremely attractive – and extremely *young* – couple as yourselves, gossiping off in a corner together? I commented upon it at the time, to my son. 'Ah, young love,' I said to Julius. 'They must be betrothed. See how lingeringly he kisses her cheek?'"

On the cheek! Kitty hadn't seen that one. *Mary Jane, you hussy!*

Constable Quill looked around the room like a drowning man searching for a lifeboat. The gap between his front teeth wasn't quite so adorable now. His mouth hung open, and his forehead gleamed as a fine sweat broke out upon his brow.

Mrs Godding watched him with calm, bland ease. "You see, Constable, we aren't in London anymore," she said gently. "Here, when a man behaves familiarly towards a young woman, she is right to interpret his gestures as a promise of matrimony, and the courts are quite consistent in their upholding the same opinion from the bench. Just in yesterday's paper there was a sad mention of a breach of promise case in Cambridge. How the man's sullied reputation must harm his future career prospects, I can only imagine."

Constable Quill ran a finger around the inside of his collar. Disgraceful Mary Jane held herself regally, managing at once to be both an image of furious beauty and wounded innocence. Kitty tried hard not to smile.

"Don't you think, Constable Quill, it might be in everyone's best interests for you to leave the education and discipline of these young ladies up to me?"

The officer slipped his notebook into his pocket and rose. "As you say, ma'am, their offences can certainly be seen as, er, high spirits and poor judgment. It's clear they're in very capable hands here with you. You won't allow them to repeat such escapades here under your watch, I'll wager."

"I'd wager right along with you," said Mrs Godding cheerfully, "except that we know what sort of trouble betting leads to."

"Quite, quite." He wiped his brow with a handkerchief and rose to his feet. "The bureau will be rather tied up for quite a while, prosecuting Doctor Snelling and Doctor Roper, not to mention Amanda Barnes," added the Constable, doffing his helmet to the roomful of soon-to-be reformed young ladies as he prepared to leave.

"Poor Miss Barnes," agreed Mrs Godding. "It's a pleasure to see you, Constable. Do come again, whenever you'd care to visit."

"We can all have *tea*." Mary Jane spoke through clenched teeth.

Constable Quill bowed, fled, and shut the door behind him with a bang.

Mrs Godding rose, rubbed her hands together, and

gathered up her plate. "This food is inedible," she said. "I'm going to warm my plate back up in the oven. If anyone else would like to join me, there's plenty of room. And, Miss Mary Jane, let me give you fair warning. This was the first, last, and only time that I will indulge you in your misbehaviour with young men. Next time, there *will* be a letter to your parents, sparing no detail."

Mary Jane shrugged and rose with her cold breakfast plate. "It won't be anything they haven't heard before."

"And," Mrs Godding added, "I will sentence you to weeks of shovelling out the pig pen on the Buttses' farm."

Mary Jane halted. "I . . . I think my breakfast is warm enough already. Thank you, ma'am."

EPILOGUE

May melted into June's dizzying sunshine, and stalks of elfin green vegetable plants rose in lovely rows in Farmer Butts's field. June brought examinations to Saint Etheldreda's School, now renamed "Prickwillow Place" by Mrs Godding. Examinations made the girls cross, except for Pocked Louise and Dour Elinor. Stout Alice and Smooth Kitty didn't mind the work but would rather have been outside feasting in the sunshine. Mrs Godding, though she lacked teaching experience, had proved to be a zealous educator. Pocked Louise, with her interest in medicine, was especially thrilled to learn all that their new headmistress could teach them about anatomy and diseases. Dear Roberta and Dull Martha gave thanks every day that they weren't in a reformatory, nor even in trouble with their parents, and tried to be content with the academic rigor.

Disgraceful Mary Jane, however, was brooding. Her abandonment at the hands of Freddie Quill still rankled her. She was not accustomed to rejection, and certainly not to losing one upon whom she'd set her sights *and* with whom she had canoodled behind the parish hall curtain. In vain could Kitty make Mary Jane see reason by pointing out that Freddie was a minor loss compared to going to jail.

They saw Julius only rarely, usually for Sunday dinners. He'd taken lodgings in the city of Ely, and was preparing to enter Oxford by studying with a tutor. There was plenty of room now in Prickwillow Place's budget for meat at mealtimes, and this without even dipping into the doubloons now stowed safely back in the carved wooden palace. Since the school's headmistress no longer needed to routinely rescue a dissolute brother, the girls' tuition payments adequately covered expenses.

Mrs Godding held a memorial service for Mrs Plackett and Mr Godding a week after the strawberry social. It was a silent, sombre day for the young ladies. The bodies now lay buried in Saint Mary's churchyard, nowhere near each other. Mrs Godding insisted upon that. "The murderer," she said, "shall not insult his victim's memory by lying beside her until Judgment Day." Dour Elinor had supervised the grave digging and pronounced it adequately executed.

One particular Sunday afternoon after a splendid dinner cooked by Dull Martha, Mrs Godding suggested that they take their strawberries and cream dessert outdoors for a picnic in the garden. She spread old blankets on the ground, and they sat and watched Aldous chase the chickens. Their cherry tree sapling, which the police had uprooted when they exhumed the bodies, Mrs Godding had suggested they replant and nurture. It hadn't died yet.

"How are your studies coming along, Mr Godding?" Pocked Louise asked Julius.

Julius leaned back and spread out his arms to capture more sun. "Very well, thank you, Miss Dudley," he said. "Do you know, I have decided to follow in my mother's footsteps and study medicine?"

"Splendid." Pocked Louise was extremely pleased. "Somehow or other, I shall find a way to do the same. I heard Cambridge University admits a few woman scholars."

"There's an opening for a surgeon in Ely," said Stout Alice. "I suggest you hurry along in your studies."

Disgraceful Mary Jane plucked the petals off a wild violet. "Did you hear the news at church today, Alice? Your odious law clerk, Leland Murphy, has received a promotion at Mr Wilkins's law firm."

"I thought he looked remarkably dapper in his new suit of clothes," added Smooth Kitty.

"I had heard the news." Stout Alice tried not to smile, and failed.

"Speaking of new clothes," said Mrs Godding, "for those of you willing to stay on over summer term, I am thinking of spending time working on tailoring skills. A modern woman should not be wholly reliant on dressmakers. When you can sew your own things, you can ensure a proper, stylish fit."

Dull Martha's ears perked up in dismay at this. "Summer term?"

Mrs Godding bit into a fat strawberry laden with cream. "No Latin, Martha, I assure you." She waved the stem of the berry at Stout Alice. "Now, in your case, Alice, I'm eager to tailor a dress for you. You have a lovely figure, and you shouldn't go on dressing like a sixty-year old widow."

Alice blushed scarlet. "I don't!"

Julius laughed. "Mother, you're embarrassing your students again."

"I'm not embarrassed," Alice said. "I just . . . think I'll go inside for a pitcher of water and some cups."

"I'll go with you, Alice," said Mary Jane.

Dull Martha and Dear Roberta pleaded for Pocked Louise and Mrs Godding to join them in a game of croquet, and to the astonishment of all, Dour Elinor joined them.

Kitty and Julius sat alone in silence and watched Aldous steal the ball and run off with it every time someone struck it with a mallet.

"I suppose we should go join in the game," Kitty said.

"Or not," said Julius.

Kitty found her awareness of every detail around her heightened, as if looking at the world through a magnifying glass, and hearing every birdsong through a trumpet. She had had no chance to speak with Julius privately since the horrid night when the bodies were found. She shuddered to think what he must think of her. And she hated noticing how much these worries bothered her.

"How are *your* studies coming along, Miss Heaton?" Julius asked.

"Hm?" Kitty looked up. "Studies? Oh. Very well." She smiled. "Your mother is an excellent teacher."

"I'm not surprised to hear it," Julius said. "I think *she* has been surprised to discover how much she enjoys this.

Taking over the school has been good for her. She was rather bored in India, except when she volunteered at her clinic."

Kitty ate a strawberry. "You must miss seeing more of her."

"I have been rather replaced." He laughed. "I suppose seven daughters for one son is a more than reasonable exchange."

Daughters. Kitty's mind caught hold of that word, and turned it over several times. Daughters. Sisters. It pleased her.

"Do you plan to stay on for the summer term?" Julius asked.

"I do," Kitty said. "Father won't object."

Julius turned to look directly at Kitty. "And how long do you expect to stay on as a student?"

Kitty steeled herself to avoid staring at his dark curls, or at the suntan he'd somehow maintained here in England. "For as long as Father lets me," she said. "If I grow too old to be a pupil, perhaps your mother would let me teach. She says she plans to take on younger students eventually."

Julius smiled. "I like the thought of that."

"Of what? Me teaching?"

He shook his head. "Of you staying on here at the school. Mother's very fond of you."

Kitty turned to watch Mrs Godding knock a croquet ball clear across the lawn. Aldous went bounding after it, and she called to him in dismay.

"I like her, too."

There was only one strawberry left in the bowl. Julius dunked it in the cream and offered it to Kitty. "And this way," he said, "I will always know where to find you."

Kitty nearly dropped the strawberry. She popped it into her mouth, stem and all.

Mary Jane and Alice came strolling around the corner of the house bearing a pitcher and cups. At the sight of Kitty and Julius sitting by themselves, they veered towards the croquet match, leaving Kitty alone to blush.

When they were fully out of earshot, Kitty took a deep breath. "Mr Godding."

He looked pained. "Julius, please."

"Mr Godding," she insisted, "I must ask you this question. Can you ever forgive me for what I did to your aunt and your uncle? For my audacity, and selfishness?"

He took off his hat and rested it on one knee. "You weren't the only one, from what I understand. If there's any blame, shouldn't it be divided seven ways?"

Kitty shook her head. "I thought up the plan and convinced the others it was a good idea. I was the ringleader."

"I'm not surprised."

Kitty tried to read his expression but couldn't, then realised Mrs Godding and the other girls had moved past the lilac hedge and out of view.

"I won't deny that the sight of them made me lose my appetite for quite some time," Julius said, with a twinkle in his eye. "But when I think about it from your perspective, I envy your daring. You had a choice between going home or building a new life for yourself. You took a chance."

"A foolish one," Kitty said.

"Perhaps, in hindsight," he agreed. "All I ask is that if you should ever come upon me, strangled on a piece of cod or succumbing to a chicken leg, that you notify the undertakers straightaway. Do you promise?"

He offered her his hand to shake. She smiled and took his hand in hers. They shook. But Julius didn't release her grip as yet.

"Friends?" he asked.

Kitty smiled. "I hope so."

Julius looked around. They were still alone, with no one in view. He pulled her hand close and kissed it. "Good," he said. "I insist upon it."

Author's Note

I chose Ely, England, as the setting for my boarding school murder mystery because Etheldreda, the Maiden Saint, was honoured in the cathedral there. I wanted to write a story about a gang of clever, loyal, scandalous maiden friends, so Etheldreda seemed like a proper candidate for my project's patron saint.

When an opportunity arose to travel to Europe, I seized the chance to visit Ely, and there I fell completely in love. Three friends and I travelled together. We were our own little scandalous sisterhood as we toured the majestic Ely Cathedral, browsed the shops and markets on streets where Oliver Cromwell once walked, strolled along the River Great Ouse, and hiked up the real Prickwillow Road. The five-star English breakfast we ate at Mrs Smith's home, our marvellous Ely B&B, still sizzles in my memory. (I asked Mrs Godding to prepare it for the girls in Chapter Thirty, and she was happy to oblige.)

Travelling to Ely, and hobnobbing with Smooth Kitty, Disgraceful Mary Jane, Stout Alice, Pocked Louise,

Dour Elinor, Dull Martha, and Dear Roberta, made this project a delight for me. Another of its charms came from researching the Victorian era, trying to understand how real people lived, ate, worked, shopped, studied, married, gambled, dressed, went to jail, died, and were buried in this fascinating period. Every quirky detail, from Mr Nestlé's Swiss chocolate, to Elinor's posture brace, to the new miracle American beauty product, Vaseline, came from research texts and books and journals published during the late nineteenth century.

Poisoning had become a serious crime problem in the late Victorian age, in part because life insurance had become more widespread. Alas, some desperate people began to look upon unpleasant relatives, if they carried life insurance policies, as worth more dead than alive. Poisoning cases were hard to prove, so many poisoners got away with murder. Methods of detecting poisons were less developed than they are today, but scientists and detectives made great strides in learning how to identify cyanide and other toxins. The details of Pocked Louise's experiment where she proved the veal was poisoned came from a book published in 1849, which was intended for doctors called upon to test evidence and give testimony in criminal cases.

When it wasn't poisoned, food in the Victorian era was a colourful concoction of dishes, some of which we might find savoury, others bland, and some disgusting. The Betty Crocker of her day was a cookbook author named Elizabeth E. Lea, whose 1845 book, *Domestic Cookery, Useful Receipts, and Hints to Young Housekeepers* is a treasure trove, and still in print today. From its helpful pages a housewife might learn how to bake breads, boil oysters, preserve pickles, discipline lazy servants, brew up salves for bunions, roast a calf's head for dinner, and mash its brains, with bread crumbs, into appetizing 'Brain Cakes.' Is your mouth watering?

Victorian middle- and upper-class parents felt a deep concern to provide their daughters with the right sort of education that would advance their prospects for marriage. Schools of every kind, both public and private, sprang up for young ladies during this time period, and manners, etiquette, social graces, posture, dancing, and ladylike arts (painting, singing, needlework, and music) were taught alongside academic subjects. While many educators were undoubtedly caring and inspiring, many others, as Charles Dickens's novels show us, seem to have been heartless and unfeeling. An education might well be an ordeal; people seemed to feel that the younger generation was best molded by harsh discipline and Spartan conditions that would save them from the sins of idleness and luxury. By these standards, our Saint Etheldreda's School pupils may have been luckier than most, even with crabby, penny-pinching Mrs Plackett instructing them.

It was an age obsessed with instilling proper morals in the young, and in particular in young women. Even popular music reinforced these ideals. Stout Alice's song, which she attempted to sing at the strawberry social, came from an 1858 collection, *The Book of Popular Songs* edited (and some of them, written) by J. E. Carpenter. In these pre-radio days, this song may well have been the closest thing to a Top Forty hit. The song, "'Tis Not Fine Feathers Make Fine Birds," compares young ladies fixated on beauty and fancy clothes to vain peacocks, and more modest, humble, virtuous girls to small, plain birds with beautiful voices. The peacock may think it's a fancy-looking bird, warns the songwriter, but its song is a painful screech. Better to dress and live modestly, it concludes, and sing sweetly. Our scandalous sisters, and particularly Disgraceful Mary Jane, saw right through such pat, simplistic nonsense. Perhaps Mr Carpenter, the songwriter, was unaware that the peacocks who strut around in their fancy feathers are the *boys*.

I include the entire song here for you.

'TIS NOT FINE FEATHERS MAKE FINE BIRDS

BY J. E. CARPENTER, MUSIC BY N. J. S. SPOBLE

A peacock came, with his plumage gay,
Strutting in regal pride one day,
Where a small bird hung in a gilded cage,
Whose song might a seraph's ear engage;
The bird sang on while the peacock stood,
Vaunting his plumes to the neighbourhood;
And the radiant sun seem'd not more bright
Than the bird that bask'd in his golden light;
   But the small bird sung in his own sweet words,
   "'Tis not fine feathers make fine birds!"*

The peacock strutted, – a bird so fair
Never before had ventured there,
While the small bird hung at a cottage door, –
And what could a peacock wish for more?
Alas! The bird of the rainbow wing
He wasn't contented – he tried to sing!
And they who gazed on his beauty bright,
Scared by his screaming, soon took flight;
  While the small bird sung in his own sweet words,
    "'Tis not fine feathers make fine birds!"

Then prithee take warning, maidens fair,
And still of the peacock's fate beware.
Beauty and wealth won't win your way,
Though they're attired in plumage gay;
Something to charm you all must know,
Apart from fine features and outward show –
A talent, a grace, a gift of mind,
Or else poor beauty is left behind!
  While the small birds sing in their own true words,
    "'Tis not fine feathers make fine birds!"

To my mind, fine feathers may or may not make fine birds,
but fine *readers* always do, and on that point I imagine
even Dour Elinor and Disgraceful Mary Jane could agree.
Thanks, fine birds, for reading along with me.

Scandalously yours,
Julie Berry

ACKNOWLEDGEMENTS

Shawn Cannon, director of the Cannon Theatre in Littleton, Massachusetts, staged British farce after British farce until finally I cried, "Enough! I must write one!" Thank you, Shawn, for keeping the arts alive in my family and community.

Professor John Sutherland, author and Emeritus Lord Northcliffe Professor of Modern English Literature at University College, London, published a series of lectures titled "Classics of British Literature" with the Great Courses company, a course I've devoured many times. A fragment he uttered in a *Pride and Prejudice* lecture stopped me in my tracks one day: "A regiment of maidens." *Oh*, I thought. *Now that's a book I need to write.*

Jamie Larsen, Julia Bringhurst Blake and Heather Marx shared my Ely travels and their lives and hearts with me. I would be lost, in Europe and in general, without such dear friends.

Deirdre Langeland and Katherine Jacobs of Roaring Brook Press had the great good humor to love this story and help it become the fizzy romp I meant it to be. Sharing this book with them has been a delight. Others at Roaring Brook, including Jill Freshney, Elizabeth Clark, and Simon Boughton, brought tremendous talent and support to the project. Alyssa Henkin, my agent, has the never-ending flexibility to roll with my ideas and champion them. Thanks also to Nicola Kinnear, for her charming artwork.

Finally, my husband, Phil, whose charms rival Officer Quill's and Darling Julius's combined, merits my undying thanks for having the courage to tell me when he doesn't like a draft, and when he does.

THE RISE AND RISE OF TABITHA BAIRD

When Tabitha starts at her new school in London, she is determined to be the coolest, most popular girl there, whatever it takes. But how will she keep her friends away from her incredibly NOT cool family?

The first in a hilarious new series by bestselling author, actor and comedian Arabella Weir.

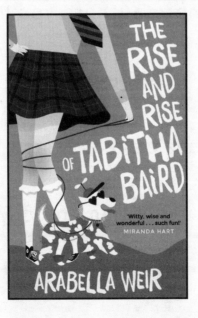

OUT NOW

piccadillypress.co.uk

Go online to discover:

☆ more authors you'll love

☆ competitions

☆ sneak peeks inside books

☆ fun activities and downloads